The System Apocalypse

Short Story Anthology
Volume III

With Stories By...

Craig Hamilton
David R. Packer
Jason J. Willis

and
Tao Wong

Copyright

This is a work of fiction. Names, characters, businesses, places, events, and incidents are either the products of the author's imagination or used in a fictitious manner. Any resemblance to actual persons, living or dead, or actual events is purely coincidental.

No part of this publication may be reproduced, distributed, or transmitted in any form or by any means, including photocopying, recording, or other electronic or mechanical methods, without the prior written permission of the publisher, except in the case of brief quotations embodied in critical reviews and certain other non-commercial uses permitted by copyright law.

No part of this book may be used or reproduced in any manner for the purpose of training artificial intelligence technologies or systems.

Books in the System Apocalypse Universe

Main Storyline (complete series with 12 books)

Life in the North

Redeemer of the Dead

The Cost of Survival

Cities in Chains

Coast on Fire

World Unbound

Stars Awoken

Rebel Star

Stars Asunder

Broken Council

Forbidden Zone

System Finale

System Apocalypse – Relentless

A Fist Full of Credits

Dungeon World Drifter

Apocalypse Grit

System Apocalypse: Australia

Town Under

Flat Out

Bloody Oath

System Apocalypse: Liberty

Head of the Class

Dropout

System Apocalypse: Kismet

Fool's Play

Fool's Bond

Fool's Last Dance

Anthologies and Short stories

System Apocalypse Short Story Anthology Volume 1

System Apocalypse Short Story Anthology Volume 2

System Apocalypse Short Story Anthology Volume 3

Valentines in an Apocalypse

A New Script

Daily Jobs, Coffee and an Awfully Big Adventure

Adventures in Clothing

Questing for Titles

Blue Screens of Death

My Grandmother's Tea Club

Table of Contents

The System Advent

This is Harry Prince, reporting from London, England. As you can see behind me, the world has come to a standstill; the snarled traffic of London streets is a tangled mess as electronics and vehicles stop functioning. There's smoke in the distance, from multiple fires and crashed aircraft.

There is currently no further information of what these blue notifications in our vision originate from. Speculation runs rampant among those I have spoken with, from government conspiracy to alien invasion. What we do know is what the notifications have stated. Earth is now designated as a Dungeon World, and that monsters and Classes are coming.

Without evidence to the contrary, without an explanation for how this is affecting the world, I can only recommend that you stay calm, choose wisely, and be ready.

As it is, I'm already recording this bulletin using my new Class and Skills as a Reporter.

The Great Black Sea

The convoy passed before them, unaware like a group of fat, lazy space mantas. Their engines burnt a dozen different colors, painting the void of space with their fission energies. In the hushed bridge, the pirates watched the projected image, waiting for their prey to cross the final boundary.

Dornalor shifted, his dandelion yellow ears lowered as he listened in, his nine-foot-tall body hunched as he waited for the Captain. He was only on the bridge because the Captain wanted a runner, wanted someone that could take word down to engineering or the raiding bays. He was fast, that he was. A tiny trickle of sweat ran down his back, somehow escaping from the tight, nanoweaved blue-black jumpsuit that he wore. Nostrils flared as the captured stink of suppressed fear and anticipation warmed the bridge, the air filters set high for methane and oxygen. He fiddled with the band around his neck, wanting to put his helmet on now. He didn't, because that would mark him as scared, and you showed no such fear. Not on a pirate ship.

Not when you were just a Cabin Boy.

His Captain was crooning to himself, the paired openings along his neck humming as his purple skin glistened in the artificial light. No one mentioned it – no one dared – but it was quite beautiful. A siren song that was utterly at odds with the vicious nature of the Captain himself. He was not known as Bloody Quinn for nothing.

If Dornalor had any other options, he would have shipped out with someone else. As a child of a space companion, one of a half-dozen spawn on the Selous pirate station, opportunities were as rare as Heroic Classes. No, you took what you could and were thankful for it.

"Donnie-boy. Get that scrawny ass down to the launch bays. We're going with launch plan C," Captain Quinn said, leaning back with a savage grin. He flicked his hand sideways, and the next second, the ship was burning fission material, power flooding through the system and coming alive. They left the grasp of the free-floating asteroid field as they rushed toward their prey.

"Yes Captain!" Dornalor spun around, rushing for the door even as he felt the Captain's Skills kick in across the ship. The engine was burning hot to get them close, but he felt From the Void mute the world inside and around the ship. It was an active Skill that used a ton of the Captain's Mana, which was why he waited till now. But it'd get them close, unless their prey had a really good sensor operator.

Outside the bridge, Dornalor triggered his own Skills. Double Time let him move faster than normal, making each of his movements thirty five percent quicker. It was a great Skill for a Basic Class as it required little Mana to keep active. It let him get down to the hangar bays in record time, his adrenaline pushing him forward. He didn't even need to use Fastest Route, his other navigation Skill, since he knew the way by heart now.

Inside, the rest of the raiding team waited, sharpening their melee weapons and checking their beam rifles. Dornalor, slightly out of breath, still managed to repeat his orders to the six raiders. The ship was low on members, the Captain preferring to run short-handed and thus having fewer shares to split.

"Har! Launch plan C. Good, good," the massive Hakarta, green skinned, tusked and uglier than sin, said, slapping the power armor he wore in the chest. His teammates, Hakarta like the first speaker, slammed their own gauntleted fists into their armor. "That will leave more for us."

"I don't like this," Bueror said, deep set eyes narrowing. The short Grimsar, with his long beard and monomolecular axe, was also the leader of the raiding team. His armor at first glance was simple scale mail, but if you peered closer, it was runic enchanted mail, as strong, if not stronger, than the power armor the Hakarta wore. "Splitting up the boarding parties is going to make the boarding harder."

"But bring much higher returns. Two ships, rather than one," Tasmaza the Hakarta said. "Come, don't show the purple of your fangs so easily."

"Caution is never harmful," Lunga said. The voice was low, languid but plush, the Movana who said it as characteristically beautiful as all their kind, with long lustrous hair, deceptively delicate features and pointed ears. Lying on her lap, a Yerrick with its big cow horns lay playing with a puzzle box. "But I'm more concerned on how we'd fly the ships back."

"Fair." Bueror stroked his beard, then his gaze landed on Dornalor. "Very fair."

***

Dornalor groaned, squeezing his greater height into the crash couches on the boarding shuttle. His greater-than-normal height at nine feet was an uncomfortable fit. Even if the chairs were rated for larger humanoids, they never fit comfortably. On the other hand, Dornalor bit off his own complaints, considering how squeezed in the Yerrick were too. Better a tight fit in a crash chair than a too loose one. That would just cause injuries during the all-too-expected deceleration.

Deceleration when they struck the merchant ships, when they boarded it. An act that he, as a new pirate, should not have been taking part in. Except, of course, he had the piloting skill and the neural link slot to allow him to control the ship, which most of the boarders did not.

Rather than think about the upcoming battle, Dornalor turned his attention to the navigation plot, hand flexing idly as he watched their ship close in on the prey. Unseen, until suddenly the ships started accelerating.

He noted the lines of fire, the shift in their shields as long range beam weaponry began impacting the ship. Their shield integrity dropped alarmingly at first before it stabilised, their Pilot taking evasive action and the Captain and Engineer shifting their Skills to a more offensive mode. They were lucky that they had individuals with the requisite Classes in the right roles. All too often, pirate ships made do with individuals who had the skill but not the Class Skills to back them up.

The ship jerked and twitched, micro-adjustments in acceleration and direction happening every few seconds as the Pilot with the aid of the on-board AI dodged attacks. Sudden acceleration pressed Dornalor into the crash harnesses, the inertial dampeners within the ship working at less than optimal efficiency. The Engineers must have taken some of the power off-line, diverting them into the shield.

A good thing too, as even if some of the attacks missed, the sheer volume of fire was sufficient to drain their shields. A combination of Galactic tech and Skills, the shields stopped before energy and physical attacks but at the cost of Mana and energy.

Even more energy was pouring into their own attacks, though *Quinn's Rest* only carried a few weapons. The ship relied on speed and stealth to win its battles, with its main beam cannon used for targeted fire. A discordant hum filled the boarding shuttle, one that set Dornalor's teeth on edge, the noise just at the edge of his hearing range.

Then, the hum disappeared, going too high. Dornalor knew what that meant, and his realisation arrived with the same flickering lights. On the navigation plot, a straight line from their ship arced outward to meet one of the other ships. He squinted, trying to tell where it struck, knowing the map's fidelity to reality was low but still wanting, needing to know.

"Direct hit to one of their engines," Tasmaza said, calling out the results. As squad leader, he had better access to the sensors than the rest of them. "Prey is slowing down. Main cannon… recharging."

Dornalor could see both last statements, but he could not help but grin. Teach those silly merch to run rather than fight. Even as they flew ever closer, catching up with each passing second, the majority of the convoy chose to run. If they had grouped together, held the line and fought the *Rest*, even Bloody Quinn would have backed off.

Merchants never thought that way though. It was all about what was best for them. Damage taken for their ships meant more cost, which meant lower profits. Better to leave the unfortunate behind. Maybe they'd survive.

Probably not. But it wouldn't be their problem.

The hum built once more as the main cannon charged, but Dornalor's attention was dragged away as the entire ship shuddered. The shrill screech of warning klaxons and escaping air rippled through the ship before the blast doors slammed shut.

"Incoming fire has increased," Lunga said, making a face. "Hopefully, the *Rest* will hold."

"Why wouldn't it?" Dornalor said, his voice quavering with fear. "It's held before."

"Well, we've never taken on so many. And you never know what might happen," Lunga said, a malicious glint in his eyes as he spoke to Dornalor. "An unexpected set of Skills, a lucky shot and a ship can come apart.

"It's what makes this so much fun."

"Fun…" Dornalor gulped.

The Cabin Boy missed the grins the raiders shot to one another at the teasing and his fear. However, before they could continue, Tasmaza held up his hand.

"Second shot fired. Hit. Too far forward. Some damage, engines continue," Tasmaza growled, the Hakarta's low voice rumbling as green skin glistened under his helmet. "Captain is sending off shuttle one. Brace for exposure in five."

On the count, the entire shuttle rocked a little as the hangar doors opened. Out a nearby port window, Dornalor watched as the second board shuttle   lifted off, its engines roaring as it left the hangar bay door at near full acceleration to swoop in on its limping prey. Moments after it left, the door to the hangar closed shut, though indicator lights indicated the hangar was not being repressurized.

"Charging for third shot," Tasmaza said.

Dornalor bit his lip, watching the plot of the first shuttle coming in on their prey. It swooped in on a parabolic arc, dodging direct fire as it closed the distance on the lame merchant. As the entire convoy and the *Rest* left the pair behind, the rate of fire slackened. Soon enough, the pair of dots connected as the boarding shuttle landed.

All the while, the ship threw itself in a variety of evasive maneuvers, one that caused Dornalor's two stomachs to lurch and twist. He kept his gut braced as much as he could, doing his best to reduce the strain on his body and curtail the pumping chemicals through his body. More than once though, the *Rest* rang out as it was struck.

"Captain should pull back. We have one already," the female Yerrick, strapped in next to Lunga, muttered. "He's gotten greedy."

"Docking prices have gone up at Spax," Lunga muttered. "Damn pirate stations, squeezing us for every Credit."

The Yerrick shook her head, reaching out to grip Lunga's hand. Another lurch, and the ship itself twisted, it's magnetized landing gears failing for a brief second as it detached from the hangar. The group shared a worried look. The hum from the charging main cannon kept rising even as the boarding shuttle reattached.

"Third shot fired. It's a—" Tasmaza never finished his sentence, as a resounding explosion threw the ship off its mooring. Flame and noise filled the surroundings of the shuttle, pulling at the raiders in their shuttle as it was tossed around. Dornalor caught a glimpse as the shuttle spun through the air and crashed into the ceiling of open space, a gaping wound in the *Rest*.

Seconds later, the shuttle was thrown out of the wounded *Rest* as its speed dropped and the pirate ship turned away. It was bleeding atmosphere and fuel, crystalised water and other sundry liquids escaping its torn hull. Point defense weaponry kept firing, doing its best to ward off incoming missiles as it shifted direction, opening up the distance between it and the suddenly hostile merchant convoy.

Dornalor's eyes widened as their own shuttle, left behind with its engines switched off was swiftly abandoned, the merchant convoy rushing after the greater prize. Leaving their craft and its occupants with its limited supply of fuel and air behind.

***

"Those vacuum-sucking sons of a naiad!" Lunga cried out, her fist crushing down on her boyfriend's. He was looking less than impressed, trying to extract his hand before the delicate bones shattered, but she seemed to be entirely ignorant of her actions. "They can't leave us! We'll suffocate."

"Pretty sure those merchant ships will be back to capture us first," Dornalor said. He gulped a little. "We could try to surrender. Take a Serf contract…"

"Never!" Lunga shouted, her roar loud enough to fill the room.

"No one is taking a Serf contract," Tasmaza growled, the huge Hakarta shaking his head. "Don't forget, the first boarding party is still out there. They'll come get us. Bueror still has honor!"

"Honor but sense too," Lunga finally finished extracting his hand. "No, we best not be waiting around for them. The kid's right, we should hail them now. Fake surrendering…"

"No!" Tasmaza said. "That way lies true dishonor. They will make examples of us for breaking the code."

Dornalor was only half listening to them. The plot, no longer updating via the main ship's sensors but now connected to the less detailed but still powerful boarding shuttles had caught his attention. A ship had shifted course, away from those pursuing the *Rest* and instead was attempting to expand the distance between itself, the pursuing ships, and the pirates. And themselves.

Fingers moved, dancing across the interface as he called up previous logs. A second later, he saw it. The update, streaming in as the *Rest* was damaged and they were being flung out.

"They hit," Dornalor breathed out.

"What was that?" Tasmaza said.

"Ignore the boy. He's in shock," Lunga said. "Now, I'm telling you, it'll work. Merchant companies won't have more than a dozen Basic Classers, only a half-dozen Combat Classers at best."

"Silence!" Tasmaza snapped, his tone of command shutting down Lunga. "What did you say, boy?"

"They hit. The *Rest*. They hit the other ship. It's trying to get away now, but they took out one of their engines. Enough for us to close in on it, if we hurry," Dornalor said, breathlessly.

"You're suggesting we keep going. Take the ship and use that to run away," Tasmaza said. "Is that what you're suggesting, boy?"

Dornalor gulped but nodded tightly.

"I like it!" roared the big, green muscular alien. He pounded the armrest of his crash pad, patching into the Artificial Intelligence that drove the boarding shuttle. In seconds, the engines roared, red-lining within seconds as they spent fuel and parts in an attempt to close in on the fleeing and injured vessel. "We take their ship and cast them to the void. Dance on their spacesuits and sup on their Mana!"

Laughing out loud, giddy with both relief at the solution and the prospect of violence, the group of raiders began the ship's chant.

"The final *Rest!* The final *Rest!* The final *Rest!*"

Dornalor mouthed alongside the boisterous Raiders, though he could not help but keep track of the plot while doing so. Not only of their own interception course but that of the merchant convoy and the still-running pirate ship.

***

The boarding shuttle plowed into the hull of their target, its ramming end tearing through the thin outer layer before deploying seals all across the new edge. Their target was a mid-sized merchant ship, a Lovano variant that was popular among middle class merchants due to their modular cargo modules, its higher than normal speed and easily adjustable features.

"Good seal achieved. Moving in three," Tasmaza said. "Vanguard to the front. We hit hard and fast. No prisoners. Two way split."

The orders were just a repeat of the plan that they had already discussed. They had all studied the layout of the ship, though being a mid-sized merchant vessel, there were only so many variant designs out there. The constraints of efficient storage and travel dictated a certain level of similarity in builds. The tricky part was, of course, the security systems in place.

The moment the boarding hatch slid open, revealing the blue lit corridor within, Gentri the Raider Vanguard exploded out of the shuttle. The elemental-troll hybrid alien hefted a shield of energy in one hand and a large rifle in the other. Head down, he turned one way even while Lunga's boyfriend, the horned and fur-clad Yerrick, took the other, hefting his double-headed energy axe.

"Clear!"

"Clear!"

The voices rang out in near unison. The rest of the team had never stopped exiting, clearing the deadly chokepoint of their breach location and splitting up. Dornalor, following along, felt himself yanked the other way by Tasmaza as the big Hakarta growled.

"You're with me. We take the cockpit," the green-skinned raider said, his assault rifle to his shoulder as he followed behind the Yerrick. A moment later, Lunga joined their team while the other group followed the fast-moving shield-carrier.

"Let's move, Arbe," Lunga said, bouncing impatiently behind her hairy mate.

"Fine," Arbe said, holding his axe close to him as he trundled down the corridor. They hit the first t-intersection and Arbe took the right, moving halfway down the corridor and bypassing closed cabin doors before he reached an access ladder. Immediately, he began climbing one-handed.

Dornalor hurried behind the group, his own smaller force shield held close by to him. Out of curiosity and feeling useless, he activated Fastest Route. It pinged, giving him a sense of which direction to the cockpit, though it felt muted. He knew then that there were blast doors deployed all along the most 'efficient' route. Hopefully they would be able to force their way through or bypass the security lockouts.

"You're up first," Tasmaza said, gesturing for Dornalor to precede him.

Eyes wide, Dornalor started climbing up the ladder awkwardly, only to grip tight and sway as the ship jerked and rumbled as the assault shuttle detached itself. The lack of escaping air indicated the temporary seal was still holding.

As Dornalor finished his climb, stopping to eye the access hatch that had swung open, new distractions arrived. In this case, over their internal comms, the snarl of beam weapons and the screams of injured pirates and crew. It seemed the other team had already found the opposition. Still, as Dornalor crouched next to the access ladder, he could not help but stare at the open hatch.

"Expected us to burn our way through?" Lunga said.

"Yes, I sort of did," Dornalor had to admit.

"Takes too long. Arbe has a Skill – Bypass Security – that he's Leveled. Opens up security hatches and doors just as fast as if he actually was authorized to it," Lunga said. "Undamaged ships are profitable ships."

"That's right, and that also means they can get us out of here. Now, keep moving," Tasmaza snarled, thumping the hatch close and dropping a small metal box next to it. It started flickering with a bunch of lights. Once Tasmaza noted it was ready, he stood and hurried after the two leads, allowing Dornalor to take the rear once more. "Scrambler. Locks everyone out. Best to guard our backs."

Another nod. The group kept sprinting forward. As a merchant vessel, the one thing the ship had was space, forcing the team to move forward at a brisk pace if they wanted to get to the cockpit in time. Already, Dornalor could imagine the Captain hastily calling for help from the rest of the convoy.

Caught in his ruminations, the young alien was the last to notice the appearance of the merchant crew's guards. They had set up behind portable barriers, hunkered down with weapons aimed at the group. While certain System fighters preferred melee weapons – the ability to create powerful, long-lasting weaponry simpler with such equipment, since a single Artisan could be relied upon for the entire production – for most, the added reach and ease of access of ranged weaponry still won out.

Traces of high-powered energy, compressed light and electromagnetic force and Mana force tore through the air. Dornalor caught one such attack on his shield, his eyes watering as the energy dispersed in front of him. The muffled grunts and sizzle of burning flesh told of more effective attacks ahead of him.

"Keep charging!" Tasmaza howled, the *whumpf* and cackle of his own assault rifle opening up nearly drowning his command.

Rather than directly following the crazed charge, Dornalor pushed himself to one side of the wall before he hunched beneath his shield and crept forward, his eyes still streaming from the initial attack. As his sight cleared up, he caught sight of Arbe hammering away furiously with his axe on the shields, the weapons of the attackers lowered to blast him. A glowing green cone surrounded the Yerrick, protecting him partially from the point-blank attacks even as fur and skin burnt.

"Not him. Me!" Screaming, Lunga taunted the group. The crew had no choice, none of them having the mental resistances to protect against the enforced targeting command. They opened fire on the Movana who threw herself sideways, a mirror copy going the opposite direction. Attacks split, tracking each of them seconds before the shield collapsed.

An axe swung, tearing through weapons, and the bark of Tasmaza's weapon striking chest and face coverings joined the resounding crash of violence. Wading through the opened barrier, Arbe swung his weapon in a furious onslaught, joined soon by Tasmaza and, finally, Dornalor himself. A small beam pistol in his hand, Dornalor peeked around his shield to take a few potshots, only to realise soon after that his help was not needed.

"Can you go on?" Tasmaza said, staring at the panting and crisped Yerrick.

"Of course!" Arbe pushed himself up, only to collapse a moment later, his legs giving way. "Goblin shit. One of them used an enervating void beam…"

"Then follow us," Tasmaza said. "Lunga, front!"

The sharp-eared, delicate-featured woman was staring down at her mate who had managed to pull a medic pack out and was slapping it on his wounds, the nannites and healing potions taking effect.

"Lunga!" Tasmaza snapped.

Lips curled in a sneer, the Movana took off, her paired guns held low and in front of her. Dornalor cast one worried look back at the Yerrick before he pushed his focus forward. While he was worried about other potential ambushes, this was a merchant ship. They had to have a limited number of crew.

Comforting himself with that thought, he kept running, following the furious Movana toward the cockpit.

***

The journey to the cockpit took longer than they would have liked. Without Arbe and his useful Skill, they had to resort to brute force to make their way through the security doors. More than once, a subtle twinge in Dornalor's Skill had him guiding the team to a more effective bypass, crawling through maintenance hatches with their simplistic security systems or hopping up a level or down two as they crossed the ship. In fact, they took so long that by the time they arrived at the final doors, Arbe had managed to catch up with them, System-healing patching the Yerrick together. Even if he looked strange with two thirds of his fur burnt off.

"Ready?" Arbe said, hand on the blast door. He was crouched low, his other hand gripping his axe, while Lunga and Tasmaza held stun grenades in their hands. The shriekers-cum-strobe system was also enchanted with a psychic attack that assaulted the minds of those unfortunate enough to be caught within.

Receiving nods from all but the nervous Cabin Boy, the Yerrick grinned and triggered the doors. Seconds later, grenades and beam attacks criss-crossed one another while Dornalor pressed himself hard against the wall. His eyes widened as he watched a pair of grenades fly through the air, falling to the ground nearby and rolling over.

No time to deal with them, not before the grenades – theirs and the crew's – went off. The explosion from the crew's grenades rippled outward, pressing him against the corridor walls, the majority of his body shielded. Even so, shrapnel and flame impacted his legs, tearing a new hole through one. He slid the rest of the way to the floor, moaning in pain.

The rest of the team were better off due to their better armor and higher health. Even so, they were frozen for a few precious seconds, the optimum time to enter the cockpit passing them by. By the time the raiders recovered and started moving inward, the crew within had shaken off the majority of the stun grenades' effects.

Beam fire took Arbe as he ducked in, explosive webbing catching him halfway through the door. Lunga gripped his frozen shoulder, throwing herself over him and spinning through the air, her paired pistols barking even as the large Yerrick shuddered and slowly collapsed. Caught behind, Tasmaza could only poke his weapon around the body, firing at the crew within.

Crawling his way forward, ignoring the sizzle of flesh and the screams of pain, Dornalor raised his own pistol to fire at those within. The cockpit was a circular configured layout, each of the seats for the pilot, co-pilot, captain and sensor personnel facing inward to one another. Automated System links and neural links fed information directly to the users, making it unnecessary for the vessel to suffer the weakness of a cockpit window.

The circular layout was efficient, allowed the ship' crew to view and talk to one another with ease and emphasised a more horizontal command chain. What it did not provide, beyond the custom moldable chairs, was cover.

Pistols blazing, Lunga landed, spinning and firing with each second. The pistols at first glanced off portable shield generators even as she never stopped moving, her attacks never ending. Tasmaza's assault rifle tore apart a chair and the woman hiding behind it, her shield failing. Dornalor's own pistol caught an exposed thigh, burning bright and tracking sideways a little as his hand shook. The blue-skinned alien twisted a little, taking its foot out of the line of fire only for his shield to fail as Lunga's attacks caught him in the back of his head.

He dropped, but so did she a moment later as the Captain ducked close, a two-foot-long knife appearing in his hand. Invoking a Skill, the attack pierced her shield and buried itself in her chest, the blade ripping outward as he traded his own health for hers.

As quickly as that, in the brief span of two score seconds, the battle was over. Lunga lay dead. Arbe twisted and frozen in the space in front of the doorway, his body suffused with rage as tears dripped from his eyes. The Yerrick had been forced to watch his lover die, even as he was unable to move.

Even so, they had won.

This fight at least.

***

"Well, come on then!" Tasmaza said, pacing impatiently in front of Dornalor, who sat in one of the only undamaged chairs. His face was screwed up tight, hands raised as he tapped into the ship's software.

"I'm trying, but they locked me out," Dornalor said.

"Of course they did. That's why we gave you the cracking software," Tasmaza snapped.

"And I'm running it. But I'm not a Hacker, I'm just a Cabin Boy. I don't have any Skills to break in faster," Dornalor said.

"Whatever. Just get us out of here before the fleet returns!" A low moan interrupted the squabbling pair, one filled with anguish. They both glanced over to the sobbing Yerrick, his arms and chest bloody as he clutched the still corpse of his lover.

"Can you get him out of here?" Dornalor said. "It's not exactly helping."

Another moan. Tasmaza looked at the nine-foot-tall Yerrick, distraught with grief, and snorted. "Whatever, just stay focused." He turned away from Dornalor, tapping his armband and switching channels. "Engineering, can you get us in faster?"

"Trying. We've got a bypass for the autopilot module which has us now turned and running as fast as possible from the fleet. We don't have access to the hyperspace module though," Gentri said, the mellow, rumbling voice of the Raider Vanguard filled with pride.

"You heard that, boy?" Tasmaza said. "Just get us into the hyperspace module." Then, he paused before calling out, "Any idea how far the fleet is?"

"Still locked out of the sensor modules. That's low on the chain of things we need."

Dornalor grunted, his eyes flicking over the information before him. As much as he wanted to help the software, he truly had little skill. All he could do was let the entire system run and wait while poking at the edges of the software to see if anything new was revealed. Thus far, outside of damage control, the entire ship was secure.

"Come on, come on…" he whispered.

A second later, the notifications and his neural link flickered to life. Hands raised, Dornalor took control of the ship from the autopilot, adjusting the details of their flight. At the same time as navigation controls returned, so did the plot that offered them a view of the world around.

Caught mid-stride, Tasmaza snarled as the plot appeared in his UI. "Green lumps in the ground… they're way too close."

"Burning photons…" Dornalor snarled. "I'm speeding up. The inertial compensators won't hold, so everyone strap in."

He gave the rest of the group a twenty-second head start even as he triggered the crash pads on the chair. Tasmaza threw himself into his own chair while Arbe ignored everything. Slapping at the chair, trying to get it to trigger, Tasmaza screamed at the kneeling horned alien.

"Get strapped in, damn it, you hairy oaf! You think this is the way Lunga wants you to go out? Squashed because you were too dumb to strap in?"

No matter how he berated the Yerrick, the grieving alien chose to ignore him.

"Afterburners engaging… now!" Dornalor said. His finger twitched just a little to engage the engines, over-revving the entire thing. The increased acceleration pushed them all into their seats, the chairs automatically shifting to provide the seated pair the best compensation for the physical pressure. Arbe at first ignored the increased thrust but eventually tumbled away, still clutching the corpse to himself. He impacted the cockpit wall hard, eliciting a pained grunt from the Raider.

"Hyperspace…?" Tasmaza croaked out.

"Still being hacked…" Dornalor grunted out. "More… importantly… can't lose them. Have to… hide… first."

A long pause, then Tasmaza nodded. "Suggestions?"

The Cabin Boy paused, uncertain. His mind swirled, searching his Skills. He didn't have many. Double Time only worked on him. Fastest Path worked on ships, but it would do nothing for the craft itself. The Right Tool gave him extra inventory space for small shipboard equipment. He had other minor Skills, but none of them directly related to flying. If not for the fact that he had manually learnt how to fly, he would have been the last choice for this position.

"I don't know…" Dornalor said, eyes flicking over the map. His gaze drifted back to where they had started this entire day. "Maybe…"

"Do it!" Tasmaza said, not even caring what it was. The Raider had no better ideas, not right now.

Nodding, Dornalor tapped in commands, swinging their ship wide as he shifted course. They would slice across the trajectory of the chasing merchant fleet, opening them up to fire about seven minutes before they entered the dense asteroid field. Where they could – hopefully – lose their opponents.

Still, seven minutes was a very long time.

"We need more thrust. Can you all do anything about it?" Dornalor said into his comms.

"Maybe!" The voice was short, strained.

"Well, make that maybe a yes. Because otherwise, we're going to so much scrap," Dornalor wheezed, yellow skin turned white as blood was pushed away from his extremities. Clenching his stomach, Dornalor forced himself to push back against the pressure.

Time seemed to pass without end to the group. In a corner of Dornalor's gaze, he noted his health dropping, the continuous acceleration damaging his body. A part of him wondered how it was for the Yerrick, though the continued, muffled moans assured him that the other was alive.

Halfway through the run, as the other merchant vessels kept closing in on them, Tasmaza growled out, "Weapons? We got weapons?"

"I can... open it. Should be... simple," a wheezed answer over the comms.

"No!" Dornalor snapped.

"What?"

"Drain them. Divert all energy to running," the Cabin Boy-turned-captain snapped. "We can't shoot our way out of this."

"Not. What. My. Father. Said," the green Hakarta snarled, but chose not to push the matter.

Dornalor would have basked in the momentary pleasure of being listened to, if not for the fact that the increased power sent to the engines made him grunt again, his breathing coming in even harsher.

Four minutes till contact.

***

"Three. Two. One." Dornalor chanted the words under his breath with each strained breath. But even when the timer went down to zero, nothing happened. Not at first. No rain of fire, no streaking, dense masses accelerated to near the speed of light. Nothing.

Not seeing anything better to do, they continued accelerating away even as the other merchant vessels trained their weapons on them.

"Pirates… buzz… Come in, Pirates." The shipwide communicator buzzed to life, the speaker distorted and tinny.

"How do they have access to that?" Tasmaza said, eyes wide.

"Didn't… hack it… ourselves," Dornalor explained.

"Pirates. I'm assuming you can… me. Stop… and give… up. We will… to you. … promise," the speakers blazed, interrupted by squealing pitches every once in a while.

"Are they idiots?" Tasmaza said, and Dornalor could only shrug.

"We shall bathe in your blood, you fools!" roared Arbe from behind the pair.

"Thirty seconds… slow."

Dornalor snorted, finding the option in damage control. A second later, he killed the shipwide speakers, leaving them in blessed silence. No one was taking their offer. What pirate would trust a merchant with their lives? Certainly none of this ship.

Two seconds after the deadline, the merchant ship rocked. Beam cannons and other weaponry opened fire, forcing Dornalor to bleed a little speed and increase the distance to their destination as he threw the ship into a series of evasive maneuvers.

Fingers danced across space as he coordinated with his own neural link, using the multiple shipwide maneuvering thrusters to throw them into radical trajectories. He relied on instinct and randomness to keep the targeting AIs from locking in on them, all the while eyeballing their shields. Shields that were fast falling.

Every other second, the ship rocked from side to side, Arbe letting out painful grunts as he was slammed around. Once, he even felt the warm splatter of blood as the one corpse they had not dragged out of the cockpit impacted the back of his chair, covering him with lukewarm, sticky liquid.

Not that he had time to worry about any of that as they entered the asteroid field. This was a dense field, with an asteroid every few kilometers. Moving at fractions of light speed, dodging the floating rocky impediments, was going to be a challenge.

"We're in!" Dornalor cried, then fell silent. He dropped their speed a little even as he wove deeper into the asteroid field. His reaction time was insufficient to keep up with the way they were moving, so he had to rely on the ship's AI and correct for it only occasionally. Balancing half-formed pilot instincts with the AIs faster calculations was the best they could do.

Even if, as the screeching impact and warning klaxons of another breach informed them, it was not enough. Dornalor felt the sudden rush of air, then the loud clang as blast doors slammed shut, sealing them off again. A blinking wireframe map showed the gaping hole up the port side of the ship, one dropping out precious cargo.

Behind them, entering the asteroid field at last, the first of the merchant ships. Not all of them, just a half-dozen. After all, taking a heavy, cumbersome merchant ship at full speed into an asteroid field would only entail additional damage to their ship. Damage that would have to be paid for. Only some, the more greedy, the more ambitious, were willing to keep chasing.

Another warning klaxon, another deep shudder. The ship spun suddenly, its impetus and planned trajectory twisted as a thruster was destroyed. Dornalor scrambled, pulling them out of the death spiral, one that threw him against his own crash harness and the Yerrick and the pulverized corpse around the cockpit. Thankfully, cleaning nannites were removing the detritus even as they were mulched.

Blood rushed to his face as they spun in a circle, almost causing Dornalor to faint again. At last, they pulled out of the death spiral, a half-dozen maneuvering thrusters destroyed, the main engine further damaged. Multiple cargo bays were broken, the contents spread across the asteroid belt.

"Two more… stopping," Tasmaza said, reading the plot.

"What for?"

"Cargo… looks like."

Cargo.

Eyes widening, Dornalor punched in a series of commands. The ship stopped dodging for a short period, cargo modules opening or ejecting from the ship like a deadly space flower, discarding metal pollen behind.

"What are you doing! That's our prize," voices from over the communicator, echoed by the Grimsar.

"Exactly!" Dornalor said, his grin savage as he leveled the ship and kept running. "It's the prize. Without it, we're just a heavily damaged ship. Not worth chasing, not with easy cargo floating back there."

True to Dornalor's guess, the ships behind had come to a crawl. Some were even facing off as they closed in on the same floating cargo container, the brief moment of solidarity giving way beneath the siren call of greed.

Even so, they did not stop running. Just because they weren't being chased just yet didn't mean they wouldn't eventually. Best to put some distance between them and their pursuers before they entered hyperspace to make following harder.

***

"Seven thousand Credits, each!?!" Tasmaza shouted, waving his hand around in agitation. "All that for seven thousand Credits?"

"Best I could do," Gentri rumbled. Dornalor, now relegated to being just a Cabin Boy again, even if he had been part of the negotiations, nodded along in agreement to the big Raider Vanguard.

"They're taking us for a star ride!" Tasmaza said. "That ship is easily a few hundred thousand Credits new."

"Exactly. New," Gentri said. "Engines shot. Hyperspace drive damaged. Significant hull damage. Then there's the docking fees and System wipe of the data. We're lucky they bought it at all."

Dornalor made a face, recalling the bumpy ride to Spax. The pirate station had been the closest place that was safe for them all but was well known for being expensive to stay. On the other hand, it was a hub for pirates and rebels, which meant finding a new ship to crew on was simple enough.

And a new ship was definitely what they needed. Seven thousand Credits would not last them long at all, not at the prices that Spax charged.

"Whatever. It's enough for a good drink." Tasmaza threw an arm around Dornalor, grinning. "And we're alive. So, let's drink, carouse and then find another ship to join."

"We?" Dornalor croaked, struggling out of the man's grip.

"You think I'm going to fly out without my lucky charm?" Tasmaza said, yellow eyes wide with mock horror. The laughter from the surviving raiders washed over Dornalor, making passerbys look at the group. Of course, the tough and glowering Raiders stared down any who paid too much attention. "No. You're one of us now, *Captain…*"

Dornalor offered a sheepish smile, even as he basked in the Title. For he had gained one, when they docked.

Title Gained: Pirate Captain of the Great Black Sea (Temporary)
Not every Basic Class manages to captain a vessel. Not every captain manages to bring their (stolen) ship back to port, especially under fire. Those that do have joined a small and elite number of the extremely lucky and extremely gifted. Much will be expected of those with this Title. Make sure to live up to it, Captain!
Effect: Reduced cost in purchasing shipboard Skills. Access to Captain and other related Classes.

Well, perhaps not just a Cabin Boy. Not anymore. And who knows, he might just become a real Captain in truth one day. And what adventures he would have then.

###

The End of *The Great Black Sea*

The First Hours

The world has gone mad. This is Harry Prince, reporting from London, England. I just saw a mischief of rats, each the size of a small cat, attack a group of Londoners. The rats didn't retreat, even after we had slain half of them.

After killing the monsters, we received experience notifications. An older gentleman wielding his cane even managed his first Level Up. The monsters seem to be swarming, emerging from walls, the sewers, or just appearing from nowhere.

In the distance, I can see flames coming from the direction of Westminster Hall. Something large and dark, filled with shadows and too many limbs, rose around there. The sounds of fighting have died off, and no one headed in that direction has returned.

There is no place of safety, not right now. Stay grouped, help one another, and survive.

Truth for Truth

I couldn't sleep. Every time I closed my eyes I heard the screams. It was the smell. Burnt metal, flesh, and something sickly sweet still clung to everything, a constant reminder of the hell we'd just been through.

I'd been with the team that attacked the Human Liberation Front's quasi-military base. Those of us who had survived barely managed to get back to the ship before things had gone from bad to worse. The Humanist, a xenophobic madman who led the brainwashed fanatics, had conquered the Trolley while we were away.

Trolley. I snorted. What a crazy name for the glorified asteroid that we were using as a ship. The name must have come from Caleb, the Teacher. Who else would saddle a spaceship with a crazy name like that?

With the battle done for most, even off-healers like me had gotten back to work. As a Dopamancer and Pharmaceutical Revolutionary, I couldn't heal as well as Penny, who was a specialist. But more people had begged, "Gerri, I need you," than had asked her for her help. It was gratifying, even if many of them stumbled over pronouns.

What my Class lacked in healing, it made up for with versatility. And Penny couldn't help them calm their nerves and sleep.

They'd cleaned me out of pills and Mana before I finally let myself collapse. I'd made the terrible mistake of not saving even a single dose for me.

So, I'd tossed and turned with the other survivors, smashed together on the hard stone floor and metal grates. Some had bedrolls and sleeping bags. Most had uniforms with scorch marks, bullet holes, and crusted blood.

I finally gave up and looked for something to distract me. Easier said than done in a spaceship sardine-packed with the traumatized. Looking around didn't help. The carved walls keeping us alive felt like a prison. And space put even Alcatraz to shame.

None of us would see the Earth again.

I tried to tell myself I couldn't think like that. Didn't help. But we were as likely to make it home as we were to wake up tomorrow and learn that the apocalypse was a bad trip. Given that I'd been drugged when this all started, I'd held on to that hope for at least the first few weeks.

When I'd realized the truth back then, it had nearly broken me. The same hopeless pressure had closed in on me then. And no amount of Levels or Stats had changed the fact that I felt like a crappy submersible that was bottomed out and ready to implode.

I'd never talked about those early days with anyone but Lee, and even he had balked at learning everything.

No. That wasn't true. He'd offered to trade his secrets for mine. We'd called it truth for truth. I'd been the one who'd chickened out and held things back. I could have told him everything, I realized now, and he wouldn't have judged me. That made one of us.

I laughed. A broken thing. And far too loud. I covered my mouth when a string of shushes and swear words hit my ears. Apparently, I wasn't the only one who couldn't sleep on this glorified asteroid they called a ship.

Still, some were managing. So I got out of there to minimize the harm.

***

I didn't realize I was looking for Lee until I was halfway to his room.

Why? To unload my budding nihilism?

Hell no. I wouldn't demoralize the person who was our only hope of surviving. But that didn't mean I couldn't talk to him. I could even offer to accept his trade to learn what he had done to the man he'd admitted he'd made an example of when the System first came.

Did I even want to know? Did I care? Not really. I knew him well enough to have a good idea. What he'd done to the aliens who'd killed his wife had been plastered across the sky for the audience's sick amusement. Somehow, it hadn't broken him.

I could still see him holding his dead wife and kids, screaming impotent rage.

His truth had been stolen from him. Could I give him mine in recompense? Or did I just need an excuse to spill my guts?

Probably.

I stepped carefully through the corridors, past the panels and tangled wires of the ship's shoddily installed AI and went to see if Lee was still awake.

I found him in the cargo hold, cycling through combat drills with brutal efficiency.

Without his shirt, cybernetics on display, his body was a patchwork of flesh and metal. His right arm, his ribs, and half his skull were gleaming steel under the lights. White, not blue—he must have already replaced them. Good. The blue lights the hexapod aliens, the Voloids, used still weirded me out. It was just another reminder that everything had changed.

I leaned against the doorframe and asked, "Do you ever sleep?"

Without turning, he replied, "Not if I can help it." His voice sounded as haunted as I felt.

"We need to talk."

He cracked his neck and turned to face me, his human eye just as cold as his cybernetic one. "What's wrong?"

I huffed. "Not that kind of talk. Why are you so pessimistic?"

Stupid question.

He gave me a flat look, which—I guess—was fair.

"I couldn't sleep, and... I think I might need to vent."

No hesitation. No judgment. Lee just nodded.

I took a deep breath and pulled on my Will—capital W—for the strength to keep going. "I never told you the whole story about the first days. You know, about what really happened."

He stood there, in what I think the military calls parade rest, and he listened. I appreciated that more than I could ever say.

That was how I knew I could go through with it. Hell, I almost told him everything. Even about my fears that we would never live to make it home.

I trusted him.

When I started my story, I kept my thoughts about the display above the gladiator fight, about his family's death, and about his thorough revenge to myself. I didn't want to hurt him more than they already had.

***

"Do you remember the party at MCAD I told you about?" I asked. It had been a while, and we'd both seen enough horror to fill up several lifetimes.

He nodded. "The one your cute blonde roommate dragged you to as a date?"

I scoffed. "I thought it was a date, yeah. Turns out you don't treat people you're interested in like that."

"Fair point," he said, with a little wave to keep me going.

"By the time the System arrived, she'd roofied me with a kiss. And that was on top of the sketchy candy and spiked punch. When I tried to confront her about what she'd done to me, she showed me her stash and I'd grabbed it to prove that I was innocent."

He started to answer, but I cut him off. "I know it was stupid, but I was tripping balls."

His lips twitched, but I ignored him and continued.

"When I woke up, things were crazy. I had System notices but not the normal ones. They were rainbow colored. Twisted. Crazy fonts. Never change your System settings while on drugs."

Lee couldn't help himself. He laughed.

I nearly smiled, but that scene was etched into my mind. "There were bodies. Humans and other things that looked like goblins from Lord of the Rings but a nasty yellow-green. The System called them Krel-Vreth, but I thought of them as snot-goblins.

"I had a dagger in my hand and there was a crossbow on the floor. I was covered in blood and healing cuts and crusted over scratches. But I was alive and everybody else in the room was dead.

"I got partial credit for them all. Even the blonde. That's the notification that I didn't tell you about earlier."

"That might not mean—"

"I know. The System is an asshole. I might have gotten in her way. Distracted her. Who the hell knows what it counts for that. But I also might have been too fucked up to tell the difference between her and them. I want to think the monster slit her throat and I stabbed it trying to protect her. Or for revenge. But I must not believe that because the Shop offered to tell me for a token price. I didn't pay it."

"She drugged you," he said, "without your permission. What happened after that was not your fault."

The guilt and strain eased slightly at his words but then snapped back with a vengeance as I saw her grinning face in my mind's eye. Her throat was traced with blood.

"You did what you had to do," he said more firmly, a mantra that we all knew well by now. On the good days, we even half-believed it.

I rubbed my eyes until they burned.

Lee just waited until I was ready to continue with my story.

"The grunts and crashing in the other room pulled me out of it. If the monsters had been quiet, I probably would have wallowed there too long. But startled as I was, I grabbed the crossbow with no bolts and got ready to run.

"Then I remembered that there were System notices and goblins and tried to loot. I got nothing, but it had tried, so it followed gamer logic.

"It got me thinking and checking things. That's how I learned I had an inventory and my first Dopamancer Skill called Secret Stash. The bag of ecstasy was sitting there in the Skill. I must have stashed it there when I blacked out.

"Anyway. The noises were getting louder so I ran. I tried to read about my second Skill as I did but fucked up like the text was, all I could make out on the move was that it was something called Handoff.

"I ran dumb. Honestly, I'm shocked it didn't get me killed. I changed floors twice and avoided the main areas. Switched directions any time I heard a noise. Look, man. I just panicked." I knew he wouldn't judge me, but I did. And he'd told me about his first day. He'd been so methodical, and I had been a wreck.

If I let myself start spiraling, I wouldn't say another word. "Sorry," I said. "It's hard not to compare how bad I screwed things up to how you handled things."

I tried to cut him off when he answered, but he talked over me. "You were a kid," he said. "I had been a grown-ass man for years. And I had training." He patted his chest. "Coast Guard."

He wasn't wrong, but from what I knew of the man and his childhood, he would have handled it better even then. I must have looked as skeptical as I felt, since he answered my mental train of thought.

"You give me too much credit. I'm still the guy who lost my leg because he was too stupid to get antibiotics, even when his wife told him to."

I couldn't help but smile.

"And that doesn't even count the time I blew myself up to get revenge." He rapped his cybernetic skull to drive home the point.

"Yeah, but that was different," I told him.

"Maybe," he said, "if that had been plan B. But no, blowing myself up with them was plan A from the start."

I couldn't help myself. I cracked up, and it helped. "Okay, you win," I said. "You're more fucked up than I am."

"You're young yet," he answered. "Give it time."

"Watch it," I said, "or I'll find a way to make your cybernetics itch."

He gave me his killer glare, though with a twinkle in his eye. "See. Suicidal already."

"Burning itch," I replied. "Probably with boils." My mind started working on the formula. Something with phosgene oxime and sulfuric acid. I let it go and decided to stop stalling and continued with my story.

"I eventually ran into monsters, but not the goblins I'd been running from."

"Hakarta?" he guessed.

"Worse. Extremists from a local group whose name's not worth remembering. All I knew about them is that they wore bronze crosses and they liked to glare or bump into me when they passed by me in the halls."

"That's worse than the Hakarta?"

"That day they were. Or at least the leader was. Troy, a dark-haired asshole with a crewcut. He'd always had a hard-on for tormenting me. Knocked my books down, spilled a drink on the table by my laptop, that kind of thing. He never pushed it far enough to get expelled.

"That day, he had a gleam in his eye, like he was savoring my fear. He was carrying a brutal jagged hand axe. Maybe from the snot-gobs or the perks. The others with him had some weapons too."

"Damn."

"Tell me about it."

"I think that's supposed to be my line."

I rolled my eyes. "Anyway, there were four of the assholes facing off with me."

***

They had the decency to look uncomfortable but none of them stopped Troy when he came for me, axe raised. One of them even backed him up, a massive hammer hefted in his hands.

I had powers now, but they were useless. Even if I tried to bribe them all with drugs, they'd just take them by force and do whatever they had planned for me regardless.

I turned to run, but I'd been so focused on the douchebags, I hadn't heard the new one coming at me from behind. He was a pale-blond man with cold eyes and broad shoulders. He wore a silver cross necklace, and he had a rifle in his hands.

"Nice," said a voice from behind me. "Good timing, Billy. This thing's trying to get away."

If he were any closer, I might have stabbed him and then run, but he was back far enough to shoot me if I tried it.

The new man raised his gun to cut me off but looked at me askance. "Doesn't seem like one of the monsters to me, Troy."

"Look closer," the predatory one whose name was apparently Troy replied, causing the new one to take a few steps back. His eyes searched me carefully, like a hunter who had a rabbit in his sights.

I tried to shift my stance like they talked about in books, but my imagination didn't line up with my feet. So, I settled on raising my dagger threateningly as I worked to edge past him. "Get out of my way," I said, trying to sound threatening. My cracking voice betrayed me. If this were a game, then I'd just rolled a one.

The stranger's raised eyebrow said that he shared my self-assessment.

"Not very scary for a monster," he said. "And they don't normally warn you before attacking." Then he scowled as he examined me. "Some kind of infection?"

"Yes!" the predatory asshole said, and I could hear that he was smiling now. "I knew you'd understand. This freak has been a stain on the campus all year long."

It stung, though I'd heard worse all my life. But these words were backed with weapons, not just shoves and fists.

Billy frowned. "All year long? It's barely been a day."

Troy laughed. He was closer now, sending a jolt of fear down the back of my neck to the bottom of my spine. "I've been wanting to do this since the first time that I saw this fucking thing."

I readied myself to stab or charge the guy who blocked my path, but he kept stepping backwards, his rifle fixed on me with practiced ease. Whether

I'd attacked or run, he would have been ready. I hesitated—just long enough to catch his sudden shift.

His eyes, bright blue and sharp, were looking past me now. His gun was no longer pointed quite dead center.

It gave me the opening I needed to attack or run, and I decided to take it when he raised his gun to point behind my head.

"That's far enough," he said.

"Or what? There's four of us and only one of you."

"I warned you not to waste your ammunition."

There was a lot of cursing from the group behind me.

"You're gonna shoot us to protect that thing? You'd be dead if not for Cody here and his Consecrated Space."

"And I thank the Lord for every moment. Doesn't mean I'm going to let you hurt, um, what's your name, mi…" He stumbled with what to call me.

That was nothing new. I'd been dealing with it my whole life—people squinting at me as if I came with footnotes. "I'm Gerri," I told him.

"I'm not about to let you hurt my new friend, Gerri. Go fight some of those demon things, or head back to the prayer room."

What followed was the strangest argument I'd ever seen. They quoted lots of weird names and numbers at each other. Short quotes that must have come from the Bible. Then they were arguing about whether or not their God had sent the System.

I was debating moving behind the good guy with the rifle, so I missed what Troy had said. But I heard the blond's response. "But you're not the one with ammunition, so you need to back the fuck up now."

I stepped around Billy and turned to face the others. From behind him, I was in position to spot the living loogies as they crossed into the hall behind the jerks. There were six of them.

"Behind you," Billy warned him.

"As if I'm dumb enough to fall for that."

But one of his friends had turned to look. "Demons," he muttered, yanking on the other man's arm to force him to pay attention.

Troy shook off his hand and whipped around.

I very nearly stabbed him in the back. If I'd been any closer, I might have followed through.

"What are we gonna do?" one of the thugs asked. "They're between us and the prayer room, and we're all out of bullets."

"He's got some," Troy answered. "He can shoot them while we all try to escape."

"There's six of them and only one of me," Billy answered. "If you run, I'm taking off the other way. Stand your ground and I'll back you all up."

A guttural, rasping grunt came from behind the monsters as a pair of giant warthogs shuffled into view.

"New plan," Billy said. "We all run."

That, of course, was when the original group of snot-goblins, the ones who'd been chasing me earlier, finally caught up to us from behind.

***

"Murphy's Law," Lee said and handed me a shot of yellow booze.

"Yeah, fuck that guy."

"I'd warn you to be careful, but it wouldn't help."

I took the shot and tried not to wince at the vile taste. "Is this the part where I'm supposed to call it smooth?"

Lee raised his eyebrow, but the corner of his lip twitched so I took it as a win.

He nodded again, with the open-handed wave that said go on.

***

"Shit," Billy said. "Charge. I'll clear a path. If we—"

He cut off as Troy fell to his knees and raised his hands above his head. The one called Cody followed suit, but he held his hands in front of him and closed his eyes. Probably, the pathetic jerk was praying.

The others had more sense and started forward. But without the first two, I didn't think we had a chance.

Bang. Bang. Bang. Each of the shots landed, one of them near the center of a forehead. I knew nothing about guns, but I assumed that was impressive with a rifle. Some System thing, or he was just that good.

With no other options, I took a tentative step forward.

I was terrified, but I was also pissed.

"You cowards," I snapped at the two who had not joined the fight.

They flinched.

Maybe I could shame them. "Fine, I'm fighting. You can both die there on your knees."

Only Troy responded. He looked up at me, eyes flat and jaw clenched. He nodded once and planted one hand on the floor. Shifting his weight, he dragged his left foot underneath himself.

One of the men was better than nothing. I wrote off his minions and charged like in the movies.

Instead of glory, I got a face full of the floor.

Pain shot through my hands, forehead, and knee as I skidded across stone. For a second, everything tilted sideways, and I just lay there, stunned.

Then heat flared in my ankle, and I just knew that fucker tripped me. I could picture him kneeling there with that sneer plastered on his face. Then he laughed as one of the boars barreled toward me, and it killed any last shadow of a doubt of what he'd done.

I nearly managed to roll aside, but a tusk slammed into my left leg. I expected agony but got crushing pressure instead. Then something tore with a wet *pop*. Heat poured down my thigh like I'd dumped hot coffee on myself.

I was terrified that there was still no pain.

Three more shots cracked out, red blooming behind the boar's ribs as it bucked, lurching as it tried to shake me loose. Finally, it slowed as the damage from the gunshots added up.

Then the agony caught up to me, sharp at first, then all-consuming. I screamed through clenched teeth as I tried to shove the beast away and failed utterly.

Desperate, I stabbed it. Again and again. I only stopped when green letters on a silver background said I got XP.

By the time the others swarmed us, the fight was all but over. There were too many of them to resist. They surrounded us and bound our wrists with leather cords.

Looking around, I saw that Cody had stopped praying. And breathing. He didn't need his faith anymore. He had his answer. Eyes wide and glassy, he was sprawled and broken on the filthy floor.

The surviving hog-beast rooted and sniffed his ruined corpse.

Snot-gobs dragged the rest of us down the long hall. The System flashed a warning in my field of vision. My purple Health triangle was turning orange, which must have been a bad thing with how much blood I was losing from my leg.

It helped distract me from the crunching sounds we left behind.

Everything dimmed, and I faded in and out of consciousness. Honestly, I thought that I was dead. But even at level three, the System had its hooks in me, dragging me back to make me suffer more. That was when the pain caught up, like a drumstick striking a cymbal every time the goblin yanked me past debris.

The halls of the University were trashed. The oddest things branded themselves onto my mind. A mural of a golden sunset vista, cracked and streaked with blood. A half-melted vending machine turned on its side. The crazy thought that I could really use a cookie and some juice.

Then the smell hit me, and I regretted thinking about food. Burnt grease and sweet, rancid meat that smelled like pork.

They'd turned the cafeteria into some kind of primal camp with bonfires and a bunch of leather-wrapped bone huts.

Before long, we were shackled with long lengths of blackened iron. The other end was bolted to the cauldron I was desperately trying not to think about. It bubbled over with something thick, foul, and brown.

The snot-gobs shrieked and barked in a language like a mix of phlegm and broken glass. Two of them fought over a half-gnawed bone like feral dogs.

The guards were serious motherfuckers. Their dark eyes were sharp, and they were all armed to the teeth.

Billy was somehow calm, breathing shallow, watching everything around us with a calculating gaze. The only hint he was worried was his left hand clenched around his silver cross.

Troy was slumped and sobbing on the floor. Even his remaining thugs looked down at him with scorn.

I followed Billy's lead, though a part of me wanted to act more like Troy. This was when I should have dropped the two unspent points I didn't realize I had into Perception—but I'd screwed up my System prompts too much for me to know. Even without it, I'd always had a clever eye for details.

The guards watched each other and the other goblins more than us. Two of the guards—one on either side of the room—had well-worn keychains looped onto their belts.

One of the monsters slapped me hard enough to sting but not to drop my Health. I turned to glare, but it shoved something solid into my hand. I looked down and saw a curved bone ladle. The creature barked something and made a twisting gesture. I didn't understand the words, but the meaning was clear.

This bastard wanted me to stir the "soup."

The heat rolled off the cauldron, soaking my clothes and clinging to my skin. The stench it carried with it made me gag. I stared at the ladle, trying not to think about what the meat chunks used to be.

I filled the bowls. What the hell else was I supposed to do?

The monsters jostled and fought for who'd be first in line. The guards were right; this whole place was a powder keg.

Could I use that somehow? Dump the soup? It would work but then they'd eat my ass instead. Throw it at them? No. They'd just kill me and find somebody else.

I was beaten, and I had nothing left to fight them with but bowls of boiling soup. They'd taken my dagger and my useless crossbow with no bolts. I had nothing. Not even my pride. Just an insulting Class and worthless fucking powers.

I ladled out another bowl of soup with a trembling hand. Acid burned inside my gut like I might puke. I forced myself to breathe and think things through.

Were my Skills still worthless, now that things had changed? *What if I dose these psycho-shits with ecstasy?*

As if he could read my thoughts, the nearest of the sharp-eyed guards turned and stared at me.

My breath caught in my throat.

Had he spotted my eureka moment? Or had he just realized I'd stopped serving food?

Apparently, it was the latter, because he went back to watching the others once I resumed doing my job.

Relief hit me like a gut-punch, and I nearly dropped the ladle.

The next snot-goblins snarled at me, impatient for a big bowl of my… *No. No! NO! Don't ever think about it.*

With willpower I didn't know I had, I forced myself to focus on the plan. Using my second Skill with the first was a no-brainer. I pulled from my Secret Stash and used Handoff to dose the bowls 'til I ran out of Mana.

Was this what they called rock bottom? Drugging store-brand trash mobs with party drugs?

***

I shook my head to clear it. Then, to stall, I sent my Skill's info to Lee.

Handoff

Allows the Dopamancer to secretly pass drugs without detection. Also allows for the exchange of currency. Functions as a Perception-clouding debuff to observers.

Cost: 5 Mana per use.

"Nice," he said. "That's the Skill you used to save my ass when you passed me a pill."

"It was," I said, surprised that he'd remembered. Then again, it was tactically useful, so I should have known he would. The man probably had it on a chart or spreadsheet from one of his Guerilla Tactician Skills.

***

My plan was risky. Would they notice the tablets or the taste? Even if it worked, did we really have a chance? Maybe. Maybe not. But I had no better options, so I went for it with fingers crossed and bated breath.

It backfired. Sort of.

They devoured the food without noticing the drugs. But when it did finally affect them, it calmed the creatures down and blissed them out. Great, now I had improved their damned morale.

They adored the soup and the aftereffects, though they didn't last that long. I didn't understand it at the time, but even at low levels, their System Constitutions were heavily resistant to the old Earth drugs.

Ironically, that flaw in my plan is the thing that saved my ass. First piece of good luck I had that day.

Apparently, the snot-goblins were fans of getting high. And they all wanted more. Demanded it. They clawed and shoved their way back toward the front.

The others must have realized that meant the soup was really good. They certainly weren't about to let that go. When the shoving turned into biting and stabbing, the guards finally got involved. I tried not to stare as the sharp-eyed one from earlier with the keys was moving toward us.

The ringleader, Troy, got jostled in the frenzy. He closed ranks with me and Billy to get safe, turning his back on me, cowering in a half-crouched pose, ready to bolt. He must have forgotten he was chained.

When the guard got close enough to pull the snot-gobs in line apart, I kicked Troy in the ass to crash him into the thing at speed.

He flailed as the guard's claws tore into him. Others around him joined in on the fun.

I could feel Billy judging me.

Troy screamed as they devoured him alive.

I couldn't look away, though the steam scalded my eyes.

In my books, they always say nobody deserves this. It wasn't true. He deserved to die in pain.

But the System was the System, and the screams went on too long.

It gave me a chance to lift the goblin's keys, but my hands wouldn't obey me once I did. My fingers fumbled at the grimy ring too long and I kept swallowing to force down acidic bile.

Billy had to take away the keys to set us free. If I'd been alone, I might have just stood there and died.

Once Billy and I were free, he let loose the others he could reach. Then he threw the keys to another group across the room.

By then I'd pulled myself together and I helped some of the others to their feet.

His better nature had taken him too long. The guard I'd robbed glared at us with rat-black eyes and stopped his gruesome feast to kill us all.

Our only hope was that the clusterfuck of goblins in his way would slow him down while we all ran.

Billy had other ideas. He snagged an axe from one of the injured gobs. "Get out," he said. "I'll try to buy you time."

Everyone took off except for me.

"Fuck that hero shit," I said. "We've gotta go."

The guard must not have liked that plan, because he shrieked in rage and drew a cruel, curved sword.

The other monsters took the hint and cleared the way.

"Run," I screamed, but Billy stood his ground and used his axe to block the first swing of the goblin's sword.

The difference in their skill was obvious and the blond man had no chance. The firm conviction in his expression said he knew that, too.

I wanted to run. Needed to. But this idiot had saved my life.

I need a weapon.

Looking around, I saw that the guard had a sheathed dagger on his belt. It was like the one I'd had before, but with a blood-red gem embedded in the hilt.

I reached for it, but the thing was strapped down tight.

It distracted the goblin, though, and Billy took the chance to slash him in the chest.

The creature hissed in rage and glared at him.

It gave me an opening, and I jabbed the monster's pitch-black eyes with both my thumbs.

It gave Billy a chance to strike again.

Half-blinded, the goblin struggled to hold him off.

I should have run then and dragged Billy with me. But I wanted that dagger. I'd felt delusionally safer with one in my hand. Irrational, but I felt the way I felt.

Since the goblin was distracted, I loosened the strap and pulled the dagger free.

It cost me a claw slash across my face.

That sharp pain was the last straw. Something inside me snapped. Fury over what they'd done to all of us exploded. I stepped forward, hauled back, and stabbed the goblin in his chest with all my strength.

Flesh burned as the dagger pierced his armor, then his flesh. The creature screamed.

The weapon warmed and tingled in my hand.

"Holy shit! This thing must be enchanted!"

From the area around us, the frantic noises hushed. Dozens of dark eyes turned to glare at me. No, not me. It. The dagger. They wanted it.

I felt like Frodo with the Ringwraiths circling me.

They wanted the weapon more than they wanted to eat me. Fuck my precious. They could have the hot potato. I hurled it over the guard and toward the largest cluster.

They all turned and rushed to dogpile the thing.

"Run or die!" Billy said, as if he wasn't the one who'd kept us here.

I'd correct him later if we lived.

I ran.

This time, he followed.

***

"Billy survived?" Lee asked, but didn't wait for me to answer. "Damn. I totally thought he was gonna die."

"So did he," I said, "but fuck that noise."

"Dying really was an awful plan. But so was yours."

I flinched, then laughed. The asshole wasn't wrong.

"I thought so, too, but that was a mistake. I wouldn't have made it out of town alive if not for him. He even made his people take me in and helped power level me through those brutal first few weeks."

"You make it sound like a sacrifice for them, but Skills like yours were priceless in those days. Even a half-assed healer was worth their weight in gold."

I smiled as I had a light bulb moment. "It's wild. I've spent years ashamed of the Class the System gave me, but from the first day, it's the thing that saved my life. And others too."

He nodded.

Then the rest of what he had said sank in and I smacked him hard. "Did you just call me a half-assed healer, jerk?"

"Yes," he said without a hint of hesitation. "But that was then. Now you're a half-assed healer and a whole-assed combat caster."

I huffed but I was smiling when I did.

He set his hand on mine, eyes sober and firm when he said, "Thank you for the story, and the trust. I know it's hard to talk about times like those."

I didn't pull away and said, "And thanks for listening and for not judging me."

"I judge everyone," he replied, and he looked haunted. "But I like you and I think you did your best. I'm glad you made it and I'm happy that you're here."

I paused and looked away. I hadn't had a friend like this in years. Maybe never, if I was being honest with myself. My voice cracked with emotion as I spoke. "You too," I finally admitted, truth for truth.

The End of *Truth for Truth*

The System Quest

This is Harry Prince, reporting from London, England, during the first day of the System Apocalypse.

I am receiving reports—and have experienced it myself—that a 'Quest' is being delivered to individuals via the pervasive blue notifications in our mind. Entitled 'the System Quest,' it comes to everyone who questions what the System is, what is controlling all these status screens, experience, and loot items we are receiving. What caused the destruction of all electronics and the spawning of the monstrous creatures that have slain so many.

Too many. The streets are clogged with bodies, many of them half-eaten and rapidly decaying.

This Quest can be ignored, but it will repeat itself till accepted. I do not know if this is an act of mockery or an automated provision in this 'System,' but the Quest is nothing that anyone can afford time to delve into. Not during the collapse of human civilization as we know it.

Whatever the case, it seems to be an intentional act of ridicule, an act of one who has an utter lack of empathy. One that will have a cost, one day.

However, the question still stands. What is the System, and why has it come to Earth?

The First Day

This is Harry Prince, reporting from London, England. I do not know who is hearing this, if it is helping anyone. I speak to the void and hope, somewhere, somehow, it reaches those who need it. The last day has been the most tumultuous period in human history, and it is not over. Not for the year promised by the Quest, maybe not ever.

We all received the notification this morning. Sixty percent of humanity has fallen to waves of monsters and further tragedy at the hands of other humans. Yes, humanity. I saw the worst in people today. Those standing guard over corner stores and other essential services, hoarding food and water and weapons.

I also saw the best. A man sacrificing himself to a goblin pack so that a bus full of school children could escape into a sanctified church, a 'safe zone.' An antique store owner who was handing out the various implements of war that his shops contained, old swords, an ornate battleaxe, and various canes and other implements of improvised death, without a care.

Most of all, I have seen aliens. Striding down the streets, casting around cobblestone pathways. Some are friends, saving humanity where they can. Others, so many others, are enemies, killing our people indiscriminately.

Though they might walk like gods, they fall like men. To monsters. To groups of enraged humans.

This is Harry Prince, reporting from London, England, a day after the System Apocalypse. Work together, stay grouped, and survive.

We will have our revenge.

Three Months In

This is Harry Prince, reporting from London, England. It has been three months since the day the world ended. Starvation, England's greatest worry during an apocalypse, has failed to rear its head. Monsters are edible, and they are our salvation. In more ways than one.

We have picked at their corpses, butchered their bodies for our sustenance, and looted their remains for the System's gifts. This loot can be used by our crafters, our non-combat personnel, to make weapons. Weapons that are more effective than the scarce guns of our police force and the tanks of our army.

The world is changing. Safe Zones are expanding as humanity locates Shops and wields their alien powers to sustain our communities. We learn to carve swords out of bones, tear down our machines, and rebuild them to work with the System. We buy new weapons from the aliens who inflicted this on us, feeding them the loot and Credits we gain in a vicious cycle of growth.

Most of all, we grow stronger. Our Levels rise, and even the most pacific grows vicious.

We have to, for the monsters grow stronger each day and they never stop spawning. New monster lairs are everywhere, and dungeons are rising when we fail to clear them. Humanity dies in the dozens.
But we survive. Somehow.

Daily Jobs, Coffee and An Awfully Big Adventure

Wendy rolled out of bed with a groan, glancing balefully at the flashing notification window that told her she was supposed to be asleep. Lack of sleep, exhaustion, low stamina – the bars all ran through the window before she dismissed it with a flick of her hand.

As she put her feet on the ground, she ran her hand through her ratty brown hair, catching on knots as she did so. She tugged on her nightdress, pulling it down across her chubby – *nicely padded* – body while she shuffled to the bathroom.

"Why couldn't they fix my hair and my insomnia? They got the wrinkles and the eyes," Wendy whined once more, her thick Devonshire accent coming through.

In answer, a small glowing bat flew down, flashing through a variety of colors and angular shapes. Wendy smiled, somehow understanding the spirit's words.

"No, I don't want to find out about the System. I studied enough about that Quest," Wendy muttered. "I've got better things to do. Like… Coffee!" The last word was uttered with a fierce exertion of will as she made it a command.

Another flash of light, this time brilliant green, lit up the small, cluttered bedroom. Clothing, scavenged from multiple houses, worn and tossed aside lay scattered throughout the room. Multiple smaller oblong boxes were attached to the ceiling and walls, reinforcing the apartment and her safe room. She still didn't have enough money to make the room a Safe Zone so she made do. Luckily, her friends were very good at helping her make do.

The little flashing blonde pixie dressed in green that appeared would be a trademark infringement if it mattered these days. It buzzed for a second then flew out the door to the kitchen where it started the process of brewing Wendy her midmorning java. Meanwhile, Wendy started casting, using her Skill to pull her friends from the nether.

"Let's see, let's see. Boom and Zoom, you've got the room. Curly, breakfast. None of that fancy stuff. I want bacon, eggs, and mushrooms. A good English breakfast." She ignored the grumpy buzzing as the summoned fairies got to work. "Nibs, outfit for the day. It'll be a busy day."

Muttering commands, more and more summons appeared. When she was done, Wendy was down to less than a quarter of her mana, but her friends were all buzzing around, cleaning and sorting her bedroom. By the time she was done with her shower, they had set right the apartment, making it sparkling fresh and leaving her coffee and breakfast for her.

Grinning wide, Wendy bobbed her head in thanks to her friends before she dismissed them once more. Better to do it now, before they disappeared of their own volition. After all, she regained a little bit of her mana this way.

"Breakfast. Then, I'll deal with these emails. I wish there was a fairy for that."

Musing about how she could create an email fairy, Wendy dug into her meal.

***

Outside, in the crisp, refreshing morning air of Devonshire, Wendy drew a deep breath. Already, she'd summoned a host of her friends before sending them out to scout for monsters. The guards had it mostly in hand really, but it never hurt to be cautious. Even the ones that wandered in past the old Roman walls that ringed the inner city of Exeter were swiftly taken care of.

But she hadn't survived the first nine months of the apocalypse by being careless.

In fact, Wendy wasn't exactly sure how she'd survived at all. Oh, she could relate everything she'd gone through, every second of it. Just like any of the other survivors. But why her, compared to the rest of humanity. Perhaps it was her naturally high luck stat. Perhaps it was her ability to use her friends in different ways.

It didn't really matter, because much as she wished it was different, it wasn't. They had managed to fight off enough of the monsters, patched together enough of civilization to reclaim Exeter. Not without suffering quite a few losses, especially among the elderly that made up the majority of the citizens. But there'd been a surprising number of old soldiers who'd taken to the System and come out swinging.

Shaking her head, Wendy continued her walk, eyeing the white-painted houses, the shops that made up the new Exeter. Gone were the old, single or double story scattering of neighborhood commercial districts. Instead, some gleamed with metal reinforced doors, reclaimed by the occasional adventurous entrepreneur. Others were left broken, windows shattered, doors cracked, waiting for their new owners.

Wendy hoped they would be more reclaimed soon. It'd make the neighborhood safer. But the center of Exeter was where the rebuilding was concentrated. She was considered weird for staying on the outskirts, away from others. But she liked her apartment and she had plans for the complex when she'd earned enough Credits.

Marveling at the robust growth of the trees, running her fingers along crisp bark, Wendy continued her saunter as the sun rose. Nine months on, the morning sun was getting late in its autumn ascent. Soon enough, winter would be here in full force. She hoped she'd have enough Credits by then, because if not, she'd have to move into town. She didn't fancy sleeping in the cold. Not at all.

Finally reaching the church grounds, Wendy looked up at the soaring Exeter Cathedral. The religious building sparkled, the worn statues of saints in the front built in the old Baroque style that had now been upgraded by the System. Now they looked just as new. And if you watched really closely, you'd notice how all the saints with their swords and the gargoyles at the top slowly shifted.

It really did bring a new meaning to the words - God is watching over you.

Pushing past the large, wooden entrance doors, Wendy stepped into the Cathedral. She paused for a second, crossing herself in respect, before she entered further. The pews within were gone, the seating replaced by cots for those Artisans and Adventurers who couldn't afford a better place to stay. Nuns moved around quietly, watching over the thrashing bodies, laying soothing hands on a few that needed it, radiating Auras of peace and serenity. The big, wooden and silver organ stood grandiosely in the back, out of place but beautiful still. Once a week, the bishop continued to hold services, and the organ would play. It brought comfort, a sense of stability to the parishioners.

"Still can't sleep?" The words jolted Wendy back into her body. She turned, to regard the speaker. Dressed in military fatigues, bright red hair in curls and a futuristic mace resting on his knees, Carl smiled back.

"No. You think they'd mind…?" she said. She knew he fancied her. But she just didn't have time. Even if the desire was there. Carl was a fetching bloke. Especially since he upgraded his Strength and started wearing those sleeveless vests.

"Nah. Just keep your lads quiet."

"Always." Smirking, Wendy moved away from the entrance, putting her back to the column like Carl before she began her summons.

"First Twin. Second Twin. Dirty bedding. Tubs, Nibs, scraps. Boom and Zoom, the organ. Quietly." Wendy started summoning, tiny little fairies appearing as their names were called, bobbing quickly before rushing to do their jobs. Unlike in her room, they all acknowledged her unspoken desire and kept their lights dimmed as they got to work.

In a few minutes, her Mana was depleted and Wendy turned to Carl. "So? How's the hoarding going?"

"It's not hoarding. I tell you, toilet paper is gold. Soon enough, they'll all be coming to me." Carl said, crossing his arms. "I got it all. Two ply, three ply. The Shop might get you some, but not in good quality, not at a good price. Somehow, they still haven't gotten it right yet. Not without teleporting it from somewhere else on Earth."

Wendy just smiled, shaking her head. For all the four months she'd known Carl, he'd had a scheme. A way of making it big. They all failed, of course. But since his schemes never hurt anyone, she and the Father never made a fuss. Having Carl around kept them all safer too as one of the few Combat Classers who would stay to guard the Cathedral.

"Less people here today," she said, eyeing the beds.

"Less need. They opened up another apartment block."

She frowned, hating the sound of that. If she didn't get a move on, her own plans were going to get scuppered. Maybe...

Biting her lip, Wendy accessed the settlement's Quest board. That was a relatively new addition that allowed anyone, anywhere in the settlement to access it without being at a settlement stone. It made finding jobs a lot easier. Unfortunately, it also meant that there was a lot more competition these days.

Good thing, she was very good at what she did.

***

An hour later, the Cathedral was clean and shiny. Everything from the windows to the insides of the organ were buffed and cleaned. Waste food, torn bandages, even holes in clothing had been patched up. The moment she completed her daily task, System acknowledged her Quest completion and deposited the funds from the Cathedral's account into hers. Bobbing thanks to Carl, Wendy hurried off, already having taken on another two assignments. There were another half-dozen that she could do on the board. If she managed to get all of them, maybe she would finally have enough to buy her own place.

Problem was, she was limited to only two additional Quests beyond her usual standing orders. So she had to hurry, if she wanted to get them all.

The first Quest was a tanning job. No one wanted to do that. Not even the tanners really, though obviously, their Skills made it easier for them. But, there were only three System tanners in the entire city. And, all but one of them had Leveled up such that they no longer did the low-Level monsters jobs. That left a gap in the market. One that Wendy and her summons were more than happy to fill.

As she hurried along, Wendy checked her Skill once more, eyeing her experience bar at the same time.

Elemental Summons (Level 4)

Summon an elemental to act as your familiar. Summoned elementals will follow all orders, for the duration of their summons.
Effect: Summon one lesser elemental.

Mana Cost: 60 per summon
Duration: 11.2 minutes

Summoner's Horde (Level 3)

Quantity over quality is this summoner's motto. Rather than a single, powerful summon, this summoner has split her strength of the summons into multiple, smaller creatures. Mana regeneration is reduced by fifteen permanently.
Effect: Summoner may split each summon instance into three, equal or lesser summons. Strength of individual summons is decreased by six times.

Wendy sighed. She was so close to another Level and a new Class Skill. If she increased her Elemental Summons ability, she increased the strength and size of her summons. Right now, she was forced to make fewer summons, just because they weren't strong enough to do anything by themselves if she split them further. On the other hand, being able to split her horde allowed her to tackle more jobs with a wider variety. Some jobs just needed a lot of hands.

Of course, completing these Quests gave her only a modicum of experience. As much as she had cursed her Class, which she did regularly, what she had was a Combat Class. She gained experience by killing monsters. Or at least, she should have.

It was the perfect method, if you ignored the screaming pain, blood and terror that fighting entailed.

Wendy bit her lip again and did the math as she started summoning her friends the moment she arrived at the former shopping mall now turned tanning center. While she thought and ordered her sprites around, she did the math. Her Leveling had slowed down to a crawl ever since she breached her last Level.

Maybe, if she just ran one kill and retrieve Quest… Get some food for the settlement. That was always in demand. Those mutated and vicious timber wolves that had appeared. They gave a lot of experience.

"What do you think, lads?" Wendy called out to her sprites, who bobbed and weaved as they scrubbed down hides, removing fur, fat, then tissue. As they dumped cleaned furs in the urine baths and then worked them out. To treat the hides, they'd had to go old school when they realized that normal chemicals just didn't work. Not against monster hides. But processing via System methods, using System processed urine, that still worked.

Well. At least it wasn't brains.

"Well?"

Silence greeted Wendy's words. As much as she enjoyed her work, she sometimes wished that she had some company. Her lads were just not very talkative.

Two hours later, she hurried out of the tanning center, making a face as she noticed that some of the other early risers had already started snatching up Quests. Wendy's next job was an easy one. A simple house cleaning job for an Adventurer party. And then afterwards, she was off to the automotive center. Out of the way but she was often the only person on duty. With her team, she could buff and fix the vehicle bodies faster than anyone else.

She hurried, only pausing long enough to send one of her fairies to pick up a second breakfast. A second fairy accompanied it to pick up a cup of coffee. Summoning and controlling her babies was hard work.

And coffee was a necessity.

***

Midday found her seated outside the Cathedral greens, enjoying the weather. You couldn't even notice where the ghouls had risen up anymore. They cleaned out all the old bodies after the last time. A good thing too. No one wanted that particularly horrid reminder.

"Company?" Carl called out to Wendy as he plopped down beside her.

"I think you just invited yourself," she said.

He flashed her a wide grin but also offered her a curry as a peace offering.

"Which shop?"

"Kumar's, off Musgrave," Carl replied.

"Is it meat?"

"Didn't ask." When she narrowed her eyes, Carl started pulling back the plastic container. "It's fine. I'll eat it."

"Give it here, you plonker." Wendy snapped at him, snatching the container back. She made her fork appear in her hands from her inventory and dove in. After the first few mouthfuls she let out an appreciative grunt.

"So, what do you think?" she asked when she finished her meal.

"The meat?" Carl said. When she nodded, he rubbed at his chin. "Dear, I think."

"Me too." Wendy fell silent, thinking of the wolves.

"Penny for your thoughts." Carl prodded. Literally, his fork digging into her knee.

Wendy yelped, slapped at his hands, and then turned to look around carefully. It wasn't as though she was worried about someone overhearing what she had to say. She wasn't doing anything illegal. But occasionally scanning the green, taking in the few trees, other empty buildings around, the lounging artisans who were taking a break from their own grind. All of it had become routine.

"Just thinking about the wolves." Wendy missed the flash of concern in Carl's eyes when she mentioned the monsters. She was too busy tracing on the ground with the end of her fork. "I just need a couple thousand more experience. A good hunt and the Quest completion and I'll get my level. Then I'll have enough money. Or I will soon enough."

Carl frowned. "You know it's not safe to go alone right now."

She shrugged. "They all have teams now, even my old group. And no one wants a scaredy-cat elemental summoner."

"You're not…" Wendy's frown made him Stop. "So, you intend to go alone."

"Probably. After my next job," she said. She glanced at the time and then stood up, brushing her hands down and making the plastic container disappear into her storage. "Which I'm late for, if I don't leave now." Without waiting for him to reply, she hurried off, leaving the man to finish his own food alone.

***

Hunting was strange. Other people had visions of tramping through woods, crossing rivers and pushing through thick fog banks. But the reality was, for most of the Adventurers, hunting happened in the suburbs. In the abandoned residential buildings and neighborhoods that ringed the city proper. Ever since humanity had lost 90% of its population, they had shrunk back into the heart of their cities. Mother nature and the System had taken over with a vengeance everywhere else.

Wendy spied a building, or what used to be a building ahead of her with trepidation. It looked like it had collapsed upon itself, the vines that had grown around the building pulling the walls down, sending the roof crashing down. And then the vines had grown over the roof remnants, burying the materials beneath it.

Of course, normal vegetation wasn't that much of a concern. Except these vines had also just eaten one of her summons. Snatched it right out of the air.

Wendy bit her lip, debating between summoning something larger and potentially destroying the monster vine or leaving it alone. The experience might be good but she'd not heard of this monster. And monsters, new monsters, always had nasty surprises in store. Maybe the grasping vines were just the start of it. Maybe it had something else like poisonous spores that it kept in secret.

After a moment more deliberation, Wendy shook her head and hurried away. As much as she wanted the experience, her goal were the timber wolves. And one of her babies had found tracks.

She hurried down the broken paved streets, moving in the center of the road so that she could have more time to react if something rose from the buildings. Wendy kept her senses peeled for her babies. She kind of wished she'd splurged on a map Skill, but it just hadn't seemed important at the time. She could feel all her babies, sense what they sensed, see what they saw if she concentrated. It was as good as a map skill.

Sort of.

Not really. But she told herself that. At least for this expedition. She continued to hurry along; then frowned at a little gray blip, a sense of wrongness that Nibs sent to her. Nibs was at her back, guarding her from potential backstabs. And thus far, that gray blip kept on following her. She couldn't tell what it was, not at all.

It could be a monster. A scavenger. One of the untransformed wild dogs or cats. Or another human, hoping to scavenge from her kills.

No way to know.

So for now, she'd ignore it.

And keep one of her children watching.

A quarter of an hour hike later, Wendy was crouched next to her Sprite, staring down at a family-sized piece of poo. She wrinkled her nose, smelling the fragrant deposit, watching as the flies landed and rummaged around their treasure.

To what would have shocked her prim and proper mother's dismay, over the past nine months, Wendy had gained a little tracking knowledge. In particular, she could tell from the consistency and hardness of the poo that it had been a recent deposit. Not dry enough or hard enough in the autumn chill to be more than a few hours old. No, this was deposited within the last half hour. That meant the pack was around here.

All she had to do was find them.

"Boom. Zoom." Wendy chanted the names, summoning her friends to her. Just as she was about to give orders, she felt the shiver of disquiet from one of her children. She tilted her head to the side and froze.

A quick switch of viewpoint, and then again, and again. Sweat began pouring down her back. She was surrounded, the wolves somehow having crept past the initial line of her children. They'd turn her from predator to prey, surrounding her.

There were four of them, and they were a lot smarter than she had thought.

"Defense." Wendy whispered her command, putting the two muscular sprites on guard duty. Next, mental summons brought half her sprites zooming back from their scouting positions. She left the ones who had view of the timber wolves where they were, adjusted the positioning of a few more.

All she could do now was summon another two to her and she should be out of Mana. A slight twitch of her hands as the wolves crept closer brought a beam pistol into her hand. It wasn't perfect, but at least she still had her shield bracelet.

As one of the timber wolves slunk out from the shadows from directly behind her, she whispered the command to her babies, "Stun and run."

Tootles swooped down, spiraling directly into the timberwolves back. The shoulder check by a four-inch sprite filled with glitter sent the wolf sprawling as it got ready to jump. Wendy ignored that byplay and the other strafing runs by her sprites as she opened fire on the first wolf to show its face to her.

The laser beam clipped the monster as it jumped aside, leaving a burning trail across its reinforced, metallic fur. The wolf was half again the size of a unmutated creature, yet it still carried the same litheness, the same agility of movement. And, just as worryingly, its level was way too high.

Timberwolf (Level 16)
HP: 218/274

No time to waste, Wendy ran, firing her pistol when she had a clear line of sight. The beam pistol only had just over twenty shots though, so she had to be careful. Reloading was likely going to be a problem. She cursed, wondering why she thought she could do this. She groaned, even as she dashed down the suburban street, rowhouses on both sides, dark and many of them trashed. She briefly considered ducking into one of the houses, using it as shelter.

But you never knew what were in the houses. She could just as easily stumble onto something even worse than the timber wolves.

Instead, she ran. If she could injure them, maybe even kill them, maybe they'd break away. And so, while she snapped off her shots, and blocked snarling lunges with the shield bracer on her left arm, she tried to focus her returned children's attention on a singular monster.

In truth, without her children buzzing in, slamming into the wolves, setting their fur on fire, she would have been caught already. Careful attacks were thrown off, nips at her heels blinded by showers of sparkles, and occasionally, one of her children would be snapped out of the air.

It hurt, in a way, to see her children die. It was different than being dismissed. She hated seeing them disappear, banished back home. It was what made being a summoner horrible. Because even though she knew they were just balls of energy, Mana given form, she still cared about them.

It was why she'd named them.

She ran, Stamina dropping with each footstep. Of course she'd increased her Constitution. No one who survived the apocalypse kept it at the base level. But she was a mage; she dumped most of her points into Intelligence and Willpower. And, she had to admit, maybe a point or two into Charisma. Vanity was probably going to get her killed today.

An unseen crack on the ground caught her foot. She stumbled, falling to the ground. Her gun jarred out of her hand and skipped ahead of her. The wordless cry of one of her children made her spin around, hunkering beneath the shield bracer as the wolf landed on top of her. Drool fell from its mouth, splattering her through the shield. She twisted and turned, attempting to throw the monster off.

She was going to die. But Wendy refused to do so without a fight. She pushed back, tense muscles straining against the monster, trying to draw breath to call upon her last summons.

Then, the monster was off. Rolling across the ground.

Surprised, she took the hand that reached down, pulling her to her feet. Without speaking, she also took the pistol that was shoved into her hand. Only then did Wendy stare at her rescuer, surprised to see Carl with his sparkling, flame-ridden mace beside her.

"What?"

"Later," Carl said. "I took out one, and the one that was on you looks pretty bad. But we're not done yet."

Wendy nodded, taking quick stock of her resources. Pistol? Check. Shield bracer? Almost out of charge. Babies? Three left. Mana? Enough for one more major summon.

"Buy me time. I'm going to summon Pan," Wendy said.

Carl shot her a look but grunted an agreement anyway. As if there were any choice, for she had already begun muttering under her breath. As the first of the wolves threw itself at them, he stepped out to meet it in battle, his mace swinging.

"*All children, except one, grow up. From the second star on the right, come… your Wendy calls.*" She couldn't help but blush; it wasn't the kind of thing you wanted to say out loud. Fanciful dreams, from the past were how she made the sprites, how she made everything work. But she needed them. Just like she needed them when she was a kid, when the branches scratched at her windows late at night. When a parent screamed, fighting over the telly's channels. Or the lack of tea.

Carl came crashing back to the ground, arms pinned by a pair of wolves. The injured timber wolf had evaded Zoom, and was charging her. Ready to finish the job.

Too late, for Pan was here.

He wasn't even that big. Just over eight feet tall. But he glowed. He glowed with the flames of youth and passion. And when he struck, he sent the monster tumbling away with just a single blow.

After that, the rest of the fight was magical.

***

Cleanup sucked. Cleanup always sucked. Even with all her helpers out, Wendy couldn't help but grumble. Dragging the bodies back, after skinning, gutting, and looting them, took forever. Especially when she kept half of her people watching for more trouble. Then, of course, it was up to her to hand in the skins. Clean them, sell them, and complete her Quests.

The worst part of it all was because Carl had helped, she didn't even get the full Quest rewards. Left her just shy of her experience needs. Nor did she have enough money, after replacing her broken beam pistol to buy the apartment complex.

"Did you make it?" Carl asked, leaning over her shoulder. Of course, he couldn't read her notification window but it was still annoying.

"No," Wendy said with a sigh. "Not enough. I'm so close…"

"Well…" Carl paused, rubbing his nose. "I'm sorry."

"It's fine. Tomorrow. I'll get it tomorrow," Wendy said. If something else didn't crop up. But, she knew, something else probably would. It's why was so tired. Something always came up, for the last four months. Then, remembering, she turned to Carl. "What were you doing there?" She put her hands on her hips, glaring at the man.

The pale redhead flushed, shifting from foot to foot. "Well, I thought that… you see… I…" He drew a deep breath and spoke in a rush. "I was following you."

"I thought so."

Carl flushed further and started edging away.

She grabbed him by the arm, pulled him around so that he faced her. Then she smiled. "Thank you. If you hadn't, well…"

There was no need to explain. They had both seen enough loss. "You're welcome. So…" Carl looked up in the sky, noting the fading sunlight. "I guess, I'll see you tomorrow."

She paused, then offered him a smile. And for the first time, she offered, "Maybe we could do dinner instead. Tonight."

Carl paused, startled, before he offered her a big smile in return. It was a start, a change in their routine. He stepped forward, offering her his arm, which, after she had one of her children clean, she took. He led her off the Cathedral green, towards High Street. And dinner.

After a few steps, he looked over at Wendy and spoke.

"You know, if you're looking for a good way to make some money, I've got this new idea…"

###

The End of *Daily Jobs, Coffee and An Awfully Big Adventure*

Seven Months In

This is Harry Prince, reporting from Dover, England. I have met with one of the alien races who have visited London. They are not invaders, but merchants, scholars, and explorers. Our change to become a Dungeon World has caught them by surprise too, and many were in-transit long before System advent.

The alien race that I have spoken to looks similar to the elves of our lore and call themselves the Movana. They are significantly more vicious. These are not the kind, benevolent, and wise creatures of our fairy tales but mercantile, political, and varied sentient beings.

It seems much of our culture has been imparted through a process known as Mana Seepage, a byproduct of the magic that permeated our existence even before we knew it. So much of what we knew—from monsters to mythologies—were just creatures from the greater Galactic universe.

Maybe this knowledge will save us. Maybe there is no saving humanity, not anymore. We need an edge. Any edge. For the monsters keep coming, arriving in a never-ending wave that swarms our walls and brings down our greatest.

My Grandmother's Tea Club

There have been many strange stories that have arisen during the process of the System Advent. The Change. The Apocalypse. What have you. If you listen long enough, the stories about heroic martial artists, crazed loners, desperate mothers, and yes, cowardly bards, permeate our culture. The growing return of our entertainment industry has seen some of these stories become established. However, of all the strange stories, I like to think the one I'm about to relate to you, that of my grandmother's Tea Club, is special.

Before we continue, I need to set the scene. In this case, Seaton Spring, Washington. You've probably never heard of it, what with us being a tiny resort village that mostly caters to tourists during the spring to summer months and the occasional city-folk during the winter. One of those one-road towns, with just enough money coming in from the tourist season and the occasional fishing and forestry people to keep itself alive, but not particularly thriving.

My grandmother now, she'd grown up there. Raised a half-dozen children who ran for the hills the moment they turned eighteen and only ever came back for Christmas and the occasional summer vacation. Not that she minded. You see, my Gran Gran was the old independent type. She might have stayed home and taken care of Pawpaw when he was still alive, but there's no doubt in anyone's mind who truly ran the house. Through the all-too-often lean years that was life in Seaton.

Anyway. I'm the unusual one. See, my mom was the youngest of the lot, a late addition to the family and the kid sister. Meant she was all kinds of spoilt, even under the jaundiced gaze of Gran Gran. Mom ran off when she was seventeen with a passing trucker and disappeared for a good two decades. Then, she made a brief reappearance about four years before the

System Advent, just to drop me off with Gran Gran before disappearing again on the back of a biker's hog.

Last I saw of her. I doubt she's still alive. Good riddance, I say.

Anyway. My grandmother and her Tea Club. It was a ritual, you see. Every Sunday, Gran Gran and her compatriots would gather around, sipping tea laced with whisky, comparing baked goods and gossiping about the latest goings-on in the city. Oh, and talking about the latest books they read. The kind that would make a more graceful lady blush.

Not that Gran Gran or her Tea Club were ladies. You didn't grow up in Seaton Springs and put on airs. There was fish to gut. Wood to be chopped. Clothes to be washed after they were soiled and the occasional wound that needed bandaging and stitching. For decades, there wasn't even a clinic about, so Grand Aunt Peggy with her wartime nursing experience did what had to be done to stitch a cut or two or hand out some much-needed antibiotics and other, well, more intimate stuff.

Yeah, things get a little wacky. It's not a surprise my Gran Gran and her friends were called a bunch of witches by the local pastor. Living in Washington, things get a little weird, you know—the clash between old-time hippies running away from society and old fundamentalist Protestants.

Still, when you'd been around as long as Gran Gran and her Tea Club, people had a tendency to learn to live and let live. Only so long you could hold a true burning grudge. Especially when you're all in your seventies and dealing with weekly or bi-weekly trips to the hospital.

And boy, was that a change when the System came. Need a dialysis treatment because your kidneys were failing? Got to drive hours one way just to get the nearest hospital, wrangling your damn insurance all the way so that they kept remembering to cover it? Not anymore! The System has you fixed and up and healthy, kidney's all repaired, liver no longer half-functioning, and those knees that didn't bend anymore? All fixed. Catch Grand Aunt Sally on a good day, and she'll talk your ear off about all the marvels of the System. In-between showing you how to shoot, disembowel, drain, and skin your latest kill.

Anyway. The start of the System's arrival caught us all early. I know some people who just dismissed the entire thing as a lucid dream. Some who went to sleep. Of course, most of those who did that never survived the day. Much better survival rates on the East Coast where it was daytime already when things hit, or even Europe.

Nah, we got hit during the early hours of the morning, and only a few people were awake. Among them, my Gran Gran and her posse. Being older folk, they'd all been up for ages, not needing the sleep the rest of us did. Or perhaps, having to deal with other, looser inconveniences.

Either way, the first thing I knew was being hauled up front of my Gran Gran and having to explain things like Levels and Perks and other shit to her. Now, my Gran Gran, she just rolled with the whole thing. Said if it was a hallucination, it was much better than the last time she took mushrooms or dropped acid. Said that the best way to handle both was just to go with the flow. So she did.

Not surprisingly, the rest of her Tea Club did too, and those that didn't, well, my Gran Gran shouted at them enough till they got with the program. Literally, in this case.

Oh yeah, sorry—that was the other thing she did. She called a Tea Club meeting, the moment she realized her hallucination wasn't going away. Having a bunch of old ladies trooping into your house in the early hours of the Apocalypse and having to set the table with the right cookies—lemon biscuit, shortbread and the kind with the half-chocolate drizzle—and get the tea sets up was both fitting and bizarre.

Either case, by that point, Gran Gran had made her decision and taken her Class. You know it, right? It's pretty damn legendary around these parts. Crone of the Wilds. Not a druidic thing—none of that heathen talk, as she'd say. Not that she'd mind it, mind you, but she was always a good Christian woman. Even if it was one of those more liberal Christian denominations. You know the ones, the ones that actually do the entire Christian charity thing, love thy neighbor bit and not just mealy mouth it.

Anyway.

There she was, with her Basic Skills, her Tea Club, and a world going to hell. Between the Perks that we got and the indication that things were going to get hectic—a Level 50+ spawn area didn't sound great, though these days we laugh at it—and well, they got to working.

A Perk and Crone of the Wilds combined made our house a Safe Zone. Stabilized Mana flows such that we could actually stay within and safe. The Game Warden Class that Grand Aunt Sally held let her set out lures, drag some of the newer spawns in for her to deal with down at the lake water and along the edges of the property too. Aunt Yow, with her Junior Homesteader Class, wasn't as useful immediately, but she'd used her Perk to update her gun collection, which she'd dragged along and well, that became useful. In-between all that, Grand Aunt Lara was busy calling everyone she could to get their ass over, which was not as many as you'd think with the phones having gone down. Her Junior Fire Warden Class on the other hand meant she could sense where everyone was, and once she got the neighbors put together, and I'd managed to explain Classes to them, well, they started bringing in more people.

Of course, even if our home was meant to hold the full family, there's still quite a difference between that and the entire couple hundred of the village. That's when Aunt Yow—having handed her gun collection off—got into it.

She wasn't the only one with a useful Class. Lumberjacks tore down trees with a few chops of their axes while Carpenters and Architects helped turn all of that into actual homes, with ground being torn up and set aside.

Of course, not everyone wanted to stick around. Quite a few people were worried about children and grandchildren in the big cities. Gran Gran had her work cut out trying to keep them from running off, and a few, she didn't even try. The fact that the MacGregors were willing to loan out their horses to anyone who had family helped, at least for the first few groups.

Mostly, that first day was a blur for me. It was over a decade ago, and you got to remember, I was still a kid. Still, I remember a few incidents. Especially the way Gran Gran reacted when the Karen arrived. Of course, she was actually called Karen but, well. She'd been a scourge on the community ever since she and her husband Bob arrived a few years ago. More than one Sunday evening was spent complaining about them, their constant leaflets complaining about everything from the beehives Eunice kept to the length of most of everyone's lawns and gardens. As though coming all the way out to live in the forest, they wanted to prune and purify the wilderness.

I still remember what Gran Gran said, a single finger raised, her Aura of the Blazing Hearth roaring off her. "Don't you 'but' me, young woman. We put up with you and your husband because that's what neighbors do, and we'll put with you more, if you'll sit down and listen. But there's consideration and there's foolishness, and pulling our people who are protecting women and children off their duties just to guide you and your husband back to the city to look for your estranged children, well . . . that's too much."

"But my son . . . !"

The wail that the Karen put out was both genuine and fake, as though she couldn't turn off that performative victimhood even now. Not that I knew all that, back then. But as I said, the entire scene was burned into my brain.

"Your son *and daughter* both ran for the city the moment they grew old enough and haven't been back since. I'd be guessing they're more than practiced at taking care of themselves." Then Gran Gran softened, putting a hand on Karen's arm. "Even if we did want to help you, there's no way to get you there. Neither of you know how to ride a horse, no?"

"How hard could it be? These yoke . . . umm . . . others do it," Bob said.

Luckily, Gran Gran left that comment alone. I know there was a little more arguing, but I forget the rest of the details, what with the next problem cropping up soon after.

See, thus far, the monsters we had to deal with were—well, they were pretty easy to stomach. You got your giant ants, your flying hornets, your slime creatures, your four-foot-tall centipedes and even more exotic things. Mutated wildlife and monsters were easy to kill. It didn't take much, to do the killing of a monster, especially not for the hunters and other roughnecks who lived around here.

Monsters were monsters. You killed them. You gutted and skinned them. You even cooked them and took their loot. It wasn't great, it wasn't fun, but it was something you did.

The first goblin party that wandered in, all pointy eared, green skinned, and looking humanoid? Well, that was a lot harder. They looked just about human enough to make people hesitate. Social conditioning and all that, you know? So while they might have taken them down, injured and tied them up and all that, the actual killing was a little more . . . well. Slipshod.

Which was when Gran Gran walked up with a hunting knife she somehow had secreted on herself, cut the first goblin's throat and then, for good measure, stuck the entire thing up under its jaw when it didn't die immediately. Aunt Henessy—the one with three ex-husbands who had died mysteriously—finished off the second by pouring a liquid down its throat and holding it still till it finished swallowing. And well, Grand Aunt Sally? She just put a couple of rounds into the last couple.

When everyone looked at them, Gran Gran just snorted and said, "What? You think they'd do anything different if you were the ones tied up? Remember, the Lord himself said that he came not to bring peace, but the sword. And we're his sword, in the here and now. Best make peace with that."

Then she took her knife back, cleaned it up, and looted the goblin right in front of them all. Because I'd told her to loot everything, and she did.

So that was the first day. The craziest day. We got everyone that we could in, organized those we could find, sent the others out to find family and friends when they had to do so. Even with Gran Gran and her Tea Club putting everything through their paces, forcing them all to choose Classes and Perks and just, you know, get organized.

We lost a good twenty people that day. Might not seem like much to you, but when the village is only a couple hundred, it was a big blow. Especially since that number included those in the outlying settlements, and we didn't get to them. Add in all those that chose to leave, and by the end of the first day, we had maybe a hundred-plus people camped outside our house, stuffed to the gills around us.

Of course, that night, we lost another dozen more to the Blood Moths. Damn things landed on people, sucked them dry of blood, and took off, never even alerting anyone else. The Safe Zone might have stopped spawning, but the sheer mass of people meant that animals and monsters came hunting.

Not that Gran Gran and the others would make the same mistake twice. We still loss more that day, as we pushed outwards and did our best to establish a perimeter. Gran Gran took my advice that day, went out to try to Level even as Architects and Handymen and the Homesteaders and Tinkerers all put their own Skills to the test, building out from the mansion. Expanding the Safe Zone by sheer dint of Skills being used in conjunction with one another, all the while being forced to fight and defend themselves.

Maybe we should have left. Lord knows, there were a few who did and who made it. If we had all left at once, maybe even more would have survived. But Gran Gran chose to stay, and her friends did too. And that was all that was needed to tip things over.

So we built outwards.

Took to the waters, fished and killed the things that crawled out of the lake, all webbed fingers and big, dewy eyes. A cross between a fish and a frog, just given humanoid form. They even talked, if you could understand their croaking speech.

We did well, for the first week. Till the ammo started running out, and the lack of reloads became telling. Things got rough for the next couple of months, and we lost even more people. Gained more too, as people stumbled over to us—guided by Skills, AIs, helper spirits or just pure blind luck. Somehow, we stabilized around sixty people, about a dozen of us kids. The village never had many of us children to begin with, what with it being more a retirement and tourist community.

Through it all, Gran Gran and the Tea Club held everyone together. I remember still having to serve tea, every Sunday. We had church meetings—the pastor managed to survive, somehow—and then, it'd be tea. No matter what was happening, even in an emergency, they'd take a few hours off and chill.

Gran Gran used to say, "If we can't stay at least a little civilized, what's the point of surviving?" whenever I asked her about it.

I still think she's right. It's why we saved the library, why we fought to keep the kids alive through it all. When we eventually Leveled—when Gran Gran did, and the rest of the Tea Club and survivors who we were able to establish a Shop connection—that's when things turned around.

Some people replaced their guns for the newfangled beam rifles. Others just kept to what they knew, but better. Bigger, nastier, more-punching-power gunpowder rifles and shotguns. A few had found a love for the spears they'd made, so they just upgraded that along with the armor everyone now wore. Armor made from tree bark and monster leather and repurposed car metal gave way to fangled Galactic imports.

Once we managed to establish that connection, expanding outwards was simple. Painful, but simple. We still lost a few people, here and there, but by that point, even the System seemed to acknowledge our little village, and we'd receive an actual settlement orb eventually.

It's why when the Redeemer and his crew finally swept through, over a year later, we were all settled. Why my Gran Gran and her Tea Club managed to keep over a quarter of the original residents alive, and a larger percentage—nearly all of us kids—breathing. Even when humanity for the most part lost one in ten, she managed to do more.

Nowadays, Gran Gran isn't doing as much anymore. She was a little old even at the start of the apocalypse, and even points in Constitution and a gene wash can only do so much. But every Sunday, every one of her Tea Club gathers together, and they drink, gossip about the latest goings-on in the village and pinch the Yerrick's bottom.

And yeah, I still serve them tea.

Because some forms of civilization, you gotta keep.

###

The End of *My Grandmother's Tea Club*

The First Year

This is Harry Prince, reporting from Paris, France. I have left England—or what's left of it—to see how the rest of Europe fares. The destruction in Paris has been widespread. The Eiffel Tower has fallen, but the Bastille stands. The French have managed to save some of their museums, art galleries, and historic buildings, preserving their history and culture through blood and sacrifice.

So much sacrifice.

If you are seeing this missive, you must have received the notification that a full Mana Integration has occurred. Ninety percent of humanity has fallen, or thereabouts. The rest are hardened survivors, bitter and deadly.

Yet, our challenges have only just begun, for the aliens who have installed this System are coming in droves now, coming to take what they believe to be theirs.

A new age of colonization has occurred and we can only hope we fare better than the native civilizations of the past.

Adventures in Clothing

Lana shuffled the stacks of System papers before once again sighing. The slightly glassy feel of the papers, rough only at certain intervals to ensure that there was some purchase to grip still felt strange to her, even months after picking up the items from the Shop. While System notifications were useful, they also had certain limitations to their use. Chief among them, the inability of an individual to carry a notification away with them, if it was not linked to themselves.

There were other issues as well, with System notifications as a managerial tool. If you had to pass on notifications to multiple individuals at once, and she was about to, you either had to upgrade your specific managerial Skill or pick the right one at the start. All those Skills came with their own benefits and hindrances, though, and there was never an easy choice. The fact that her own Class was a combat Class and not running a settlement, especially one as large as the free province of British Columbia, was a pain and a half.

The tired redhead ran a hand through her hair, once again cursing John. It had been nearly a year since his disappearance, and the war effort down in the States had stalled. Rather than continue to throw herself into violent, foolhardy situations, Lana had returned to Vancouver, picking up the task of managing his settlement in his stead. She'd still help out — as one of the higher Leveled individuals, she had to. But she would not lose track of the fact that the settlement needed managing. Life was more than war.

For a moment, she considered the man, considered all that she had lost when he left. It still hurt; the death of her pet, the loss of her boyfriend when she needed him the most. She was still reeling, to some extent, from the death of her brother, the only family that she had for so many decades. To lose Anna on top of that had been too much.

For a time, she, Mikito and Ingrid had tried to do what John had done for the United States Army. They drove themselves and their alien enemies to the edge, acting as the spearhead of the group. It was only a close call, one that nearly cost the life of Sam, the Technocrat, and herself, that she realized perhaps those choices weren't the best.

What was it that Mikito had said? Oh yes, "just because you miss the baka, doesn't mean you should act like one, too."

That was the reason she was back up here, in Vancouver. Katherine Ward, the secretary and manager that John had hired, along with the AI, had done well at keeping things running. But neither one had much of a vision, and neither one did more than keep the settlement running.

Today's initiative was Lana's first attempt at fixing that gaping hole in the settlement development strategy. She smiled to herself as she leaned back in her comfortable, swivel chair in the office that was in the back of a public library, overlooking the various streets below.

If things went well, today would be the start of her special-teams.

***

The four individuals that stood before her, holding up the sheets of paper before them, were nothing special, at least in terms of their Levels. All Basic Classes, all of them in their mid-20s, and none of them so far had exhibited any particular specialty or gift. They were, in other words, entirely mediocre.

Even worse, none of them were combat Classes by nature. The highest-level member of the group was the Tailor, whose level of 29 came entirely from her work as another underpaid Artisan. The problem for many Artisans in Vancouver and British Columbia was the lack of suitable material. Specifically, for a Tailor like her, they lacked cloth. System generated, System marked cloth or other clothing materials. There were rumors that in China mutated silkworms had been evolved, and over in the north, there was a dungeon filled with mutated spiders that spat silk. But all of that material was out of reach for your average Basic Class Tailor.

As for the other three, there was the Model; tall, tan, very pretty and desperately in need of a pair of hamburgers who flinched at every loud noise or sudden movement. Of the other two, one was a five foot four blonde female, dressed in a Sailor Moon dress, fringed and green, while the other had the unfortunate class of costume designer. The designer had once worked on a few well-known DC tv shows, but was now out of work, having little else to do with her skills as production of entertainment venues were at an all time low.

Lana knew that none of them other than the Tailor would have reached level 20 if not for the training programs that John and herself had put in place. Artisans and noncombat personnel were carried through combat missions by volunteer groups, allowing them to level up as necessary. Items produced by them, when it was possible, were also distributed to groups on the regular, providing for the needy, while giving a minor experience boost.

In truth, there were still ongoing arguments about the carry program. Many pointed out that combat Classes could gain much more experience if they were not constantly babysitting Artisans and noncombat Classes in the dungeons or the outskirts of the city. The counterargument, that all individuals were important, and needed a minimum Level of 20 ensure that they could survive an unfortunate encounter with a roaming monster, were often dismissed and set against the concept of personal responsibility.

Thankfully, the counterarguments came from only a small subset of the population. Still, Lana and Katherine kept an eye on that group, because you never knew when they'd hit an argument that could sway the minds of the general populace.

Not that either Katherine or Lana intended to run the free provinces of British Columbia as a democracy. For one thing, the System did not generally register democracies as a viable government form. To make it viable, one would have to purchase the necessary Skills and options from the System, and thus block off the penalties in forming a democracy. However, neither Katherine nor Lana had the money to undertake such action.

More importantly, unless they intended to boot John off the city settlement orb, he was the settlement owner, the provincial Lord. And for reasons both personal and practical, neither party felt the need to force the issue.

"Ms. Pearson?" The first to speak was the Tailor, holding aloft the sheet of system paper. "Are you serious about this?"

"Ms. Williams," Lana's eyes flicked up quickly, so quickly that it was easy to miss how she checked Hana Williams' status bar ahead of her head, "I am deadly serious. I would like all of you to form a party and complete a Quest for me."

"Why us?" This, from the old model. He flashed Lana a smile, one heartbreakingly soft and winsome. Unfortunately, his charms had little effect on Lana, her own charisma well above his, and thus providing her a small degree of protection. That, and he was just not to her liking. Too pretty and lacking in certain rough edges.

"Mr. Obrav, we spent quite a bit of time searching for a mixture of classes. We believe, together, all four of you can form an unconventional but effective questing team." Lana said.

"I don't fight," the costume designer said. "I'm not a combat class."

"I never said you were," Lana said. "There are more types of Quests, more objectives that need to be completed, than just combat. While there might be, probably will be violent encounters because we live in a Dungeon World, it is not the goal of putting this team together."

"And what do we get for working together?" The cosplayer asked. Meg raised an eyebrow, completely at odds with the sweetness she normally displayed in her videoclips.

"Page five of the document lists your expected benefits, but in short, you will work as direct government employees with salary and benefits. In addition, you will be eligible to receive your quest rewards. It should be sufficient, even for you, Ms. Hillhouse."

"And what if we don't like the offer?" Meg said, then, side-eyeing the rest of the group, she continued. "Or the people you chose for us to work with."

"Then you may decline the opportunity and inform Ms. Ward. In either case, you might or might not be assigned to a new team," Lana said. "You are not the first nor the only individuals this offer is being made to."

When Meg moved to speak further, she felt a hand land on her arm. To her surprise, she found the male model pulling her backward with a surprising strength for his lean frame. When she opened her mouth, he glared at her further.

A slight increase in Aura pressure from the seated Beast Lord before her reminded Meg of who she was actually arguing with. That Aura was not a friendly, managerial aura but a combat aura. As if to remind her further, a low growl emanated from the floor, where to her – and the teams- surprise, a giant husky sat, cloaked in his own, moving shadow.

How did she miss that? Gulping, she backed out, leaving the Beast Lord alone. Anyway, she still had the documents and those could be resold if she needed to. It wasn't a complete waste of time.

***

The group of four reconvened at one of the numerous public tables located on the lower floor of the ex-public library. The fact that there were still tables had been one of many battles between the librarians and the new management, one that the librarians had won. Sort of. Even now, you could spot them moving from stack to stack, storing away books after using their Skills to store the information within. Even more, deep in the bowels of the library, the archive section brought back new books to be catalogued and stored in the libraries shared storage space.

Though the System had marked much of that information and even kept an on-going storage of it all, what it did not do was provide such information free. Rather than purchase that information – and then break the System locks on sharing such information, librarians over the world had taken to storing what information they had to continue to serve the public good. Talks were already underway about the set-up of a global library network, to ensure that such information could be spread globally, providing a boost in education and information resources. Other talks were already underway to recreate or purchase System-stored information, Class information and Galactic information to expand the library services to the System-Age.

All of that, of course, was unimportant to the four non-combat Classers who sat in silence, perusing the data sheets provided to them by Lana.

Eventually, it was Obrav who spoke up, breaking the silence around the group. "This Quest doesn't look too hard."

"What do you know?" Hana said. "You're not the Tailor who has to make it."

"Har! You think it's just tailoring that's going to be needed," Meg said, shaking her head. "This is going to need some creativity in it."

"Definitely," Cassidy said. The costume designer ran her finger down the sheet, speaking out loud as she read. "Create four blueprints of minimum Tier IV quality, for non-combat personnel that maximises Skills of non-traditional combat classers."

"What does that even mean?" Hana said, shaking her head. "I can make clothing, but blueprints?"

"Don't you use blueprints? Tailoring guides?" Meg said, frowning. "I always did when I was working on my outfits."

"Sure, but that's not what they mean here," Hana said. "At least, I don't think it is. And even if we do register a blueprint, what's this about maximising Skills? Is this for combat? Or just in general?"

There were a series of group shrugs at that, before Obrav continued. "It sounds like we've agreed to try this at least?"

His pronouncement made the group freeze. They eyed one another slowly, uncertain about such a statement. They'd only met one another recently after all. And this seemed like a big project. On the other hand, it was a Quest and free Credits.

"I'm game," Cassidy spoke up first. When everyone looked at her, she shrunk back a little, waving a hand as if to distract them. "It's... good Credits."

Obrav nodded. "Me too. I could do with a job. I'm getting really tired of hauling around stuff for other people."

"Is that what you've been doing?" Meg said, her lips half-smirking.

"Oh, as if you've done better," Obrav snapped.

"I've been going out fighting," Meg said, raising her chin.

"Not very successfully it seems," Obrav said, eyeing her Level. Meg flushed, but didn't refute his comment. Even if her Skills as a Cosplayer gave her some benefits, it wasn't a pure Combat Class. It made finding pick-up groups who were willing to work with her hard. Either that or she was consigned to working low-Level zones, harming her own experience gain.

"Well, at least I'm trying!"

"Enough, please you two." Hana said. "Or just drop out if you want, Meg." The Tailor gestured down to the documents. "We can probably make do without you in this."

"You think so?" Meg said. "Because I'm pretty sure Ms. Pearson chose all of us for a reason."

Hana shrugged. "Maybe. But I don't want to be in a team that keeps fighting. So unless the pair of you can tone it down…" She trailed off, leaving her choice unspoken.

Obrav glared at Hana and then eventually looked over to Meg. He searched her face for a few long moments, before he sighed. "Fine. I can work with the amateur."

"Ama-" Finding a hand on her arm, Meg looked over at Cassidy who gave her a pleading look. Simmering slowly, Meg nodded. "Fine." She said, mimicking Obrav's tone. "I can play nice."

Hana rolled her eyes at the pair, since their definition of nice was certainly not hers. Still, at least they'd agreed. And, she had to admit, she was intrigued. "Then, perhaps let's start by finding out what a blueprint is, in terms of the System. And what we need to do to get one."

The group nodded, before falling into discussion on the how.

***

Hours later, the impromptu team had re-grouped at the same table. A short discussion later, Hana was holding up her hand, raising fingers as she spoke.

"Let me summarise what we've learnt. Blueprints are System-registered designs, sort of like copyrights. Anyone can make them or create them, but it requires either a Skill to register them with the System or you need a specific organisation. A corporation or the like."

There were nods all around at her words. Meg smirked, having been the one to learn that.

"The easiest way to do that, the most cost effective one, is for us to set-up a System-registered clothing company. Once we pay for the set-up, it'll give us the right to register clothing blueprints for a fixed price, rather than varying depending on the individual," Obrav added. "Or we could find a System-registered Clothing Administrator or Blueprint Merchant, but that might be a little harder."

Hana grimaced at that. Generic merchants might be able to do that, depending on their particular Skills and their System Shop access that they gained. However, it was much more costly to work with a generalised Merchant than a specialised one, and registering through a generalised Merchant would be nearly as expensive as just doing it direct via the System.

"I doubt there's any Galactic specialized Merchants like that," Meg said. "At least, they're really uncommon."

"Compared to Earth specialised Classes?" When Meg nodded, Hana echoed her. "Yeah, makes sense. But that leads us to the next point, to make a company, we need a minimum of an Advanced Classer to head it or three Basic Classers." She pulled out the System-sheets, flipping through the information before she came across the portion she was looking for. "And it seems Ms. Pearson's bonus Credits for signing and accepting the Quest is equal to the amount for three such individuals."

"We still need materials," Cassidy said, piping up.

"Manipulative," Obrav said. He sounded almost admiring.

"Annoying," Meg said, crossing her arms. "So, what? We have to work together to build this company? Or do we try to build the blueprints first, then register it later, if we have Credits?"

The group fell silent. Hana played with the sheets of paper, reviewing the Quest and the information provided. Obraz watched the group and those around, while Meg took out a pen and paper, sketching some ideas. It was Cassidy who spoke up, hesitantly.

"There's no real experience gain for a company, so maybe we should try at least one blueprint first? If it works, we can register the company," she said hesitantly.

The hesitant suggestion brought quick nods from the group.

"So, what do we make?" Obrav said, brightly and innocently.

***

Of course that agreement led to another, much more heated argument. Eventually, the group broke apart, to come back the next day to restart the conversation, armed with reams of research and solidified positions.

"If we make a single core blueprint, then modification for each Class afterwards is simpler!" Meg said, slapping her hand down. "It doesn't matter what kind of magic girl costume it is, it's still a magic girl!"

"Magic girl?" Obrav smirked. "And mass-produced work is never going to be as strong as custom made work. We should choose a single Class and then tailor our work to them. That's the way the elites do it, in the System." He thumped his hand down on the stack of System paper, financials and articles before him.

"That's if you have the Levels. Which we don't," Cassidy said, piping in. "Also, we've got so many variant Classes that building custom work for all of them would be a ton of time. And limit our customer base. They can't afford it anyway."

"That's the point!" Hana waved her hand in the air. "Why are we targeting humans? They don't have funds. We should be going after the aliens. The Movana and Truinnar all are roughly humanoid, so reshaping for them is simple. And they've got Credits!"

"You might as well suggest we make clothing for the orcs!" Meg said, shaking her head.

"They're Hakarta, not orcs," Cassidy butted in. "And they're quite nice too."

"Oh, really!" Catching something in Cassidy's tone, Obrav rounded on her. The other two fell silent too, smiles growing as Cassidy grew ever redder under their observation. "I think we'd all love to hear about how these… Hakarta… are *nice*."

"It's not like that!" Cassidy protested.

"*Really*," Meg said. "Because it sounds exactly like that."

"That's not true." Cassidy whispered.

Taking pity on the poor girl, Hana broke in. "Look, working clothing for humans are nice and all, but if we target the aliens who are on Earth, a single sale would make us enough to Level and earn a ton of Credits."

"But why would they buy from us," Meg said. "We don't have the Levels, like I pointed out. Humans will though, if nothing more than because we'd be able to do it cheaply."

"If we can work out a variable blueprint!" snapped Obrav. "That's much more difficult than customised, individual Class blueprints."

"Well, I'm up for the challenge!" Meg bristled.

"Gods, you Americans are all the same," Obrav said. "It's not just about will."

"Oh, you Americans," Meg mocked Obrav. "I've been in Canada for nearly a decade!"

"Enough you two!" Hana snapped. "Arguing isn't going to get us an answer. We need to decide on something, or else we might as well give up."

"Well, I think…"

"We should…"

The argument broke out again, even if it was a little more civil. Hana did her best to keep both Obrav and Meg in-line while Cassidy fell silent. Eventually, Obrav caught sight of the silent young lady who was studiously sketching on one of the pieces of paper and pointed at her. Startled, Meg looked over followed soon after by Hana. Together, the trio stared at the silently working Cassidy who slowly grew aware of their regard.

Peeking over the paper, light pen in hand, Cassidy stared at the group with wide eyes. "What?"

"What are you doing, Cassie?" Meg said, her voice growing wheedling.

"Yes, what are you doing?" Obrav said, hands on his hips.

"I'm…uh…working?" Cassidy said, uncertainly. She stared down at the sketches, watching as her Skill – Design Optimisation – overlay suggestions. It was rather distracting, especially when she was attempting basic sketches.

Before she could react, Meg snatched the paper from her arm. She stared down at the sketch in hand, frowning. Obrav leaned over, staring at the barebones sketch, trying to envision the final product, only to hiss when Meg swiped to the next image and then the next.

"You know… these are good," Meg said, tilting the paper down at Hana's insistence. On it, a stick figure outline sketch was seen of an outlined figure in what could be only described as a butcher's smock. However, unlike the traditional smock, this one came with multiple side pockets and extended arms, closer to a surgical gown in design – if more stylish – than a full smock. In highlighted notations, recommended materials were highlighted such as 'mutated bear muscle fibre' or 'ocra skin'. "Though your material choice is horrible."

"Agreed," Hana said. "And you could adjust the line and cut for those sleeves. They're a little shallow for full range of motion." Without asking, Hana flipped backwards and tutted as she saw the sketch for the dress that next appeared. "And that's just wrong."

"Sorry. It's not what I'm used to making," Cassidy said, ducking her head.

"Still, these are pretty decent," Hana said, biting the edge of her lips as she continued to flip it backwards. After a bit, both her and Meg spoke up at the same time.

"You're using a single major design!"

"Well, that's what we suggested," Cassidy said defensively. "I just… thought I'd get started."

"We haven't decided on that yet," Obrav said snootily.

"But she's got the basic plans for one… and look…" Hana stabbed a finger down. "The recommendations are mostly minor changes in cut and shape… simple enough to do…"

"And materials. Don't forget materials," Meg said, eyes gleaming. "You could alter the material types and the lining form, to give those bonuses they're looking for. This is exactly what we're talking about. Good job Cassie!"

"Thanks…"

Rolling his eyes, Obrav stared down at the work for a little more before he shrugged. "Fine, so we've got a sketch. But that's not a blueprint, is it? What else do we need to do?"

Hana pursed her lips, then pulled out another piece of paper. A short while later, she waved it in front of the group. "Now, we get to work. We've got to create samples of them all."

"Sounds good," Meg said, rubbing her hands together. "I can get started on finding the materials. I've got some contacts."

"I can do the initial roughing out of the designs. Cassidy, can you clean these up a little more?" Hana said.

"What am I supposed to do?" Obrav said, frowning.

"You can find your friends a better place to work in." The voice caught the group unawares, making them all jump. Appearing from behind them, the man stood there with his arms crossed. "While we don't mind you doing research here, actual work is not permitted."

"That's—"

"Fine. Not a problem," Hana nodded, cutting off Obrav. He glared at her but fell silent when the librarian walked off, exiting the privacy bubble their tables created around them. "Don't piss off the Librarians. They'll ban you. And you don't want to know what Library fines are like these days."

Obrav frowned and opened his mouth.

In unison, all three girls chorused together, "Don't ask."

Startled, they look at one another and then burst out into laughter, giggling and guffawing. At Obrav's continued chagrin, they burst out into another round of merriment.

***

"What about group four?" Lana said, one hand down by her chair's side where she idly stroked Shadow's head. The immense huskie pushed its head into her hand, nuzzling it while looking up longingly at her. She kept scratching his head, mentally telling him 'later'. The biggest issue with owning a husky was their endless energy. It was luckily tempered by the System providing the dogs increased intelligence and willpower, giving them the ability to handle the long periods of boredom as Lana was forced through paperwork. Still, extending her senses, she felt the other members of her group rushing through the local wildlife in North Vancouver, tearing apart monsters as they spawned. Even Roland was out tonight, though he prowled Stanley Park, scaring both joggers and hunting down the elusive Shadow Badgers that had made it their home.

"They've rented a building in Gastown," Katherine, the settlement manager, said as she flipped over to the particulars. "The hint we sent put them on the right course. Obrav has good instincts when it comes to negotiations. That Costume Designer has a good eye for design and is working hard on the base blueprints while the Tailor is attempting to make prototypes with the materials provided by the Cosplayer."

"And the blueprints?" Lana said, pursing her lips.

"Unsuccessful thus far."

Lana shook her head in regret. "They should have aimed lower than an integrated blueprint."

"It is difficult, but they are Leveling," Katherine pointed out.

Lana nodded. "But will they manage to get it done before they drive each other apart? Or run out of funds?"

To that, Katherine could only shrug.

Lana sighed and flicked a finger, pulling up information on team five. She read over it for a second, a smile pulling at her lips. "Team five seems to be doing well. They're already onto the sampling stage…"

***

"System-integrated cucumber and mint kombucha sample, miss?" The man thrusted the bottled drink forwards, the handmade label already beginning to peel as condensation gathered. He looked hopefully at Meg who paused, taking the drink and turning it over. A slight squint and thrust of will and the System provided her details.

Cucumber and Mint Kombucha Beverage

This Artisan creation is formed from System-grown mint and cucumber vegetables and processed for fourteen days in a welded tank. The drink is further enhanced by a Beverage Maker, making it taste barely palatable except to certain idiosyncratic groups of human and alien society.

Effect: +12 base Mana

Duration: 9 hours and 6 minutes

Costume Synergies: Steampunk Alchemist

Meg wrinkled her nose, then popped the top off. She swigged it down quickly, pausing as the first mouthful entered her mouth. Her eyes widened, and she looked at the drink for a second more before chugging the rest of the drink down. A moment later, she had her own Status open, eyeing the increase in base Mana that her Mana regeneration was filling.

"Nice!" Meg said. "Though, 12 Mana is a little low, isn't it?"

"Sure. We expect that as we keep working on the base materials and Level up our Skills, we'll increase that. But we're also targeting more people like you!" the man said, beaming at her.

Meg eyed the beanpole of a man with his mustache and vest, trying to decide if she was supposed to be insulted.

As if seeing the look she was giving him, the man hurriedly spoke. "I meant Artisans. We're working on another formula that gives an increase to base Mana Regeneration that will be even more useful. But this way, you can channel a higher amount of Mana for enchantments."

"Huh," Meg said. She knew what he was talking about, since even with her hybrid Class, she too had a Skill that relied on channelled Mana to make her costumes work better. She opened it to peek at the description again even as she continued speaking. "So, can I get a half dozen samples? I have colleagues who would love to test this out."

Class Skill: The Costume Maketh the Cosplay

Authenticity is the name of the game for a good cosplayer! The closer your costume, the more believable you are as the character. Being believable for your adoring public is the most important thing. Effectiveness of Skill depends upon fidelity of detail of the costume to loaded Cosplay. Note that channelled Mana can help
*Effect: User gains x (where x equals Mana cost*costume fidelity/(System Mana differentiation level)) Skills of cosplayed individual for use.*
Cost: Varies

"Sure!" The man smiled, handing over the bottles and taking back the empty one from Meg. "We also do deliveries to your work location and we'll be selling them soon on the regular. Just check the System-link for more details."

Meg nodded, waving goodbye after storing the drinks and hurried off to their office. They were in week three of their current quest, and thus far, had yet to produce a single acceptable blueprint. They'd produced a bunch of blueprints, but none that met the requirements of the Quest and worst, none that would likely ever make their funds back. Certainly, building a blueprint was easy – but unless it was sufficiently robust, there was no way it would ever sell.

As it stood, most of the human Tailors and other clothing designers on Earth bought and modified alien blueprints. Those were guaranteed to work, often had better base stats before and after modification for the human body. Until they could match that, it was a losing proposition to even attempt to register their blueprints with the System. No one would buy it.

Cassidy refused to give up, producing blueprint modification after modification. From those blueprints, it was Hana's job to turn it into a physical product, often with Meg's help. Then Obrav and Meg would take turns wearing the design, using their own Skills to modify the clothing to suit themselves better. The fact that Meg could cosplay as a Class meant that they could verify bonuses for specific Classes, while Obrav's own Skills like Perfect Fit and Work It gave them an idea of the maximum benefits that a particular prototype could provide.

From there, it was a matter of passing that information to both Hana and Cassidy, allowing the two to modify the blueprint and prototypes further before a new piece was made. Once that was done, it would be up to Meg and Obrav to sell the product – Meg by taking it into the dungeons with other groups and Obrav on the streets.

Of course, that required them finishing up a working prototype.

"Goood morning," Meg called out after shouldering the entrance door open. It was dull grey steel, heavy-built and required a significant amount of her improved strength to open. No more glass doors – these days, most entrances were modified with heavy security panels or ultra-high-tech System materials, depending on how rich the landlords were. In their case, their landlord had chosen the cheaper option of having a Builder or

Workman or something similar to fix up the building for habitation. "I've got drinks."

Cassidy looked up from her drawing board, glanced at the drinks that Meg was holding aloft and sighed. "Kombucha, right? Put it on the coffee table with the rest."

"Rest?" Meg said, only to spot the pile of bottles.

"You weren't the only one who conned them out of a few bottles." Cassidy grinned, then shifted her demeanour a little, batting her eyes and smiling sweetly. She even dropped her voice a little as she added. "Oh, sir. This would be so useful for my team..."

Meg snorted at the caricature but had to admit, she wasn't wrong that the man had been an easy mark. And it wasn't as if they weren't going to use it... "Any progress?"

Cassidy made a moue of a face at the question. "There's a new prototype that Hana's working on right now, but..."

"Not close?" Meg said.

"It's a good costume. But I can't make it fit into the configurable blueprint..." Cassidy muttered. "The zippers are in the wrong place, and if I adjust the seam for the shoulders, it knocks out the other option. The System is only allowing a tolerance of 0.2 cm adjustments, which is just..."

Meg tuned out Cassidy as she blathered on about her problems. By this point, Meg knew that she spoke more for her own benefit than anyone else's. At some point, both her and Hana would look over the next blueprint and offer their own suggestions, but Cassidy preferred to take the first pass herself.

Walking up over to Hana's station, she traded greetings with the Tailor. She picked up a hung piece, judging the work critically and once more, finding it more than sufficient. Both Skill and skill helped Hana cut, sew and adjust the pieces to exact levels of standards. Standards that had fallen to the wayside during periods of mass consumerism, where clothing was bought, worn for a month, and tossed aside. If that long.

"New prototype?" Meg said, holding the short-sleeved dress up to her body. "Why the short skirt?"

"It's a skort," Hana said, distaste in her voice. "You wanted something a little more maneuverable, right?"

"And fashionable! Always fashionable," Obrav thrilled as he flounced down the stairs. Meg frowned, eyeing his clothing and the state he was in.

"Did you sleep here again?" She demanded.

"Yes!"

Meg paused, stymied by the unashamed statement. She worked her jaw, before she left it alone. Whether Obrav just had no place to go or preferred the office, she was just not sure. Sometimes, it was best not to ask. The wounds from the System's arrival were rampant and as unexpectedly deep as puddles on a potholed alleyway in Gastown. Before its recent hippiefication, at least.

While she was working all that out, Obrav bounced over to her, grabbed the dress and held it up to him. He twitched his fingers and the next moment, the clothing had replaced his current wear as he activated his Skill – Quick Change.

"Oooh, I like these. Do you think they make my butt pop?" Obrav said, turning his head around to stare at the aforementioned part. He stuck his back out a little more, shimmying a little before he grew serious, his eyes glazing over a little as he accessed his notifications. "27% fit change. Not bad, though it's a little loose in the chest region. And a little tight on the sleeves. Move that down maybe an inch. I've got a… hmm… +2 on Agility,

+4 on Constitution and physical resistances, and chemical?, yes, chemical, resistances."

"It's meant for the Painters and Alloy Makers," Cassidy called out from her seat. "Of course there's chemical resistances."

"Then why the physical resistances?" Meg said, frowning. "And give me that!"

"Of course, girl. You only had to ask," Obrav said. He snapped his fingers, triggering another Skill and the pair swapped clothing, his Perfect Fit Skill upscaling Meg's plain brown t-shirt and grey yoga pants to his own form. "Mmm…. So pedestrian."

"It's comfortable! And easy to change out of," Meg snapped at Obrav. Ignoring the Model, she twitched the skort and the top of the dress, triggering her own Costume Skill. "Ooooh, I get a choice of Skills."

Both Hana and Cassidy perked up at that. With some careful regulation and change of materials, potential Skills that Meg found could be added to the blueprints which would provide even more versatility to the work. Of course, it made the generic blueprint option even more difficult, but many would pay more for a clothing choice that provided new Skills – or bonuses to existing Skills.

"I've got Fast Coat which seems to be a sped-up application Skill. A little boring, but probably generally useful and, Full Body Coverage." Meg didn't need to explain the second Skill. It was a common Skill that sometimes appeared as an enchantment, one that basically allowed an increase in resistances or lackluster physical coverage to actually take effect over the entire body. It even worked with certain armour types, letting people walk around with helmets.

"Again?" Cassidy said, groaning. "I swear, I think your Class is affecting the Skills we get."

"I tend to agree," Hana said. "There shouldn't be a reason for us to get it with overalls and a skort."

"Except that helmets suck," Meg said, sticking her tongue out. "They mess with your hair and you lose major cool points."

"I have to agree – there is very little fashionable about masks." Obrav said, tapping his lips. He'd changed back to his own clothing, having racked Meg's clothing for her. "Even with the best art. Not when one is as handsome as many have become."

"Bah! That's because you just don't want your adoring public to miss your face. A good mask design can be just as characteristic. Like Darth Vader!" Cassidy said, waving the pen she had been using to sketch on the paper before her. "But still, Full Body Coverage seems to be a decent basic Skill. We could use that as the base…

"And the kind of materials it seems to use include coastal seaweed, iron cotton…"

Obrav leaned over, whispering to the two other girls. "Did she just forget about us again."

"Yes. Now, why don't you two try out the other options I've made, make some notes and test out the full limitations while I finish up," Hana said, waving down to the piece she had been working on.

The pair of non-craftsmen traded glances and then nodded in unison. There was little direct work they could do right now. But in time, it would be their chance to shine. Once they'd done their initial jobs, they would head out to gain experience and take further tests.

"Oh! And hand me one of those kombuchas before you go!" Hana called out as the pair left to change, bundles of clothes in their hand.

***

"And you're sure this is the right call?" Hana said, biting her lips. The entire group were clustered around Cassidy and her tablet, all of them staring down at the five blueprints. Each of the other four blueprints were linked to the main one, the customisable main blueprint that allowed any purchaser access to the other specialised four.

"Yes!" Cassidy said, exasperatedly. "You all agreed to this. You've seen the stats." Then, realising what she said, she shrunk in a little before she shook her head and sat up. "No. I'm right. We did talk and agree on this."

"Sure, but the cost…" Meg said, trailing off as she stared at the Credit amount. Between the corporation registration they'd paid for already and the registration for the combined blueprints, it would wipe out their savings — including the grant-cum-salary that Lana Pearson had given them.

"Once we complete the quest, we'll be swimming in funds again," Obrav said confidently.

"No we won't," Hana corrected. "We have next month's rent to pay."

"Shit," Obrav said.

"Yeah, my rent is coming due," Meg said, frowning. "I was kind-of counting on the quest rewards. I can't afford to pay it without the quest rewards."

"And if we don't register this, we won't have any money for next month," Cassidy said, throwing her hands up. "We already took three months to get this done. I've been working on this day and night. I'm seeing blueprints in my dreams. Are we doing this or not? If we aren't, I'll just sell it."

"Sell it?" Obrav said, frowning. "What's this about selling it?"

"And what do you mean, you'll sell it. We all worked on this!" Hana protested.

"But it's my design and my hours," Cassidy said. "And you know, it's not as if I was going to keep the entire payment. I'd share! But just sitting on it is not doing anybody any good."

"I just… that…" Hana fell silent, biting her lip.

"She's right," Meg said. Her eyes twinkled a little and she reached out, pinching Cassidy's cheeks. She pulled her hand back after it got slapped, laughing. "Look at our little Cas. All grown up."

"Hana, can I borrow your scissors?" Cassidy said, glaring at Meg.

"No! No one touches my scissors." Hana stared at Meg, then grinned. "Though I could buy a set just for stabbing Meg."

"Hey!"

The group laughed at the annoyed cosplayer before sobering up after a few moments, their gazes drawn back to the System-paper that held the blueprints. Eventually, Obrav spoke up. "Just do it."

Hana put a hand on Cassidy's shoulder and gave it a squeeze before Meg nodded. Receiving their confirmation, Cassidy's hand hovered over the registration button, hesitating for a brief moment more, before it plunged down.

The data blipped, and then after a few seconds, a big 'Registered' notice appeared on the blueprint. Moments later, the party received a quest confirmation along with the rest of their rewards. One advantage of System-rewards was the lack of wait times.

After finishing perusing the notifications, Cassidy looked around at the group before breaking the silence.

"So… uhh… what do we do now?"

****

"Finally!" Lana rolled her eyes as she read the notification. Group four really was the slowest of the groups she'd put together. Still, she had high hopes for the team. If they could keep producing blueprints, they might actually be able to start the formation of a new industry in the region.

Though, she had to say, as she sipped on the kombucha drink with one idle hand; the other groups were much further ahead of them. But humanity could not rely just on producing unique foodstuffs and combat Classers. They needed to branch out.

"Now, what else do we need…" Lana tapped her lips, flicking between the notices and messages she received. There had been something from the General, something about clothing. There! Their uniforms were becoming an issue, with the majority of their pre-System uniforms destroyed. In the field, they were working on purchasing System-enabled armor that was adjustable, but during non-duty periods, the General had begun complaining of a lack of uniformity.

Hee. Uniformity.

Lana cracked a grin at her own pun, before sending a quick message to the General's aide. A few minutes later, she had her confirmation. A few more minutes, and the local Quest board had a new notice. One for an off-duty uniform blueprint and a second one, set to trigger afterwards, for the production of a few thousand pieces of said approved uniform blueprint.

Leaning back, Lana nodded. Sooner or later, group four would spot it. And hopefully take on the contract. In the meantime…

"What am I going to do with you?" Lana said, calling up the details of group eight. Converting vehicles to Mana-fuelled transportation methods were common. But group eight had chosen to convert construction equipment instead, figuring it was a good idea. Except, with the fast-increasing Levels of those around, the need for human-made construction equipment was quickly disappearing.

She sighed, considering how best to shove them in the right direction. Or whether to just leave them alone…

Beside her chair, a low growl erupted from below. Placing a hand down, Lana scratched Howard's head while considering. Work for the wicked was never over. And if it was not as thrilling as killing xenos and taking back cities, it was just as important.

"You better get back soon, you lunk…" Lana whispered, almost unconsciously.

###

The End of *Adventures in Clothing*

Sixteen Months Post-System

This is Harry Prince, reporting from Lyon, France, on the state of Europe after the System Apocalypse. Earth is a Dungeon World now, and the monsters are stronger and more vicious than ever. Aliens—creatures in the shape and form of our myths—have arrived, and they claim our cities by dint of strength and the System.

The System shapes our lives, gives us Classes and Levels. More and more Basic Classes have broken through the barrier of the first 50 Levels. Others, having received Perks that allowed them to skip the initial tier, are powerful Advanced Classes that lead the vanguard of the battle.

Humanity has allied and fought our alien overlords. They claim our lands, our Shops, our buildings. But they bring with them new resources, new Adventuring Guilds, and knowledge on how to survive in this changed world.

Europe is no longer ours, not solely. Not in the majority. The Truinnar, the Movana, the Grimsar, and more have claimed it, and humanity lives on the edges of what was once ours, driven to do battle over and over again in dungeons and against monsters of yore.

I can only hope that humanity has redoubts of greater strength elsewhere.

Interdimensional Window SHOPping

The normal process of being teleported through time and space—and potentially dimensions, Nick was never entirely sure—was instantaneous. You placed your hand on the Shop orb, which was often linked to a Settlement orb, though not always, and then *bam*! You were there.

Not this time.

Instead, Nick felt his body twisted and pressed, the very fabric of his reality torn apart and put together, microseconds stretching into an eternity each. In his mind's eye, or perhaps with his real eyes, he saw portions of his old life flashing by. A loving wife, working on a trailer with his father, long hours playing poker with friends.

Then, his present one, mixing in. The poker players transformed from his friends into monsters from the deepest myths. Adam grew long, pointed ears, his naturally ombre skin darkening even further to the color of a cloudy, moonless night. Leo suited his name, growing fur and fangs, his nose and mouth elongating into a muzzle, his ponytail transforming into tawny mane. Down by his right, Sam turned into a pixie, shrinking so she was barely taller than the wooden table.

Monsters crept along the edges of the table, hiding in the shadows of cheap IKEA lamps. Goblins, guai, werewolves, harpies. More. So much more. In the distance of the half-solid room, the windows of this dream world silhouetted even larger, nastier creatures. One shadow in particular kept coming, closer and closer.

Just before the windows broke apart as a jabberwocky crashed through, reality snapped back into place... Nick staggered, hand raised in fear to deflect the massive monster.

Reflexive motion turned into swaying nausea, and he had to breathe fast and deep as he struggled to control his body. Thankfully, Class Resistances came into play moments later, snapping into place and stabilizing his physical form. Interdimensional Shopper, for all its various negatives, was meant for such trips.

Not his first Class, but resetting from "Junk of All Trades" was no big loss. If he had a choice when the apocalypse started and the System arrived, he would never have taken it. The fact that there was a choice, but he hadn't known to take it, Nick ignored with ease and practice.

Some regrets weren't worth returning to.

Anyway, the Class reset was part and parcel of his new career.

Interdimensional Travel Shock Resisted!

"Are you doing well, valued customer?" The voice was filled with concern, perfectly tuned and pitched to set one at ease. Female, older and matronly and midwestern, it was like a warm hug of a voice.

Auditory Charm Resisted!

Too bad he was ready for that kind of trick too.

"Who are you? Where am I?" Nick cried out, shrinking back from the woman. Tall, beautiful purple hair that reached her shoulders, and not one but two pairs of tits. She was offering him the most sympathetic smile he'd ever seen and was even clutching his arm, pulling so it pressed against her.

"You're in the Smallest Big Bang Supermart, the Galaxy's Premier Shopping Destination for the Discerning Shopper," the alien lady chirped. "I'm your *personal* shopper, Vi, and will be happy to guide you around, Nick."

"How'd you know my name?" Nick said, startled.

"I scanned you, of course. We do that for all our esteemed customers," Vi said. "It's not every day we get a *Gambler* in here, though. It's not the most popular—or survivable—Class choice on a Dungeon World."

Nick grunted. That had been his other option when the apocalypse came, and he'd agreed with her. Getting automatic attribute points in Luck was one thing, but Luck wasn't going to stop an enraged overgrown hamster from eating your face.

Not that Junk of All Trades was much better, but at least he had options with the Class Skills, including the ability to swap them out for even worse variations of a Skill's other Classes used around him. It had given him at least some combat options in the beginning, along with a lousy heal. Good enough to keep him alive until he got his lucky break.

Probably why he chose to use Gambler as his cover Class too. He was lucky after all.

"What can I say, I'm lucky." Nick narrowed his gaze, standing straight. He did not, however, pull his arm from hers. Being woozy and a little out of it was part and parcel of the act, after all. "But this isn't my Shop. Mine's a lot more green. And a lot uglier. Has an orc with a scar and an eye missing too. Don't even know who he was kidding—you could get that fixed by the Shop super simple."

"Hakarta."

"Orc. Same thing."

He noted Vi's eyes flickered with suppressed anger. One thing Nick had learned was Galactics didn't like casual speciesism. Deliberate speciesism was fine, but casual ones? Not a chance. Certainly not directed at groups that were considered more established, like the Hakarta. Annoyed or not, though, she kept the smile on her face, even leaning in deeper and purring a little more.

"Come, come. Let's sit down. I'm sure you're still feeling a little nauseous? You do seem to have recovered well though, Nick, my dear."

"Good Constitution, I guess." Nick made sure to stumble a little as she led him away from the teleportation pad to a nearby open awning. He flopped down into the swinging chair, which was floating in midair, a metal base beneath utilizing powerful magnets to keep the entire thing aloft. "Had to put quite a few points in to survive Earth."

"Of course, of course." She looked at him a little suspiciously still but moved on as she brought out a yellow bottle. "Have you tried Esvan alcohol yet? I understand it's similar to your world's whiskey."

"More a bourbon fan myself, but sure…" He took the alcohol from her, sipping on it carefully. It was sweeter than he would have expected from the description.

Debuff: Mild Alcohol Poisoning!

"Oooh, this is the good stuff. Hard to get a buzz these days." Nick made a face, a grimace that Vi echoed.

"Shall I add a bottle to your bill?" Vi said.

"Uhh…sure. I got a bill?"

"You will. We just need you to confirm the opening of an account," Vi said, smiling. She conjured a datapad for him, showing him a bottle of Esvan on it for only twelve Credits. "If you put your hand on the pad, it'll authorize us to start a bill and debit your System Credit account later."

Nick sipped on the drink again, frowning a little. "Only what I buy, right?"

"Of course." Big eyes as she leaned over to give him quite the view. She kept that smile on her face, even as her finger poked at the terms beneath. "See?"

Nick scanned the legalese. It was, surprisingly, quite short and clear. Only authorization for whatever he bought today, no ongoing debit or added charges. Basically, everything she had said. Which marked them as somewhat more scrupulous in Nick's estimation.

"Yeah, sorry. Can't be too careful, you know?" Nick said, placing his hand on the datapad. He felt the connection being created, then the prompt from the System. A quick scan showed that, no, there was no additional legalese added on this side, either. Taking his hand off the datapad, he picked up the glass and swirled the amber liquid before sipping again. "Let's make it two."

"Of course, dear Nick."

He didn't miss how she shifted the pad so he could not see it anymore as she punched in the addition. Then, she slipped the pad away into a front pocket that hung just beneath—uncomfortably close to—her bottom pair of mammaries

He was fast getting an idea of how this was going to play out, but his buzz was getting going now, and she was talking again.

"What did you say?" He didn't even need to feign confusion this time.

Hidden disgust—not that well-hidden, not to him—sparked in her eyes. "I was asking what you were looking for that you couldn't purchase direct from the System."

"Oh, that!" Nick leaned forward, glancing around. "Yeah, shit. I meant...well."

"A problem, dear Nick?"

"No, just. Well. I had something that was a bit...unusual."

"The broken card dealer strapped to your other arm?" Vi said with a slight smile. "We have our own Artisans who can fix that for you. It looks like it's been modified a little?"

"I…" Nick coughed. "Look, it's not that I use it all the time. Just sometimes. Mostly, it's for the knives, you know? Got to stay safe. It's a Dungeon World after all." He shifted his left hand, twisting it in a certain way for the throwing blade to pop into it. "Works the first time, mostly. But…" He dropped the knife to the side, flexing his muscles again. This time, a whining crack echoed rather than an actual weapon appearing. "Well, that happens."

"Ah. We can't have you defenseless, now can we."

"Also, you know, the card dealer itself, it doesn't switch out anymore. Or let me slip a card in, when I need it."

"I'm sure our people could fix that."

"Great, great." Nick grabbed at his glass and took a deep sip before he lowered the now-empty vessel. "Just need to be able to slip the knives in, you know? Subtly and easily and all that."

Vi refilled his glass without prompting. "If you'd take it off, we'll get it fixed. At the Smallest Big Bang we do not judge the needs of our clients, of any kind." She squeezed his hand, which she still hadn't let go of, kneeling as she was next to him to emphasize her point.

"I, well…" Nick smiled a little tightly. "Maybe later. I got, you know…" He was unsure how to decline her advances. This was a little more blatant than usual. Correction, a lot more blatant as she brushed his arm up her body and then let it go with a pout.

"Of course, Nick. Just tell me what I can get you."

"Ummm…I guess, the usual?" He flushed a little, ducking his head as he breathed in hastily. What was wrong with him? Why did he feel so disappointed at her changing how she called him? He wasn't into her. Sure, she had a nice pair of tits—an amazing pair—but he wasn't a nineteen-year-old.

"The usual?"

"Yeah, you know, I need replacement Mana batteries. A knife, a good one. Lost the last one I had. Armored jumpsuits for protection. Food, enough for two weeks. Real food, not the monster meat, you know? I don't know how people eat that stuff. It's creepy…"

Nick let himself ramble on as he pulled up his notification log. It'd been suppressed at some point, and he hadn't even noticed it, even though he normally kept it rolling in his vision. He knew some people hated that, wanting only the most important notifications to appear. In his job, though, keeping it running was important.

"Anyway, yeah. Just the basics."

"Easily done." She had pulled out the datapad again at some point, was keying in everything he said. "Did you have anything to sell?"

Trying to keep his eyes focused on the glass, on the liquid within, he sipped. Hard, because he knew he was a little drunker than he should be. But more than that, he couldn't let her see he was reading his logs, so it all had to be controlled mentally.

Tricky, tricky, tricky.

"Nah, I just got some basic stuff. Nothing you'd be interested in, and I'll get a better deal on Earth."

"Ah, well, I wouldn't be so sure of that, dear Nick." He found himself smiling as she blinked up at him and lowered her voice. "I could get you better rates on a barter, you know. No Credits, so we don't have to pay the System."

"Really?"

"I would not lie to you."

"Well, okay then. I guess I could…" He waved his left hand, the one holding the glass to the side. Monster loot fell in a rain, forming a small mound. Meat, claws, organs, venom sacs, hide, and scales. Basic stuff, nothing over Level 30.

In his mind's eyes, he saw it. There.

Pheromone Attack Resisted!

Debuff Received: Alcohol Poisoning (Mild)!

Pheromone Attack Resisted!

Perhaps it was better to say the repetition. Damn, she was good. Looking at the timestamps, it was clear he wasn't resisting all of it. In fact, maybe only half. Which meant the longer he was here, the more susceptible he was going to be.

There was a limit, of course. It was a charm, not mind control. It'd get worst until it stopped, and then it was just…what influence she had. But it wasn't good either way. Not fair at all, to play these games.

"Well, I…Here?" Vi grimaced, but then flicked her hands. The loot he dropped began to disappear, falling into the ground one after the other with surprising speed.

Nick lurched upward, then slumped backward, the drink still clutched in his hand spilling a little. His head was spinning as he croaked out, "What's going on?"

"I'm inventorying your loot, of course, dear Nick. You are selling it to us, right?"

"I…" Nick blinked. He needed to figure out how to get out of here. Fast. Being actually drugged was not the plan. "I guess. Yeah." Again, he sipped the Esvan, drawn to consume more. It tasted like honey and fire, sliding down his gut and warming him, driving away his worries. "Got to get it sold. Need more of a stake when I…get back."

"Of course. Let me." Vi refilled his glass of Esvan, then propped the bottle next to him as she slipped back a little. "I'll just put the rest of your order in, yes?"

"Sure, sure." Nick paused, then added with a little smile, "I got to say, the customer service here is great. Better than the bastard fox…"

"Of course, dear customer." Something in the way she said that bothered him. Chasing that idea, he drank more. Damn, but that was going fast…Good thing he had the bottle. Reaching for it, he tried pouring more, missed, and spilled the liquid on himself. Vaguely, he could see her working the datapad, the loot nearly gone.

Whatever. He didn't need a glass. He just started using the bottle itself.

When, exactly, he slipped into oblivion, he was not certain. Somewhere between three-quarters and four-fifths of the bottle.

***

Waking up was a pain. Literally. Someone had hired a team of tiny dwarves, all of whom had been given pickaxes and bright lights, and then hid them inside his skull. Now they were hard at work, and the only good news was they weren't singing that blasted song. Didn't matter, though—they were pretty damn industrious at slamming those picks.

How it was possible for his body to heal from grievous wounds that would have crippled and killed him in minutes and still, somehow, manage to give him a hangover the next day, he was not certain. Maybe a cosmic joke played by a teetotaler of a System.

Or maybe the kind of drugs and poisons required to make a System-enhanced human drunk was a tad on the very toxic side.

"Wake up." A shove, a push, made his stomach lurch. He threw himself forward, only to find himself bound around his chest, which meant he'd ended up clotheslining himself on the rope. The chair wasn't moving from its position, and a hand came along to grab at him at the same time, the grabber's reflexes lightning fast. Not quick enough to dodge the vomit, though, as Nick spewed the contents of his stomach all over splayed feet. Large, slappy, kind-of-like-a-duck feet, with the way they were shaped.

"Disgusting! These humans are all the same." A hand pushed Nick's face up, and water splashed over him. He shook it off, spluttering, as his mind cleared under the shocking coldness. He managed to even get some of it in his mouth and down his throat.

"Now, who sent you?"

"Sent me? No one. You're the one who grabbed me," Nick snarled, shaking his head gingerly like a wet dog. He opened his mouth, hoping they'd get the hint and feed him more water, but no luck.

"We never talked about that." Vi's voice now, coming from the side where she sat, legs crossed. Not friendly at all, the way she was looking at him.

Shit. She was right. The pheromones had thrown him off his game and the script. But… "Not hard to guess, right? I didn't come here on purpose, so it had to be you."

"Nice recovery. I don't believe it." The slapper leaned down, putting his face right in front of Nick's. Which was quite the feat, considering Nick was five ten, and a lot of it was in his torso. Still, his assailant was even bigger.

Big eyes, eyes the size of dinner plates, looked at him, unblinking. Soft down around the eyes themselves, a hooked nose, and a mouth with razor-sharp teeth finished the visage. Maybe duck wasn't that far off. He'd even be cute, with that silver-gray coloration of his feathers and skin, if he wasn't looking at Nick so predatorily.

"I don't care. Let me go. This isn't how you treat a customer."

"And that's why. Too late. Also, not panicky enough." The hand came down on his shoulder. It was webbed too, with talons on the end that uncurled and punched into his skin as the hand on his shoulder tightened.

"Shit. You want panicky? I just came out of a damn apocalypse. This ain't the first time I've been tied up. At least you ain't cannibals." A slight pause. "You're not cannibals, right?"

"Why would you humans eat each other? You're on a Dungeon World. There's monsters everywhere!" Vi said, exasperated.

"That's what I said too," Nick said, trying the bonds on his arms. Tight, though there was a slight give. He might be able to slip out, but they'd tied him to the arms of the chair, and since they were right in front of him, it wasn't as though he'd slip out unnoticed. "Guess what they said."

"What?" Vi said, curious.

"They liked the taste."

Now she was looking nauseous too. Nick didn't blame her. The cannibals were still high on his list of repeating nightmares, especially considering it was over a year since the start of the System when he'd run into them. He couldn't even count—and refused to find out—how many humans they'd killed.

"Enough." The hand squeezed again, and Nick hissed, looking at the birdman. "Tell me who sent you. Otherwise, there's no point keeping you alive."

"You can't. The System logs transports to and from Shops. If you kill me, you're in trouble," Nick said hastily.

"And how do you know that?" birdman said, softly.

"You think I didn't look it up?" Nick said. "I'm not insane. I get transported into a seedy two-penny dimension, I'm going to check what it means before I do that the next time, you know."

The birdman frowned and Nick exhaled, wincing in pain as the talons shifted. Stupid, stupid, stupid. The pain in his head and the aftereffects of her pheromone attack and the drink were still leaving him two beats behind the dance. He was saying things he should never have, giving more hints. Breaking character. But they were still buying it.

"Smart man. But I got something even better." His shoulder was released and Nick couldn't help but sigh in relief. Moments later, though, that hand was back with something glimmering, something that snapped around his neck. Cold metal tightened around the muscles, strong enough to dimple the flesh and make it uncomfortable to breathe.

"What the hell, man. Consent is key! You didn't even ask for my safe word," Nick said.

"No safety, not anymore." Those eyes staring at him—they hadn't blinked. Not once. Maybe they couldn't blink. "You think I haven't dealt with spies like you before? I don't care which of my competitors is doing this. The lesson will be the same."

"Lesson, what lesson?" Now Nick was worried, because those eyes…they weren't fluffy-cute-birdman eyes. Those were predator eyes.

"Boom." Taloned hands near his neck moved apart as the birdman showcased what he meant.

"Torak. I didn't agree to this," Vi spoke up. "Killing…"

"He came in here trying to trick us. Scope out the competition? Nah. No way." Torak bent down, and Nick heard the soft click of magnets releasing the chair. Moments later, he and the chair were lifted, the whole contraption being carried along. "I didn't last this long being weak."

"Look, wait. Let's talk about this…" Nick said, struggling in the chair.

"You should have talked when you had the chance."

"Torak…"

Sadly, the room they had dumped him in, which was just inside the actual—and only—building in this dimensional space, was not far at all from the teleportation pad. Each of Torak's steps took Nick closer to it.

"Make sure you finish the sale before he leaves. Add all the junk he asked for, mark it up appropriately. Drain him." A slight pause, then Torak turned his head, rotating it on his frame without shifting his torso at all. "How much did he have anyway?"

"Forty-seven thousand and change."

"Definitely a spy."

"What? Why?" Nick cried.

"Perfect spy amount. Not too much to be surprising, not too little to make us skip on grabbing him when his 'port came up."

Nick belatedly remembered to scan the man. In fact, he'd forgotten to scan Vi too. In seconds, he had their information filed away in his logs.

"Teleport Bandit?" Nick squeaked as he read the man's Class. Also the high Mana and hit points, which meant he was at least an Advanced Class. "And Devilish Shopkeeper? Who are you people?"

"Torak, he really might just be…"

"Doesn't matter. I don't take chances." Torak dropped Nick and the chair on the platform and crossed his arms. "Add the chair and collar as a gift and finish the bill, Vi. Now."

"This…"

"Do it. Or else you can join him." Torak let out a low squawk. "Or I could just sell your bond back to Spec'bid."

Now Vi looked fearful, paling a little and hammering on the datapad. She spun it around and showed it to Torak. "Done. It's done, all right. Damn you."

"Good girl. You might be useful for something." Torak pivoted his head back and grinned wide at the stunned Nick, never bothering to move his torso.

"What do you mean—"

The birdman wasn't listening, his talon-hand waving in the air, triggering the teleportation. That same twisted wrongness of dimensional manipulation threw him into the membranes of reality once more, spinning him through multiple dimensions of space and time.

***

"—man!" Nick shouted out, only to find himself back. Reality stabilized, with his body feeling a lot less abused this time. No surprise since the return journey was being reinforced by the System and his own Class Skills. As existence reasserted itself, a low, insistent beeping had him jerking his hands to his throat. Only to be caught, once again, by the rope holding him still.

"Easy there, Mr. Kilen. We see it. *Temporal Field.*" A voice, soothing, calm. The kind you expected to come from a British butler. Which made it all the funnier when it came from a pink-skinned, feeler-headed, Northern Irish–accented Galactic called Ijj,hh12'ss, or Bob as he allowed others to call him.

Also known as…

"Boss! This isn't the time for all calm and mannered. Get the bomb off me. Now!" Nick said, freeing his hand. Now that he wasn't actually trying to hide all his Skills, escaping the bonds was easy. Weird how a lot of Agility combined with a lifetime of bartending, card sharking, waitering, and other manual jobs had given him quite the flexibility.

Never mind his small Perk of being "Slippery."

Hands free, Nick darted them to his neck, only to find them struck aside. The movement was so fast he never even saw it, and it left his hands smarting, down by his side.

"This is a Tier I slave collar. Illegal on most planets. Quite expensive and normally quite stable, but this one is secondhand. I'd say its stability is only at forty-seven percent of the original." Pink hands hovered next to his neck as Bob turned his head from side to side, examining the collar and information only he could see. "Correction. Forty-one point six percent."

"Just get it off, will you?" Nick pleaded, cold sweat on his brow.

"There!" A click, and Bob grabbed the now-open collar. It disappeared moments later into his Inventory. "All done." Hands dipped, and the rope around Nick's chest parted, the flicker of light of a knife conjured and then put away going by too fast for him to properly lock upon it.

"I take it you failed."

"Depends on your definition…" Nick groused as he stood up. He gripped the chair back firmly, shaking his head a little. "I got records and evidence of a Shop dimensional transfer hijacking, the sale of overinflated goods, and the use of a chemical and pheromones to induce purchasing behavior outside of allowable limits." Lips pursed, he added, "Also my attempted murder."

"Then they completed the sale?" Bob said intently.

"They did," Nick confirmed.

"Then we have confirmed jurisdiction." Bob grinned and stepped aside. Behind him, a creature that Nick could only describe as a jellyfish given humanoid form floated forward, suckers reaching for his head.

"Hi, Stue. Be gentle with me, will you?" Nick leaned forward, keeping a hand on the chair. "It's been a hard day."

No answer. Stue never did, not auditorily. Not when he had a choice. Sure, Stue had a voice box that translated his thoughts into words, but he hated using it. Said it didn't sound like him, not even after hours of tuning.

Which didn't surprise Nick at all, since telepathic communication was so much more detailed and rich. No voice box—no matter how sophisticated—could mimic the myriad emotions and thoughts that a single moment of communication could provide.

Nick felt Stue's tentacles on his head, digging into his memories. It wasn't painful, just a little uncomfortable as the last hour of his life was replayed. Everything that had happened, everything he'd felt, everything he'd sensed. All repeated, recorded in Stue's mind, and later downloaded to an external recording for the Galactic courts.

His entire trip was just for that, a way to entrap Shop bandits who waylaid humans during the transfer to their System-designated Shop. Most cases, the transfer was just a little bump, a shift of who was going to receive a customer when they either requested a new Shop or were being assigned one on their first usage. That had been the majority of cases during the initial year as humanity was integrated.

Those kinds of infractions were a fine. Fines those Shops were sometimes happy enough to pay, what with the potential for ongoing profits from their stolen customers.

Nowadays, even if those cases still made up the largest number, the actual bandits, the outlaws and gangsters and conmen who made their livelihoods cheating dimensional Shop transfers, were coming into play. After all, humanity was finally making enough Credits to become worthwhile targets.

That, of course, was where people like Bob, Nick, and Stue came into play.

"I do wish you'd take the Neural Link. This would be a lot simpler," Bob said when Stue drifted off, leaving Nick to wash his mouth of the dryness and taste of blueberries that telepathy always left him with. The dry mouth was entirely psychosomatic, of course, but it wasn't something he managed to shake.

Yet.

"Give the targets even more reason to be wary of me? No chance," Nick said. "One of these days, one of them is just going to kill me and call it a risk worth taking."

Bob just smiled at Nick's protest before he turned to Stue. The jellyfish bobbled in its version of a nod as tendrils wrapped around a cone-shaped structure that was the guild's memory-storage device.

"Well, once again, good job. The Guild of Dimensional Shopkeepers is grateful for your service. You'll receive your usual seven-day furlough before you are sent on your next mission," Bob intoned in his usual officious tone. "Our enforcers will track down the rogue Shop and their personnel and enact appropriate punishments."

What exactly those punishments were, Nick had yet to find out. Nor did he intend to. Galactics had weird ideas about appropriate punishment. A flicker in the corner of his vision showed Nick his Quest had updated.

Quest Completed!

Visit the Smallest Big Bang Supermart. Verify its legality and collect evidence of wrongdoing for the Guild of Dimensional Shopkeepers.

Reward: +3,238 XP (Bonus XP granted due to increased difficulty of Quest). Continued employment with the Guild of Dimensional Shopkeepers. +11 Reputation with the Guild.

Nice! Close to a new Level then, with this. One more good investigation and he'd Level again. That is, if they had more work for him.

"Hey, Bob. Question. Why not just use the System to find them and punish them?" Nick said. "It knows everything, right? So why use people like me? Not to say I don't want my job, this is still—overall—safer than getting shot or clawed at on Earth."

"Cost, of course." Bob looked surprised at the question, then swiftly irritated. "You and the rest of your human cohort are much cheaper to utilize than constant information requests from the System. In addition, we never know what particular form of lawbreaking is occurring. Then there are the more sophisticated scams, which need to be validated and punished. They are, in and of themselves, unworthy of the price of a single question."

Nick grunted. He liked those jobs, really. Swapping out one kind of ammunition manufacturer for another, using a lower-grade power cell, or reselling Mana batteries that weren't rated for Dungeon World use. The Shopkeepers, when found out, rarely made a fuss and paid their fines. Rarely tried to kill him even if they figured out whom he was working for.

"Whatever." Nick rubbed his face. "I'm going to get some R & R."

He was nearly out of the room before Bob spoke. They'd set up a bunker in the side of a mountain somewhere in the Appalachians that some unfortunate prepper had never managed to claim.

"For your next cover Class, what do you think you're going to choose? We should begin building your identity now."

"How about Ballroom Dancer," Nick said just before he exited the room. He couldn't help but chuckle to himself as the doors slid closed behind him, cutting off Bob's words of indignation.

Small victories like this were the pleasures he lived for these days. It made his job worthwhile. Well, that and the chance to keep a portion of humanity safe while receiving a steady paycheck.

###

The End of *Interdimensional Window SHOPping*

Wee Timorous Mousie

Sun dappled down on their fur, like the gentle caress of a long-lost parent, soothing the two mousekin in their deep sleep.

The dew barely had a chance to form, brief little gems glimmering into life and fading into oblivion a moment later, leaving only an echo of petrichor to mark its passing. The wind was echoing the lazy pace the morning was shaping into, barely ruffling the fur of the pair.

It was enough, though. The fading coolness of the evening, the flickering light, the rising warmth, and the gentle touches of wind all gathered together into Holland's sleeping mind, and roused him to wakefulness before he even opened his eyes.

Holland didn't want to wake up. The warmth was perfect. Selene nestled into his back, her little claws buried just right in his fur. He could feel her whiskers tickling the edge of his ear, and the contentment was a deep little ball of perfection down in his belly, making his tail curl into an even tighter arc.

Heaven, if he believed in such things.

A sharp twitch cracked through his arm. No reason for it, just a memory of an injury long healed. No real cause for the twitch, aside from the memory, but for whatever reason the memory insisted on itself. Not a full memory, not a real memory.

Pain, darkness, gunfire, blood. Always blood. A tiny hand, grasping at his, blood on the pin-thin claws, driving into the pads of his paw with urgency.

He twitched again; the memory hitting him like a flash. Confused. He wasn't grasping that little hand; it was his little hand, his paws, grabbing at his father, before...

Holland's eyes popped open. He couldn't help the minor hitch of his breath as he woke fully up, but he slowed it down right away, falling right back into his sleeping rhythm. Didn't want to wake up Selene, didn't want to lose the moment. He closed his eyes again. Maybe if he faked sleep hard enough, he'd fall back into it.

Selene's arm slipped over, under Holland's arm and across his chest, hunting for his hand. He met her halfway, holding her hand tight and pulling it into his chest, and let out a long sigh.

The reward for the sigh was a tight squeeze of support, and the gentle nuzzle of Selene's nose and whiskers alongside his jaw.

That made him smile.

Selene must have felt that, because she gave him one more quick hug, and then disengaged her arm and got up.

The sudden cold was unpleasant, but Holland didn't bother trying to cling to the remnant warmth. The past was eternal unto itself, and didn't need his efforts to make it last longer. Gods grant, someday he'd elevate, and be able to traverse all along the conscious moments of his life, dwelling as he wanted.

 Not today. Today was just another day of earning his place in the moment, for future him to enjoy. His choice, to make every moment a heaven or hell.

Holland rolled over onto all fours, stretching all along the length of himself, arching up until his back cracked in five places, a rippling snapping that seemed to echo off of the trees. Selene laughed in response, shaking herself into a giant ball of fur, and then letting all the fur settle back down along her compact and curvaceous body. When she caught Holland's gaze on her, she laughed and gave him an extra shake before squatting down to unpack the camp gear.

Standing up brought even more fresh air into Holland's lungs, and he rolled his shoulders and took in what the morning had to offer.

Breakfast on its way, judging from Selene's actions. Clear skies. No threats nearby, not that he expected any here. The forest glade was serene and protected, even with the slow-moving river that ambled through at the edge of it.

A bath might suit the morning, but the flicker of dream still hadn't quite left Holland as yet. And they still had work to do. Vacation work, but still work.

With a gesture, his storage space opened, and he pulled out all of his gear, laid it all out nearly in front of him.

Under armour, rigging points. Long, laced boots, open at the heels for mobility, tough hide all along their length. War skirt around the waist, pleated armour falling down to just cover his knees. A little flare of it, with a quick spinning step, to get it to settle just right and let his tail out through the gap in the back.

Uniform shirt, with its cooling tech and other support weaves built in. Duty belt with holsters and pouches, set just so. Gaps at the back, an old habit from his patrol days, to avoid awkwardness when sitting in a chair for long periods of time. Armoured vest on top of that, chameleon and beam repellent weave integral, supporting defensive tool and enchantments.

Pistol in its holster. Rifle up, slung across his shoulder. Holland stared at this helmet for a moment, and then decided against it, tossing it back in storage.

After all, this was a vacation.

"Shall we eat?"

The smell hit him, and he turned around. Selene had outdone herself. Nothing fancy, just a little grub stew with boiled, beetle-stuffed buns. Nothing special, but just about impossible to get that particular blend anymore. The Cadre had moved far past those worlds, long ago. She must have been saving them up.

Selene wasn't waiting for him. She'd already broken out the camp chairs, and was chowing down on a bun, with a bowl of the spicy stew held in her other paw.

Somehow, Selene had found time to gear up. She wasn't part of the Cadre Armed Forces, so she wasn't in the modern military uniform that Holland wore. She preferred the old-school adventurer look, custom plate armour and a two-handed glaive that radiated a menace that always made Holland a little fearful.

Every Mousekin was a warrior. Even those who only served at home. Selene was one of the best, and Holland let a wave of pride add to the warmth of the day as they settled down for breakfast.

***

The glaive went through the neck of the Alpha with a slight popping sound, a faint ring of steel pinging into a soulful harmonic. The monster's howl of rage was cut short, but as Holland watched its head slowly tumble off, he could see that the beast hadn't given up its life just yet. Its mouth was still trying to chomp down, its eyes blazing as it looked for something, anything, that it could deliver one last bite to.

Selene wasn't one to take a chance, and less than a heartbeat later, she'd sliced the head in half with a follow-up backhand.

Holland popped his rifle magazine out, replacing it with a fresh one. Tapped it hard against his thigh in habit, seated it in place, slapped it back in. Tapped the charge switch, flicked the safety with one absent claw, all while looking around.

The Alpha's lair was empty of everything except corpses, gore, and the varied stenches of combat. Even the glow of the ambient light from the glowing fungus on the walls was tainted into twisted shades, covered as it was with viscera.

Selene was grinning ear to ear. Her armour was pitted and scarred, acid burned and clawed, barely hanging on. There was a huge gouge running the length of her thigh, and the blood dripping down it was still foaming in reaction to the toxic stew on the Alpha's claws.

Holland wasn't much better. The damn thing had been tough, and even in a support role, he'd been hard pressed to keep from getting disemboweled twice. One hell of a challenge, but not enough to level up. Not enough for Holland.

More than enough for Selene. The glow on her face was all the notification Holland needed.

The vacation had been a successful romp for them before this, a brief escape from the cares of life, but this was all it took to push it up to being an unmitigated success.

The grin soared across his face, and they were in each other's arms a moment later. One last sweetness to finish a week of happiness.

***

"Cadet Holland. How was your vacation?"

Holland grinned as he sat down in the chair the major was waving him into. "Excellent. Selene managed to level-up after a boss kill, so we've put in a request for a litter."

That got a raised eyebrow and a grin back from the major. "I've no doubt you'll see that approved. You've both been in the top ranks of your generation since you graduated. I think I can speak for the whole of the forces when I say we've been waiting for the day your reproduction licences came through. I look forward to training your whole brood!"

"Thank you, sir! I look forward to the challenge of being a parent." Someday the Mousekin would settle enough worlds that population control wouldn't be an issue. Until that day, everyone had to fight for the chance to be a parent.

Major Brigs smiled back, and a distance came over his eyes. Holland sat back, giving the old mouse some time to get to whatever he was preparing himself for. Holland wasn't worried. If it was something really bad, Brigs would have cut to the chase with no pre-amble. Brigs wasn't one to rush when he was trying to say something serious, though, so Holland let his gaze wander about the office for a moment, to give a polite opening for Brigs to gather himself.

A part of Holland wondered if it was time for him to be promoted. He wasn't due for a promotion, but he'd been jumped from captain to cadet a year earlier than anyone had expected. Holland knew he was good, but he also knew that the promotion was a result of sheer luck and a mission near gone sideways. He'd had good practice at repressing the shudder that came with the recollections of it, facing down an actual giant, watching three other platoons wiped out in a heartbeat. Their deaths had given the rest of his company enough time for one final cataclysmic strike of prepared weapons. It had been far too near of a thing, and Holland had expected a court martial at the end of it instead of a promotion.

But the Mousekin forces rewarded luck as well as proven skill, so he knew he was now on track for greater commands. He just had to put in his time.

As the silence grew, Holland was starting to doubt that it was good news. He couldn't help himself and shifted just a little in his chair.

The Major looked up from whatever distance had captured him, and for a moment, Holland could see the age in Brigs' whiskers. The desk between them seemed to grow a little, and Holland found himself noticing a few other things.

The awards on the walls, the holograms of different units. A tattered old battle flag on the wall over the window. The row of ribbons on Brigs' chest. A bit of a ring on the wood of the desk, from whatever beverage Brigs had been drinking before Holland arrived.

And the shrouded blur of an official orders communique.

Holland sat up straighter and looked up to see Brigs staring right at him.

"I'm sorry, Holland. I know the timing is terrible. But you're the only available force at the moment, and this is a now job. And you are back from your vacation."

Holland said nothing. They both knew the problem. The reproduction license was probably going to come through soon, and no one sane wanted to wait on that. Holland was back on active duty, but even a week more on base would probably give him a window pass on his genes, in case the worst happened. That was a set of dice they all rolled, every mission.

Brigs didn't let Holland wonder too long what this was all about. "It's an informal tradition to keep Mousekin home for a rotation when they earn a reproduction license, but we can't do that at this time. This is a big money contract, and it presents a rare opportunity. For you, and for us. It's a Dungeon World. A new one."

Brigs caught the look on Holland's face, but was ready for it. "It's settling down a bit, but still growing. We're getting signs that it might evolve into one of the most dangerous ones yet. The natives are ruffling some feathers, too. Nothing too major yet, but the portents are skewing. So when they saw a contract, the powers that be decided that we needed to send someone

ASAP. Both to fulfill the contract, and to scout out this new Dungeon World. To see if there is a place there for us."

"The mission is straightforward. Some kind of coming-of-age ceremony for a youth. He's been given a Quest. You will be going along to act as bodyguards and mission support. We've already polled for volunteers on this one. Can't assign a line unit to something this risky, not with our current taskings."

Holland nodded. It made sense. High risk, but high reward. A new Dungeon World meant untold opportunities, especially if someone on that world had survived enough to be able to afford hiring mercenaries. Some mitigation of risk…and it was unlikely that some rich parent was going to let their kid face a truly terrible Quest. It should be fine, as long as Brigs didn't say the magic words…

"Should be a cakewalk, though. I'm not seeing any major risk for you. Two dungeon locations. The first one is already established but hasn't been cleaned out yet. The second one is a much higher rating, but you only need to make a quick raid into it, and retrieve some rocks. Couple of weeks, tops. Some tough native beasts, but we aren't seeing anything super high Level in the region. At least…not within your operational area."

Holland sat up a little at that, hesitated, and then decided to just push ahead. "And out of that area? I will need to know about any potential issues that might pop up."

Brigs' whiskers did that little wobble that snuck out when he was trying to waffle on something. "Stick to the planned area, and you should be fine. It is a new Dungeon World, though. At least one dragon, but it's north of your operating area."

"A dragon."

"Small one. Hundreds of kilometres to the edge of its noted hunting range."

"And that's it?"

More whisker wobbles. "Well. You should expect new threats at any time. And some part of the second dungeon seems to have been protected, but again, no reason for you to hit that area. Quick raid. In and out. A few days, tops."

Holland leaned back and crossed his arms. "This is a bad idea. Especially when you're already holding something back from me."

"I am not!"

"Brigs, I still remember Nova Secundas Beta Three."

"A onetime glitch. And full regen was covered for your whole team."

"For my remaining team."

"Details. But fine. Yes, it's going to be a shitshow, but it's your turn in the hot seat. I can cut you some slack. What do you want?"

"I get to pull from my teams, if they didn't volunteer."

Brigs popped his remaining ear back and forth a few times. "Any other mission, for sure. But this is a *new* Dungeon World. You know your contract as well as anyone else. We can't order anyone to go on this mission if they don't volunteer."

Holland snapped his teeth together in dismissal. "Joining up is volunteering. All my teams know that. They'll follow my orders, if you allow me to issue them."

Brigs was quiet for a moment and turned to look out the window. Holland was content to wait him out. It wasn't like he was asking for anything too untoward. Besides, he knew his teams. They'd come along, no matter what. All of them, he expected. And if he was going into the fire, he wanted his best with him.

Hell, half of them were crazy enough that they'd probably love the idea.

With a sigh, Brigs turned back from the window. "Fine, but that's it. We'll give you enhanced armoury access for your loadouts too, but that's it. Nothing more."

Holland stood up to attention. "In that case, I accept. When do we leave?"

"Tomorrow. Your teams are already emptying out the armoury. They've got your kit sorted as well, so you have tonight to say goodbye to Selene."

Holland started to salute, and then Brigs' words hit him. "They already volunteered."

"Everyone one of them. As soon as we announced the brigade's' cadet was leading the mission, they all demanded to be assigned."

Holland was only a little surprised by that, but the warmth that filled his belly rose up to his eyes pretty quick, and took an effort of will to hold back.

Words felt risky, so he just gave a quick nod in reply, saluted, and went to tell Selene the news.

***

Dinner was perfection. Holland's favourite grub, a rare little speckled quinote, was the centre of the meal. Selene had ordered a half-dozen of them, baked into a fragile cloud of pastry that served as the lid to a stew of eggs, spicy little dough balls, and a sweetly sour wine broth. Puffed cheese balls for a side, street food from the world they'd both grown up on, and two frothy mugs of a heavy Hakarta premium stout. Chilling it was probably a crime on any Hakarta world, but it made the heavy brew a perfection of creaminess to Mousekin palates.

"Tomorrow?"

Holland glanced up, only just realizing he'd been staring into the dregs of the stout. The question was wistful, but with an edge Holland had learned to pay attention to.

Selene was looking at with the intensity he'd expected…but there was more to it. The shining luminosity of her eyes had a little extra edge, and if Holland didn't know better, he would think his spouse had been wrestling back tears.

He didn't answer. He didn't need to acknowledge what was on her mind. Didn't need to say anything. Death was always a companion to life for Mousekin. Since the dawn of the System, since the first clan lost to waves of giant monsters, they'd only known war, with brief periods of peace.

Holland had been the one to watch Selene head out for her own missions, more than once. It had been his turn to curl up in their nest-bed, all alone, reaching out to her side in the middle of the night, fighting back the demons that whisper of her doom into his head. It was a burden they both shared, and they'd been together long enough to know that the universe wasn't big enough to hold the right words to soothe each other.

All they could do was cherish the moments together that they stole from the universe. Cherish the moments, the feel of each other, the sounds of each other's breath, and the little bits of the smell of each other that rose up when they buried their noses in each other's fur.

That was all Holland wanted, for this moment. He started to get up, and reached for Selene, but she held her hand up, stopping him before he rose. He cocked his head to the side in question.

"Not yet, love." The glimmer was still there in her eyes, but there was something new in it, as well. Something almost like mischief. "I have something for you, and I want to give it to you now, because once I do and we go upstairs, I want you to make sure I'm sound asleep when you leave."

That put a new fire into Holland, and he sat back down. "I think I can promise that."

The glimmer in her eyes turned positively molten, and she reached back, opening her personal storage space.

Out came a sword. It looked plain, but Holland could feel an almost restless hunger coming off of it. It was in a sturdy, plain leather sheath, but wrapped in a shimmering white cloth.

Selene set it on the table between them, but held up another finger when he started to reach for the blade.

"In a moment. It's an energy sword. You'll find out the specs when you put it on tomorrow. You can wait that long. And that's not the important part, anyway."

She reached out and unwound the cloth from the blade. It wasn't a bolt of cloth, but rather a long strip of smooth fabric, with a short row of white tassels at the end. She held it in front of her as she stood, and entirely without thinking, Holland found himself next to the table, kneeling in front of her.

"Brigs told me a bit of the world you are going to, and I did a search for their warrior traditions. There is a story of a man, a poet and a swordsman without peer, a leader who never relented on his principles.

"The story goes that when he was in a war, under the leadership of another, that other was flawed. As a symbol of his noble birth, the leader wore a white scarf like this one on his arm. But when he went into battle, the warrior noticed that the leader took it off. When asked, the leader said he didn't want to make it easy for the enemy to notice that he was a noble, and single him out for attacks.

"The warrior took up the scarf himself, on hearing that, and leapt into battle, putting himself at the forefront of every engagement, slaying every foe that came up against him. Then he returned to his lines, went back to his leader and gave him back the scarf."

Holland nodded. "A true and good warrior…"

Selene stopped him again. "When he gave the scarf back, the leader took it back with delight, and waved it where the remaining enemy could see it. It was a signal he had arranged, that would call the enemy down and surround his own forces. I admit the translation was terrible, but I got the impression it was done so that the forces of the leader could be sacrificed, the leader as well, as a distraction so that the overall battle could be won."

Holland sat back, thinking about that. Selene leaned forward and tied the scarf around his arm. "You keep your panache with you, but I want you to remember the balance. Both the leader and the warrior called Cyrano were brave, but one sacrificed for pride, the other duty. So this scarf is to remind you of both of those things. The sword, though. The sword is for love."

And that made it clear to Holland. Pride and duty were the Mousekin watchwords, what drove them forward. But real heroes, those who transcended? Those were driven by love.

His eyesight got a little blurry. "I love my duty, and I love my pride, but Selene, I will remember that I love you more. I promise you I will always find a better way. I will find my way back to you."

***

Holland wasn't sure if the whole world was wet, or if it was just this part of it. The west coast of the northern continent they were on was as deep and twisty a maze of fjords and razor peaks as any Holland had ever heard of, and twice as wet. They'd arrived late in the evening, and the rain hadn't stopped since then. If anything, it was even fiercer this morning.

And they'd been standing out in it, in full formation and at attention, for over an hour. In a big world, surrounded by big sapients who were clearly un-troubled by what was, to them, light winds and puddles. Nearly ankle deep on the Mousekin though, and threating the solidity of their grip in the buffeting winds.

Waiting for Roger.

The leader of their expedition. The person Holland and his troops had been hired to protect. A person they were very likely to die for.

Roger, who was having an extra serving of breakfast while they waited in the rain.

At attention. In formation. Because no one had bothered to tell them not to after they'd been called to formally bind themselves to Roger at 9AM sharp, local time.

Most of the troops, at least, had turned out in all weather gear. Holland's formal cadet uniform included nothing so practical. The cadet rank was a rare one, assigned only sporadically to soldiers who rose above and beyond their duty, and managed to do so with style. Enough style that command felt they could reasonably represent all of Mousekin armed forces, under any circumstances.

Except rain. Formal uniform was meant for formal situations and being assigned to a new commander was as formal as it got. The gravitas of being a cadet meant that such situations were always of exceptional honour and formality.

No one told Roger that, apparently.

Holland's beret had started to soak through a few minutes before, and once that had happened, it had started to dampen the fur on his head. At least now it was as wet as the rest of him. He bit back the urge to sigh. Again. Even a deep breath might shift his posture a hair to one side or another, and that would be enough to ripple down through his soldiers. He'd been still as stone for an hour, and he would be, for as many more hours as he took.

The weight of all their eyes bore into his back, of all their expectations. The next few weeks, they would all face death and pain, and it wouldn't be discipline that carried them through.

It would be Holland.

His hand itched to hold his new sword. Selene's gift had been perfect for him, and in his mind's eye he could see himself with the sword strapped to his hips, the brilliant white scarf tied to his arm. That would be an image his people could focus on, could believe in. It was an image he'd be happy to project, because it truly felt like him.

No room for that in the formal issue Cadet Uniform. Soon. As soon as Roger finished his breakfast. The schedule was to head out before lunch, so a uniform change would be almost instant, barring any other quirks of the patron.

The door to the canteen banged open, a loud crash even across the hastily organized parade ground that the Mousekin had occupied for their ceremonial review.

Three of the humans burst out of the door. The largest clearing the way with a loud, braying laugh, and swatting the second largest on the shoulder, nearly sending him tumbling down the steps.

Holland snapped his hand up in salute, heard the rustling crack of that echoing from behind him. One of these three was the principal.

The smallest was a true hunter. Their outline was indistinct, shrouded with loose bits of fabric and intricate collections of bones of all sizes, undoubtedly from prey. They gave off the scent of chaotic magic. The next largest was solid, stoic, clearly the tank of the group, with all the focus of a stone wall. He carried a nearly oversized shield, with a short sword on his waist. It was an odd contrast, and Holland was looking forward to seeing the utility behind that choice.

The largest had all the signs of being a lout. Bulging with muscles, but with the softness that comes from growth and not use. Exuberant, without an ounce of care showing in any of his motions. His gear was all of top quality and looked shop-fresh. It couldn't be, of course. This was a Dungeon World, and the thought of any youth growing up without considerable combat experience in the last few years was unthinkable.

Unless they'd be surrounded by babysitters the entire time. And that looked to be the case, because the soft lout was clearly the Roger they'd been sent to escort. Bodyguard.

Babysit.

Holland could tell he was the one in charge, because when the big male turned to look at the Mousekin, the other two followed suit.

It wasn't possible for Holland to firm up anymore, but he stilled his centre as much as he could, and bore his eyes into Rogers, so that their new commander could get a proper measure of who would be leading the forces at his command…

Roger didn't meet his eyes at all. He just skimmed over the group of them and then went back to talking with his friends. More laughter rolled out, and they walked off and away from the parade grounds, leaving Holland to slowly drop his salute, and to feel his own shoulders betray him by slumping down.

✳✳✳

Holland pulled the sword belt a little tighter, gaining one more notch, and then wiggled his hips a little to check the fit.

"You think you're going to use that thing?" Blossom growled from the other side of the short-hop aircraft that was going to take them on the first leg of their journey.

Holland cocked his head a bit before he answered, and then gave a curt nod. "I'm not planning on it. I'm planning on you getting up and close with all the fearsome beasts. And I don't plan on you screwing up. Why? Are you planning on screwing up?"

The grimace on Blossom's face had the effect of making it look like the scar that ran down one side of his facing was folding in on itself. That had taken Holland a bit to get used to. Blossom cherished that scar as his favourite memento of a past battle, and knowing the effect it had when he scrunched his face just right, it had become his smile.

It wasn't a pretty smile, but it suited Blossom. Grim but not humourless. "Screw up started when we took this mission. Not our fault, and we won't be the ones to screw up past this point."

That got a grim little laugh out of Holland. They were the last ones to pack and load up, so they had the field to themselves. "Fair enough. And yes, the oversized pup is going to be a problem. So yeah, I think I might probably use this thing."

Blossom muttered something under his breath. At least, mostly. Holland caught enough of it to know better than to reply directly, but he also knew that he should stomp on Blossom's errant thought before it spread to anyone else.

"No, he's not going to fall on it, Blossom. He's our charge, and we will do well by him. You see this thing on my arm?"

Blossom glanced up, and Holland was pleased to see there wasn't even a trace of resentment on the older Mousekin's face. It really had been a joke. In poor taste at the start of a contract, but still meant with no malice. Still, as Blossom's gaze ran across the white scarf, Holland followed up with what had been on his mind.

"Panache, my friend. Even if we die in a stupid cause, we will do so with style. That's what this represents. I'll promise you this, right now. I'll keep this scarf spotless, no matter what happens to us, no matter what we go through with this pup in charge, I'll keep it pure. That will be our way, just between you and me, of ensuring that no matter what, we'll have this symbol to fight for. If nothing else, we have ourselves and our panache."

Blossom snorted, but nodded his head. "I suppose that's as good as anything else to fight for. Alright, you've got a deal. We are the best, after all. Gotta die someday, happy to die being the best. But…you sure you can keep that thing white, in the middle of all of this?"

Holland looked around. The rain had finally let up, but the sun was only fitful bands of false promise shiny through the damp. It was pretty, though. He had to admit that. The actual clouds had lifted enough that he could see the staggering height of the mountains all around him, massive walls of green with hard stone caps. There was still a rumble of boisterous laughter and horseplay coming from the smaller vehicle that held Roger and his two friends.

He turned to look behind him, and the rolls of the deep green ocean crashing on the rocks, across the strait to the mountains that rimmed all across the way, to the distant empty darkness of the farthest ocean, a minor sliver all that was visible.

It was a big, distant, terrifying world.

Big enough for anything to be possible.

Anything at all.

Holland turned back, looked at Blossom, and shrugged his shoulders. "I don't know. But I know I'm going to try. I'll add one more thing, though.

I'll keep this white and pure till the end…unless something better comes along. Something better worth fighting for."

Blossom shook his head at that, and then turned as Rogers's vehicle shook again, with a shriek and a laugh at some sort of prank. Then he turned back to look at Holland. "You really think that's possible?"

Holland turned his gaze back up on the nearest mountain.

"Maybe. Anything's possible. And in the end, isn't that what we're born for? To find out what's possible, and to try to make sure it's always something good?"

Blossom burst out in laughter at that, and clapped Holland on the shoulder.

The engines bumped up from a faint purr to a throaty roar, shaking the frames of the suddenly fragile-feeling craft. Something good from all this possibility? Juvenile shouts cut across the engine howl, and Holland found himself staring across the airfield to the other craft. The side doors were open, and he could see Roger slapping the upraised hand of one of his companions. Just before their door closed, Roger turned aside, and caught Holland's eye.

For a brief, fleeting moment, something cut through the bravado on that alien face, a brief something, between one breath and the next, gone in the blink of an eye.

An uncertainty, a hesitation, a touch of fear.

The door slammed closed, but Holland could still see that brief touch, that flash of truth.

He kept the sigh silent, but he still let it out. The warning chime sounded, and he pulled himself back from the door before it closed. The engine roar was cut down, but the vibration increased.

A moment later, the small cluster of craft rose up into the air, and they were on their way to the city of Prince George.

156

###

The End of *Wee Timorous Mousie*

Twenty Months Post-System

This is Harry Prince, reporting from Barcelona, Spain. The historic city is destroyed, large tranches of buildings leading up to the water missing. The Sagrada Familia is the only building still standing near the water in its original form, the Shop that manifested within having protected it from destruction.

The Zarrie occupy the city, with merfolk patrolling the shores and battling the constant horde of fishmen that emerge from the warmer waters. They kill and kidnap any living being they can get their gilled hands on, dragging them into the water to consume. We are told they are sentient, but only marginally so. Much like the ubiquitous goblins.

I have gained access to a new Skill, a Class Skill that allows me to receive information about happenings across the world. I will be providing short updates when I can, though I'm told other Reporters are covering their regions as well.

There is hope, even if it might not seem like it.

In North America, the Truinnar have established a foothold in the Yukon. However, a group of intrepid Adventurers have managed to recover a significant portion of British Columbia and some portions of Alberta, with a push further south beginning. Meanwhile, disparate clusters of American military personnel and civilian survivors battle monster hordes and alien invaders to keep the United States of America free, even as multiple competing 'true' governments compete for loyalty amongst the remaining army personnel.

In Asia, Africa, and South America, their larger population has seen to even more widespread deaths. Though bodies dissolve faster, the monsters have spawned in greater number and strength as well. In some cases, the pressure of death and destruction has crystalized in powerful individuals leapfrogging in Levels and strength. Monster swarms are both a catastrophe and opportunity for these groups.

Such individuals have become the linchpins that hold their society together, the Champions of their settlements.

Humanity is recovering, if slowly and inconsistently.

A New Script

Morning brought with it the noises and smells of a small, badly ventilated building crowded with sleeping men and women. Overnight, the air had grown stuffy and rank; the stink of bloody, uncleaned weapons, dirt encrusted clothing and the exhaust of humanity roiled and congealed. The space itself was a previous retail clothing store, once filled with thin, cheaply made female clothing. That clothing had been torn apart and raided for bandages while the once clean, cream-colored walls streaked with blood, soil and ash. Clothing racks and mirrors had been propped in the corner to make way for bunk beds three levels high, offering their occupants no more space than a coffin motel.

At least they were better than actual coffins, Jin admitted to himself. That had been a bad night. And waking up these days was no longer a long, torturous process of convincing his lazy body to move. Weeks of living in fear of the slightest sound had engrained new habits. Now, Jin first brushed his hand across the beam pistol by his side and then, he eyed the other occupants of the store.

Most were dressed in the eclectic pickings of a sci-fi and medieval flea market, some already stirring like him even though the morning was still young. Directly across from him, Fatima slept in a dark steel, scale mail jacket. A nano-woven head-covering kept her hair hidden and her ears protected from damage, while a pot helm rested beside the team's Actor and their only front-line fighter.

On the bunk below Fatimah, Ian was dressed in a nanowoven jumpsuit in gray and black, the tightly woven material keeping his once-portly frame together in a tight package. The jumpsuit was one of the more common designs – both practical, self-cleaning to a degree and cheap to purchase – available from the System Store. It was what Leo, on the topmost bunk, and

Jin was dressed in too. Isabel their Director and team leader, on the other hand, had chosen to stay in floral dress and tights, though Jin could not see her from his spot. With the System's enhancements to her Charisma, she looked more like an international model than the fresh-faced college student that she had been, a bare few months ago. Back when they were all just students. Before the System. Before the apocalypse had taken any kinds of normality or sense with it.

Now monsters roamed the streets, they all had Classes and Skills and aliens called themselves their overlords. Now, the surviving humans had to fight, kill and Level.

Satisfied that his team was still here and alive, Jin rolled out of bed, beam pistol sliding into his shoulder holster the moment his feet hit the floor. A second later, the shriek of unoiled metal grates erupted through the room, signaling the official start to the morning. Early morning sunlight bathed the room, revealing other occupants on their feet; some with breakfast in their mouths.

"What time is it?" Ian complained, rubbing at his eyes. The short, bulbous nosed Editor was a night owl, constantly preferring to stay up late. Even the apocalypse had yet to change his behavior.

"Time to get your lazy, human asses out of my building," the grating voice that called to them originated near the doorway. There, Kaerius the aqua green merman stood, tapping one finned foot. The merman was clad in a green and blue diving suit, clear tubes floating around Kaerius's neck where water flooded into and out of his gills.

Considering Kaerius's voice was artificial, it made no sense that it was so grating and rude. Then again, it did not matter. The aliens treated humanity like dirt, and they... took it. For now. All around, Jin sensed the pull of Mana; that strange energy that powered both their Skills, their spells and their bodies; as other occupants triggered Cleanse spells. The simple and cheap spell washed away the accumulated funk in the room and their targets, relieving many from the need to wash. Or brush their teeth.

"Two things," Kaerius called out as some of the occupants began to make their way out. "Rent for tonight's fifty credits per person. Also, reservations and curfew expire at eight from now on."

"That's outrageous!" A female from the back shouted.

"You're banned. Get out." Kaerius didn't even bother to argue with her. The shock on the woman's face was matched by the looks of pity she received. Without a Safe Zone to sleep in at night, her expected life expectancy had dropped to days.

"Anyone else?" The challenge saw no takers. The fluid around Kaerius's gills turned purple and swirled away before the alien jerked a webbed hand to the door. "Then get out."

One by one, the occupants streamed out, stopping only long enough to pay their reservation fee to Kaerius. By this point, Jin had learnt enough alien body language to confirm that Kaerius was literally gloating.

Outside, the team moved down a few doorways carefully, watching the abandoned retail complexes on Lynn Valley road as they headed for open space and the residential neighborhood up the street. As they were in the North Shore of Vancouver and thus close to numerous greenery and the mountains, zone levels escalated rapidly. And while monsters generally kept to their zones, it only took one out-of-level encounter to make the group wary.

Worse, most of the neighborhood had consisted of single detached housing filled with older residents. That meant there had been a higher than normal number of deaths during the System advent, leaving a large number of monsters to roam unchecked. It was why the team chose this place, why they worked the surroundings on a daily basis. More monsters meant more Credits and experience.

After so many weeks, the group was used to working together, taking turns eating, drinking and swilling coffee as they walked. Once they were a couple of blocks away from the shop, they took station in the middle of the crossroads, each facing a different direction. Only Ian stayed in the center, watching over the group as a whole.

"God damn it. Fifty credits each? We'll barely be able to save anything," Fatimah said.

"Language!" Leo chided. He rubbed at the small cube at his side in nervousness, checking that the folded shield was in place.

"Bite me." Fatimah replied. Jin turned to the right and watched as she twirled her short sword around her hand, the plasma conduit in the center off. Like the circular particle shield on her other arm, Fatimah only triggered the noisy equipment when needed. As their main tank, Fatimah used melee weaponry exclusively while the rest of the team armed themselves with a mixture of beam rifles and pistols.

"Please!" Isabel said. "Let's not fight among ourselves."

"Yes, ma'am peacemaker," Ian teased. "It'd be nice if you could just edit Kaerius and make him less of an ass."

"You know Edit Lines doesn't work that way," Jin said.

"Be nice if it did though," Isabel said wistfully.

"Eh, I'd be scared of Jin if he could change people like that. In either case, Fatimah is right," Leo said. "The price raise hurts. We're still a couple of thousand Credits away from getting our own place."

Their own place. That was the dream for everyone stuck in Kaerius's slumhole. Every team, every group talked about it. But, thus far, only one team had managed to make it out. They had so much to balance, between buying Skills, spells and equipment from the System Shop that saving was low on the list.

"Jin?" Isabel called out. Hearing his name called, Jin turned to see Isabel regarding him steadily. Ian, caught in the middle swirled his finger around, pointing them back to their lines-of-sight.

Jin considered for a second. If what they were earning wasn't enough, then…"New script?"

"Yes, please," Isabel replied.

"Ian. Switch," Jin asked his friend.

In short order, Jin was in the center of the group, readying himself to trigger his Skill. Script was a strange Skill, allowing him to create a modified quest that gave bonuses to those who had a part in the script. Jin had to lock down certain aspects of the script like the protagonist and antagonists, but could also leave other aspects to chance. He could, in turn, designate a live scripted event or a play. Like most things to do with the System, it was part magic and part acid-fueled game mechanics given life.

Data swirled around Jin as he worked, eyes half-closed as he perused the streams of information made available to him. It was not easy though, the information fragmented, written in multiple languages and filled with extraneous data. But eventually, Jin had a new Script to forward to Isabel.

New Script: Lynn Canyon Park

There are rumors of a new monster in Lynn Canyon Park. A party of adventurers, out of their depths in the new System Apocalypse, travel to the Park, in search of the rumored monster and financial gain.

Script Quality: Mediocre

Script Bonus: +15% to production

Produce this script? (Y/N)

Isabel and Jin shuffled places, allowing their erstwhile leader player producer and director, to slot them into the appropriate place in her production schedule. Each choice updated the entire team in real time, glowing blue script appearing before their eyes.

Scriptwriter, Jin Long. Director, Isabel Groves. Cinematographer, Leo Houston. Fatima was their principal – and only – talent. And Ian Gibbs their Editor. If they had a larger party, they would have been able to fill out more roles, but…

Jin shied away from that thought, too raw still. Once, they had been able to fill all those roles. Once…

"Oooh… a 15% bonus. You added a Skill point?" Leo crowed, rubbing his hands together. "This will make my Freeze Frame even better."

Jin grinned. "Yeah. Last Level."

"A new monster?" Ian asked, concern in his voice. "Isn't that dangerous?"

"What about our life isn't?" Leo said. "We might even get a bonus for finding a new monster."

"Maybe." Jin shook his head. "You know how my Skill works. Details are a little fuzzy."

"I don't know about this…" Ian protested.

"Stop being such a damn scaredy cat," Fatimah said.

"There's going to be a nice Credit bonus. If we want our own place, we're going to have start taking quests like these. Waiting just means letting them up our rent again," Isabel said. Jin risked another look over to Ian, only to see the blond man flush.

"Yeah, okay. Just… let's be careful, 'kay?" Ian said.

"Always. Now, come on. We've got to go if we don't want to be late back," Isabel said.

"The New Reel is on the go!" Leo crowed, drawing a snort from Fatimah.

The group fell into familiar formation, Fatimah leading the way while Leo hovered just behind her. As always, Ian and Jin held back, allowing Isabel the center position.

***

What would have been a brisk fifteen minute walk in the past became a grueling hour of hiking and enforced caution. Twice, the team passed other groups who were engaged in frantic battles. They paused only long enough to ascertain that the fights were energetic but non-lethal before moving on. The new convention in the apocalypse dictated that each team was left alone, so long as no one was in mortal danger.

Soon enough, they left the residential houses and paved roads to trudge along the gravel roads leading into the northern rainforest. In the distance, Jin could hear the flow of water in the canyon, feel the increased humidity on his skin and the regard of hidden creatures.

"Everyone ready?" Isabel called out as the group passed the wrecked entrance sign, the wooden board lying abandoned where an oversized beaver had chewed its supports away.

"Ready. Any directions?" Fatimah asked.

Isabel hummed for a second and then triggered a new Skill – Scene Directions. Jin saw the flicker in the corner of his eyes as the notification appeared and disappeared. No surprise there, since the Skill was targeted at Fatimah herself.

"Got it. Quest marker and all," Fatimah crowed. "This way."

The group followed the Actor, watching the slowly encroaching forest warily. All around them, the normal forest quiet had warped; punctuated by the trump of heavy feet on forest bed and the screams of unending battle. The canyon was no longer a tourist friendly walk, but a battleground of competing monsters, each attempting to stake their claim.

Ever since the System arrived and Mana overflowed, both animals and vegetation had flourished. In three months, the once clear path was choked with vegetation, forcing the group to close ranks and cut their way through. If not for the passage of earlier groups, the path would have been no better than a deer trail.

Worse, the vegetation had a bad tendency to mutate. Sometimes, the mutations were benign. Branches shifting coloration from brown to purple, or the addition of small thorns to upper branches. Other times, like the moving, grasping vines that attempted to wrap around the team or the poisonous, exploding mushrooms, it was less so.

The squirrels hit them as they finished rushing out of the field of exploding mushrooms, choking on the cloying spores in their lungs. The poison within doubled their vision and made them gasp for clean air. The first mutated squirrel, now a foot tall with razor sharp teeth and bushy tail of serrated fur threw itself from a tree at Fatimah, only to be intercepted by her shield. A follow-up thrust skewered the falling squirrel, ending its life.

That was just the first of many. The scurry of squirrels emerged from the dense undergrowth, to nibble at ankles, or launch additional airborne attacks. Isabel caught one on the body of her beam rifle, while Jin missed his own grab. The squirrel latched onto his chest and tore into his collarbone without mercy.

"Freeze Frame!" Leo called out. Not that he needed to use his voice, but the boisterous cinematographer enjoyed it. The Skill froze the attacking squirrels on one side, giving both Ian and him a chance to shoot the frozen creatures.

In the meantime, Jin managed to yank his attacker off and stomp on it. At the forefront, Fatimah used her gift of Improvised Acting to borrow skills and wield her sword. To Jin's chagrin, even after stomping on the monster a couple of times, it would not die. Rather than let the monster escape, he set his entire bodyweight to pin the creature and fired his beam pistol point-blank into its head. Only then did it finally die, leaving Jin to wrinkle his nose at the smell of burnt flesh and fur.

It was because of these ridiculous damage balancing aspects of the System that guns – human made guns and explosives – had become defunct. If something wasn't System registered, it did little damage. The weaponry, the spells, that they wielded had to be purchased at the Shop in the center of town or be worthless. And since Jin had no special unarmed combat Skill, his stomping had done little to the overpowered squirrel monster.

"Damage?" Isabel called out as Jin got back up after looting the squirrel.

"Another suit," Jin called out. The bleeding on his chest continued, but by now, all of them had learnt to ignore minor injuries. The System would heal them, and anything short of dismemberment or death could be healed in ten minutes.

"Need an edit here," Leo said, trying to hide the pain as he leaned against a nearby tree. "Got my Achilles heel."

"Hold still," Ian said. The once heavyset editor crouched beside Leo, peering at the ankle. He twitched his hands, framing first the ankle and then pulling back with his hands. An image of the damaged and bleeding ankle detached from the leg, allowing Leo to breathe easier. Ian clapped his hands together and then made a tossing motion with his hands, discarding the image. A second later, Leo was bouncing on his now pristine leg. "Fixed."

"And you're sure that's not a time aspected Skill?" Leo stroked his goatee as he peered at his now fixed ankle.

"I'm sure. I can only do small edits right now. And I got to catch it fast too," Ian said. "It's just like Jin's Edit Line Skill. System idiocy."

"Alright. Enough. We should get going. And keep an eye out for more monsters," Isabel commanded.

As they got ready to go, Jin could not help but smirk internally. They might not be your regular combat team, but they had learnt to make do with their Skills. You just had to get a little creative.

***

"This the spot?" Jin asked Fatimah an hour later. If it was, the location was less than impressive. From the ridge the team was currently occupying, they could look down into the canyon clearing. The current canyon clearing was carved from the river overflow, leaving it dry in these summer months. The entire space was around thirty feet wide from ridge to the sloping hillside where the monsters resided. Running along the edges of the cliff and both ends of the clearing was a variety of small, normal-looking green bushes. The area around the entrance to the lair, a small cave had been flattened through repeated movements.

"Unless the quest marker's wrong, I'm bloody sure it is," Fatimah said.

"I'm not crawling in there," Ian said.

"I don't think any of us are," Jin remarked. "I'm not fighting anything on my hands and knees."

"Except a cute girl, eh?" Ian elbowed Jin who rolled his eyes.

"Don't remind me. I haven't gotten laid in… Ow!" Jin cut-off and rubbed his head.

Leo pulled his hand back while hissing. "Language! We have women here."

"No one's going into the hole," Isabel said. "But we do need a plan."

"If something's in there in the first place," Jin added. When the others looked at him, he explained. "Whatever is in there might be hunting."

Almost as one, the group turned around to check their rear.

"Right. Find out what is in there and then…" Leo said.

The group of city folk stared at one another, before Fatimah offered. "Lure it the hell out."

"So, we watch?" Jin said.

"We watch," Isabel confirmed. "Let's spread out a little though."

"You got it, ma'am" Ian said.

***

The first sign of movement came two hours later. The creature emerged from the bushes in a low crouch, followed by two smaller companions. At first, Jin thought that it was a wolf. It had the same body shape as a wolf, if twice the size, with those spiky, pyramid shaped ears, the long bloody snout and wispy gray fur. But that initial impression disappeared soon after, for the monster stopped crouching and straightened. Upright, the monster still did not look right — its shoulders and chest region hunched and warped, the limbs hanging from it not really meant for use as arms nor as legs for running. Yet, for all its strange appearance, when it turned to review its lair, there was a malicious viciousness in its eyes.

The bigger creature — the Alpha — waited until its brethren entered the cave, making a full circuit about its home and marking its territory before it joined them. A tap on his arm by Isabel and the group snuck away, to put themselves out of earshot. Jin absently noted that the others not on overwatch had fought a few, quick battles in the interim, keeping other monsters away from their lookout.

"Level 14 Adlet Alpha. The pair are Level 9," Isabel announced to the group after Jin finished describing their opponents. Production Plan allowed her to slot each of them into their appropriate place in her production, and in this case, the Adlet's were cast as the antagonists.

"Only three?" Ian said, relieved.

"Abilities?" Fatimah said.

"Checking," Jin said. He closed his eyes and pulled out the script that he had initially created. It was a swirling mass of post-it-notes and notecards, with only the first few pages written, detailing what had happened. Those, Jin ignored. It was the post-it notes, especially about their antagonists that he was curious about. One by one, Jin plucked the notes and reviewed the data, doing his best to parse the machine code, alien words and short-handed gibberish. "Medium strength. High speed. Low cunning. Hungry carnivores. The basic types are just minions. The Alpha has a… spirit, uhh… thing?"

"Thing?" Ian said.

"It's not in English."

The group sighed but by this point, they understood the limitations imposed upon Jin.

"Alright. It sounds like we go with the usual plan then." Isabel cleared a little space on the ground and using a stick, drew a rough map of the clearing. As she spoke, Isabel added to the map. "Usual formation. Fatimah in front, everyone else backs her up. We throw in a plasma grenade, wake the Adlet up. Fatimah tanks the Alpha and one other Adlet, we focus fire on the other one. Take it down as fast as possible and then switch."

"To the Alpha or…?" Leo asked.

"Play it by ear," Isabel said. "Assume Alpha if I don't change the orders."

A few more questions and adjustments were made before the team trooped back to the lair. As they approached, Jin watched as Ian kept drawing and sheathing his knife and licking his lips in nervous anticipation.

Lowering his voice, Jin slowed down a little to give themselves a little more space. "You okay?"

"Sure. Sure. Just our first Alpha, right? Nothing to it," Ian said.

"Right. There's just three," Jin said. "We got this. And if you don't, we'll just edit it out."

"Right. Right." Ian nodded, but his face grew even more strained.

Uncertain what else to add, Jin was saved by Isabel gesturing for them to hurry up. Relieved, Jin hurried after. It was going to be fine. They'd fought monsters before. Tons of them. An Alpha wasn't that different.

*****

Even after the group trooped into the clearing, making not a little noise, no Adlet rushed them. Low growls erupted from the small cave, but no creature exited, allowing the team to spread out and ready themselves. Jin, placed in the back with his pistol drawn, looked about the canyon clearing one last time.

Down here, the cliff they had been watching the lair from was much steeper and more difficult to climb than it had seemed up top. The vegetation that was not tramped down was even lusher than expected, cutting down their line of sight even more. Thankfully, the ground was mostly dry, offering great footing but for a central muddy section.

"Aaaand... roll!" Isabel called out.

Isabel complied, tossing one of their few plasma grenades into the hole. The small oblong explosive pulsed red as it was activated and bounced perfectly into the hole. In seconds, all sight of it was lost. The cave suddenly vomited a volume of superheated air and flame as the plasma grenade exploded. The group cowered and hid from the heat, feeling it wash over them and singe eyebrows and toast hair.

As the team recovered, Fatimah drew her short sword and activated the weapon, seconds before the Ablet launched themselves out of the cave with a howl. The first monster crossed the ten feet between itself and Fatimah in three bounds, hitting the particle shield with its snapping jaws before bouncing off. Behind, its brother swerved around Fatimah, allowing Leo to catch it mid-jump with a Freeze Frame. The remainder of the group open fired on the frozen monster, trying to take it down. Beams of energy tore into the monster, crisscrossing one another and burning away skin and fur. One, too short arm, was burnt down to the bone while fur smoked, revealing thick flesh. Unfortunately, the Skill gave way after three seconds, releasing the monster to limp after Leo who had deployed his shield in the meantime.

Jin and Ian spread out, trying to keep the creature in sight as they fired more carefully now, worried about hitting their friend. Isabel disengaged, hefting her rifle as she eyed the lair.

"Alpha's missing!" Isabel called out.

Her words startled the group. Leo let his shield drop a little too low and paid for it, clawed fingers from Ablet's remaining hand slipping through the slack defense. Ian triggered his Skill, editing out the attack, allowing Leo to return to shield bashing the monster and shooting it around his shield.

Jin looked away, searching for the Alpha. Only to see it appear from behind a nearby bush and charge the group.

"Look out!" Jin called out, too late.

His directionless warning did nothing more than distract the group. Loping forwards on all four feet, it hit Isabel low, throwing her to the floor. Even as the director fell, the Ablet Alpha dug into the ground with its claws to turn, scrambling over to clamp down on her flailing hand with its jaws. A moment later, white light shone from the Alpha and surrounded Isabel. Each pulse of the light drained her health, whitening her skin and slowing down her struggles.

"Help!" Jin called out as he targeted the Alpha. A couple of shots with his beam pistol were ignored, barely scorching the creature's flesh.

Isabel weakly beat on the monster with the butt of her rifle with one hand, each blow only serving to annoy the Alpha. Fatimah was fighting her own opponent, trying to break away but cut-off at each turn. Leo was focused, unable to look away from his own Ablet, barely hanging on with Ian's help.

Jin shivered as another pulse of white light flowed from Isabel to the Ablet, healing the creature of the wounds his own attacks had made. He had to make the monster let go of Isabel somehow. Somehow…

Drawing a breath, Jin triggered his Skill, targeting the Alpha. Edit Lines allowed him to change aspects of the script, altering behavior or aspects. It only let him change a few things, a few words here and there. Worse, he only had enough Mana to make two edits.

But that should be enough.

First line. Edit the monster's Spirit Skill. It was obvious that the second word was drain or the equivalent. So, swap it out. Now it was Spirit Gift.

Jin dropped out of his Skill, fired another shot at the Ablet that was ignored and then watched as the pulse of energy surrounding it and Isabel reversed. Instead of taking away Isabel's life, it gifted it back. The Alpha released Isabel with a growl, jumping back as it was startled.

Another shot by Jin's beam pistol annoyed the monster, and it turned to glare at Jin. Freed, Isabel drew its attention back by firing her rifle, before she struck the monster just below its crouched chest. That action drained the very last of her energy and Isabel slumped to the ground.

"No. Me!" Jin snapped. Another Edit. This time, he focused on another aspect of the script – who the monster was targeting. A swap of names, from Isabel to his made the monster turn around. But Jin was not paying attention because he was already running for it.

It took a good ten feet before Jin dared look back, and realize the foolishness of his plan. Even if the Ablet was not made properly, the creature's higher attributes and four-legged lope was faster than his own two. At the last minute, Jin threw himself to the side, narrowly dodging the leaping monster. Skidding along the grass, bare his skin tore on the ground as he came to a stop. Before he could rise to his feet, the Ablet had made his way over to leap at Jin's throat. Raised hands managed to ward the creature off, holding the monster away by its thin shoulders. Together, the pair fell to the ground with a thump.

The Alpha crouched over Jin, snapping at his face, attempting to tear him apart. Again and again, it lunged, and Jin twisted and jerked, dodging against the ground. A bad dodge had canines tearing at his cheekbone, drawing blood. As the creature lunged again, a sudden burst of inspiration made Jin throw his arms around the Ablet's neck and hug it to him. Tiny arms, with distorted claw fingers tore at his body as it scrambled against his chest, but the more dangerous mouth was kept away. Together, the pair thrashed about the clearing, grappling for dominance.

"Jin. JIN!" Fatimah screamed.

"He's not listening." Leo snapped.

"Break apart!" Isabel cried, triggering her Scene Direction Skill. It made Jin throw his hands apart, made him scurry away while kicking at the surprised monster. Before it could recover, his friends attacked.

"Freeze frame!" Leo cried.

As Jin attempted to roll to his feet, he took in the clearing. Around him, his friends were gathered and focused on the Alpha. In the background, the dead bodies of the other Ablet lay, their flesh sizzling. Tired feet gave way as Jin made it up halfway, blood and pain finally making their way past the adrenaline and Jin sat with a thump.

The Alpha unfroze but Fatimah stepped in its way, bouncing it off her particle shield. Together, the reformed team worked to kill the monster. This time, their teamwork worked perfectly and the Alpha fell, keening in death.

"Good job," Ian slapped Jin on the shoulder, making the man groan. Already, the torn skin on his chest and stomach was patching itself together.

"How… Isabel…?" Jin said, shaking his muzzy head.

"I Edited the damage. Between that and regeneration, she got back on her feet," Ian said. "I'm out of Mana, though, so we'll need to do this old school."

Jin touched his face, feeling the torn flesh and then looked at his torso. Exhaustion washed over him and he let himself lie down. Ian snorted, pulling out bandages and a squirt bottle of water. "Just got to clear the debris. Regen will take care of everything else."

To distract himself, Jin watched as his friends moved around the bodies, looting the corpses via the System before taking out hunting knives. As bad a job as they might do cutting the creatures apart, the bodies would be of use to the craftsmen. A moment later, Jin rolled his head to look away from the bloody task.

In the corner of his eyes, another notification. Latching onto that less bloody distraction, Jin was surprised to see that he'd Leveled up. Fighting Alphas seemed to be worth it at the least.

***

"How much did we make?" Jin asked as the group finally reconvened. After the fight, they'd made their way back to town, stopping off at the small office building the craftsmen had made their own to sell off the torn body parts. Meat would be used for the stew pots, the bones, teeth and claws for crafting weaponry. Most of the weapons crafted by the craftsmen were of low quality and thus, the prices they were willing to pay for the materials similar. But it was better than nothing.

"Just over seven hundred Credits for the pot," Isabel said.

"What?" Leo exclaimed.

"The Alpha got us a bonus, same with them being new monsters," Isabel explained.

"Does that mean…?" Fatimah asked, eyes wide with hope.

Isabel shook her head. "One thousand two hundred more."

Silence fell over the group at her pronouncement. Even if they threw in a few Credits each, they wouldn't have enough. If that was the case…

"Guess we're staying at Kaerius's again," Leo said, fatalistically.

"But we're hunting Alpha's tomorrow. And the next day, till we get enough for our own place," Jin said.

His words were met with silence at first before wide grins broke out among the group. Maybe they couldn't buy a place yet. But every day they survived was another day they grew stronger. One day, the struggles would end and they'd remake their lives.

One day.

###

The End of *A New Script*

Valentines in an Apocalypse

The Vancouver Public Library's central branch building was an iconic structure. It had been modeled on the Coliseum, giving it a cylindrical appearance with a freestanding, elliptical, colonnaded wall on one side that contained the offices and reading rooms. It had been built with a total of nine floors including the subterranean storage locations. Unlike the real Coliseum, floor-to-ceiling glass windows dominated the structure offering a view of the books and tables inside while contrasting with the light brown granite walls. It was an iconic building, made even more by the broken and shattered earth buildings in the distance and the gleaming, twisted metal alien structures surrounding the structure. Even after six years from the System apocalypse, Vancouver was still recovering, a mish-mash of recovered and rebuilt buildings with the new System created structures standing side-by-side. It was only because Vancouver's Shop had been located in the central branch that it had been spared from damage.

Damage, but not change. Dotted around the library square were beam turrets, the automated weapon systems constantly shifting and tracking potential threats. Shield projectors, barely taller than a man and looking like old-time phone booths – one painted an iconic blue – were strategically placed around the perimeter, ready for activation at any moment. Luckily, Vancouver itself was now a Safe Zone, leaving the weapons to lock and dismiss the never-ending slew of unmutated pigeons, and the occasional flying individual. Teddy Loh barely noticed any of these sights as he hurried in to begin his work shift. Even after the fall of civilization, it seemed the 9-to-5 workweek was still honored.

A misstep, an unseen slope in the ground had Teddy stumble. He splashed a little of the coffee he clutched in one hand on his black jumpsuit, and watched as it fell off without leaving a single stain. The apocalypse might have brought many things with it; death and destruction on a level that he had never even imagined, magic and aliens in vast numbers and this strange System and character sheet – but it had also brought sci-fi level adaptive clothing that refused to take stains, that refit themselves to their purchasers on command and regulated body temperatures better than anything that he ever had. It'd also brought small conveniences, like the muscular, fast-regenerating body of his and supposedly, an extended lifespan. The System had even taken away his need for glasses, leaving Teddy with 20/20 vision for the first time in four decades.

Eyeing the empty spot where he had stumbled, Teddy flagged the anomaly on his System. As he swept a hand through his slowly greying, shortcut brown hair, he let his gaze rest on the clock in the corner of his vision. 8:55. No time to verify the issue. Just another mystery in the System. There were others who would deal with it.

Inside the enclosed atrium of the building, Teddy took a right turn and entered the main foyer of the ex-library. Even now, numerous individuals browsed the remaining stacks, though most of the first floor had been transformed. These days, instead of a group of helpful attendants, a bank of computers and the popular news section; the library had become the closest thing to an adventurer's guild that the city had.

Where librarians used to work, city attendants stood, taking questions, offering advice and generally directing newcomers and struggling citizens to jobs that best suited them. Even with all the technology and the System on-hand, a human touch was still needed for some. In another section, more attendants and a select few merchants stood around, accepting quest rewards, System registered items and minor crafts. Unregistered corpses and items were all dealt with outside of the library, since those could not be handily stored in an inventory. But all those were just sideshows to the main attraction of the library.

Dominating the main portion of the first floor, flanking the escalators and staircases that led to the next floor were multiple floating spheres, each of them a linked entry point to the Shop System. Every few seconds, Teddy watched as a newcomer would touch the sphere and disappear, teleported to the Shop instance that they used. And just as often, individuals would reappear, nearly hitting other users before walking off, having finished their business. If not for the fact that the Shop was generally more expensive and bought products at a lower price, it'd have killed the local economy a long time ago. Still, there were many things only available in Galactic Shops or items that could only be sold there.

Teddy took all of this in with practiced ease, gauging how busy the city's hub was this day. He let his gaze track over the individuals within the building, eyeballing them for potential threats. He didn't even blink when he noticed the four legged, two armed lizard creature that stood to the side, arguing with a minotaur – more properly called a Yerrick –, or the cluster of two foot tall, brown furred creatures rolling along one side of the building. They were just the start of the weirdness. The aliens that had flooded the city were just another part of daily life now.

Judging the city to still be quiet, he took the escalators up, heading for the third floor where he worked. He didn't even pause to look at the second floor, which was much of a repeat of the floor below but with fewer shop spheres and more attendants and merchants. The second floor focused on crafts and local businesses, with a small but busy section dedicated to the Northern Lights Venture Group. One of the introductions of the settlement owners, the Group financed loans and a very small number of grants to anyone who could show the willingness and ability to progress their craft.

Rumor had it that they had a stake in a good forty percent of the businesses in the city, including some of the larger fishing fleets.

Finally reaching his own floor, Teddy sighed. All that hustle and bustle was tension inducing, which was why he was glad the third floor was still quiet. It's role had changed a little, but it was still a repository of knowledge, a filter for information. Here, Teddy worked, with a large group of other administrators and researchers, all of them pulling information from branch offices throughout the province, gathering and indexing data. Data that turned into information under their skilled hands, the very same information that those attendants below gave out. Even after six years, the number of monsters - new and mutated – quests, and galactic aliens just kept increasing. Of course, all of this information was technically available in the Shop. But no one wanted to pay the prices they dictated, and so, Earth was building their own database. One that was publicly available, one that would benefit all of humanity. It'd been the brainchild of some kid in South East Asia and been taken to with vengeance by the city.

As Teddy walked over to his desk, he spotted Kaylee seated at hers already. The heart-faced redhead flashed him an absent smile, fingers twitching as she triggered screens that only she could see. She paused after a few seconds, turning to him with excitement bubbling in her eyes. "Did you hear?"

"I just arrived. Also, morning."

"Oh right, good morning!" Kaylee, the ever-persistent gossip leaned close and whispered. "Lana managed to close the deal with the Bebrex's. We're going to get access to their library."

Teddy's eyes widened, and a grin split his face. That was good news. Lana had been working that deal for the last three months, negotiating over interstellar communications to get access to the Bebrex network. The flood of information from their library, combined with what they had, would fill in a lot of holes in their Galactic knowledge. It wouldn't patch all the gaps, just like the other three deals they'd made, but it would help. It would help a lot.

"That's really good news."

"You going to tell Janet?" Kaylee said.

Teddy hesitated. His wife would like to know, but… She was coming in, in about twenty minutes anyway. Somehow or another, she'd negotiated a later start time than him. One of the advantages of being a linguist in this bureaucracy. Not that he resented it. Not at all.

Kaylee shot a glance at Teddy, when he shook his head in the negative. Taking his own seat, Teddy got ready to start the day, pulling out the latest data feed as he sat. As a Librarian, one of his Class Skills was information sorting. Combined with some basic Skills, it allowed him to access the interface, sort through all the data that arrived at the speed of thought – and sometimes a little faster - and categorize it, collating the data with previous reports to begin an analysis of trends.

It was a good thing that they all had Skills to do their jobs, because what took entire departments of the Federal government to once before was now sometimes the part-time job of a single individual. Weather patterns over the entirety of BC? Joe did that, when he got in in the morning, assessing models and tweaking them before he got onto his real job – watching for Mana shifts. Needed population numbers of monsters in the Comox Valley? See Kate or Jim.

If they got lucky and had the time, they could look for trends, analyze when a dungeon or an Alpha Boss might appear. If not, you got the base summary. All so that the adventurers who were relying on the information had as close to real-time information as possible. It was an impossible task, but when they failed, and that happened all too often, people died.

Caught up in the flow of work, Teddy soon lost track of time, his attention drawn into the streams of information that flowed past his eyes. Janet, the news and Kaylee all forgotten.

*****

Janet yawned, staring at the mug held in her hands. Jim had forgotten his own, again. Some reason, even though he asked her to make coffee for him every morning, he still forgot to drink it. He'd then go out and buy a cup from the barista's that lined the downtown core. She knew she didn't have the Skills those baristas had, but still… It was Credits. She sighed, looking around the room, eyeing the poor and meager furnishings of their new home. They lived only two blocks away from the library, in one of the first fully functional, safe zones the aliens that created. The proximity came with a cost though.

They'd both felt lucky when they managed to find a place in a safe zone to stay, but now, they were paying for it. The pale blue paint on the walls – but it wasn't actually paint, Janet knew, but a sheen of the metal itself – and the slightly off-center visible light arrays always disturbed her. They could fix it – would fix it – but first, they had to save enough.

She missed their old home, even if it had been smaller, lacking in all the high-tech functions of this room, and now, but rubble. Of their home, a single photograph had managed to survive, hanging slightly askew on one wall with its cracked frame. Their wedding photo. They'd both been so young, so hopeful back then. Now…

Now they just were. Just getting on with it.

It wasn't as if they were unhappy. In fact, she had to admit, they were both feeling more fulfilled in their jobs than ever before. What they did mattered. She, as a just graduated linguist from UBC, now working with aliens and trying to grasp, interstellar nuances of societies and languages. He, as a librarian, collating data for everyone. No, it wasn't their careers that had her maudlin today. It was…

It was them.

They just did not talk. Each of them scrambling from one crisis to the other, one urgent task to the next. When they got home, they were as likely to collapse, conjure some food from their inventory and eat in silence, than just, talk.

Connect.

It was funny, how all this important, lifesaving work could still leave her feeling slightly down. A quick sip of her coffee and then she looked up, eyeing the time in the corner of her vision. If she didn't get moving, she was going to be late.

Janet ran a hand through her hair, peeked at the light red coloring that she'd chosen yesterday and frowned. Time for another change. It only took a thought, just a simple command before the nanobots in her hair altered the coloring to a more vivid purple. She eyed the florescent coloring and winced, making the base color darker until she was satisfied. A quick application of makeup — normal, human makeup because the alien stuff was still hit and miss on human skin — and hurried out the door, coffee forgotten.

***

Lunch arrived, all too soon. Teddy made his way down to the concourse, grabbing a seat near one of the ubiquitous sandwich shops. He took one glance at the menu and ordered two sets of the daily special. A part of him felt guilty about eating seal meat, but the swarm of seals that attacked the city a few days ago had been anything but normal and peaceful. They lost half a dozen people, noncombatants just like them, before the adventurers and the guard managed to control the situation. Ever since then, mutated seal meat had been the special all over town.

It didn't help that like most mutated, monster meat, the System had managed to make it so very, very tasty.

Even with the delay, and the constant flow of customers, the food arrived before Teddy a good ten minutes before Janet arrived, hurrying over with quick steps and an unapologetic smile.

"Sorry. Had to jump on a call at the last minute. The Poosken chief just kept trying to talk my head off." Jenna dropped into a chair beside Teddy before she noticed his gaze had fixed on her hair. She touched it self-consciously. "Like it?"

"Sure." Teddy said. He didn't manage to sound very convincing though, so he immediately pushed the seal meat sandwich over. "You should eat, before it gets cold. It's a bit fatty when it's cold."

Janet just shot him look, one that made Teddy know that he had not managed to pull off his distraction. Not that he'd ever managed that, not in decades. She always seemed to see right through him, even on their first date when he'd tried to hide his dislike for boy bands. Still, Janet didn't say anything and started eating.

They were halfway through their meal before Teddy spoke. "Good news, isn't it? The Bebrex treaty. Though, I haven't seen the data flow yet." With the way the System worked, they should have started getting that information immediately.

"That's because we sign tomorrow." Janet wiped a splotch of mayonnaise from her mouth, before she continued. "They don't sign treaties on festive days. Cultural thing."

The researcher in Teddy perked up, and he leaned forward. "What festival are they having?"

"Not them. Us." When Teddy's brow furrowed, she added. "It's February 14."

"What? Valentine's Day isn't an actual festival. It's a manufactured, capitalist moneymaker." If there was one good thing about the apocalypse, it had certainly gotten rid of a vast majority of these foolish events. Who cared about diamonds, when a beam pistol was a more appropriate gift. When everyone was busy trying to survive and make it through the next day, celebrating a silly thing like Mother's Day or even birthdays seemed trivial.

Janet frowned, but ducked her head and focused on her sandwich before her, biting into it resolutely. Occasionally, she looked around, focusing on too loud voices intently before returning to her meal.

"Sorry," Teddy said, noticing his wife withdrawing into silence. When she didn't answer, he gave up and turned back to his food. They ate in silence, and when done placed their serving trays away to free up the table for another.

Together, the pair walked over to the entrance, the brittle silence still hanging between them. Teddy reached out, touching her hand with just the back of his fingers, only to feel her pull away. He winced slightly, only to see Janet turn, offering him a half–smile.

"I should get back to work," Janet said. She gestured upstairs and then to the side where the bank of elevators sat. "I think I'll take the elevator."

Teddy nodded, watching as she left, leaving him at the foot of the stairs. He always preferred the stairs, it gave him a chance to look around, to move and not be enclosed in a metal death trap. Even if he had the treatment from the Shop for the claustrophobia, it still made him uncomfortable.

Alone, Teddy turned to survey the surroundings and could not help but notice the signs of the 'festive' day now. A few cards, a few roses clutched in hands. He wondered how he missed the signs, but it was sparse. Nowhere near the same flood of red as before.

"It's a stupid festival. Not even a real one too." Muttering, he took the escalator up, headed for his desk.

***

Janet slumped, staring into space. That last message had been a pain to deal with. Most people thought her job was simple. Buy a language pack from the Shop, you're good to go. All that information, downloaded directly into your brain. A new language, without the study. No problem.

Except, you never knew who made that pack if you didn't check. You didn't know what biases they had. Nor did most language packs contain information on the full range of social and cultural cues, not unless they were of the highest quality. For day to day conversations, the average language pack was functional. But not diplomatic correspondence, where making a mistake on one word, on one assumption or missing an allusion could stall a negotiation for weeks, even months. Maybe forever.

The worst kinds of messages were from the Movanna and Truinnar. The damn elves, white and dark, were so full of themselves that they felt the need to write messages with layers of meaning. And if you missed it, well, you missed it. Even something as simple as the word 'dance' could have numerous cultural meanings behind it.

Janet quickly made a note for Teddy, a slight small smile crossing her face as she considered his reaction. He'd get so excited, learning something new about the two societies that she'd been negotiating with. That silly man.

After a moment, the smile disappeared she remembered his tirade. Wasn't as if she didn't know to expect the rant but… well. A woman could hope. But not a lot. Turning back to her files, she sent the quick message off to Teddy with a flick of her fingers, already forgetting about it.

***

Teddy heard the chime of the incoming message. It was very familiar, mostly because he'd made sure it sounded that way. Altering his Status Screen and his link to the System had cost him some Mana regen but it had been worth it. A quick flick of his eyes brought up the message, and his smile grew as he read over the information. Who would have thought that the Poosken's were a matriarchally led theocracy in the past.

His smile quickly faded, as he remembered the way Janet had shied away from his touch. Ever since six months ago when they'd nearly died from another damn random attack, she'd been careful about touching. How she'd wake up late at night, screaming. Of course, she didn't remember any of that, all the times he'd held her while she sobbed her heart out until she fell asleep again. And even if she did, they all had their own nightmares.

As he dismissed the message, his attention was caught by a nearby conversation. Curiosity made him turn to check, to see Kaylee flushed red as a tall, gangly goth proffered a bouquet of roses at her. Teddy watched as the young man stumbled over his words, professing his infatuation to the older woman.

"I... I..." Kaylee stuttered, unable to come up with an answer. Still, she clutched the bouquet of flowers tightly to her chest.

"Just think about it. I know we are not, you know. But, it's the end of the world. And I think you're the most awesome person." The goth replied and then immediately dashed off, heading down the stairs at speed. Teddy could almost swear that he triggered a Skill, the way he moved.

"Admirer?" Teddy teased Kaylee when she turned around and caught him staring.

"A former student." Kaylee ducked her head and took a surreptitious sniff of the roses.

"From college?"

"Yes."

"Well... What are you going to do about it?" Teddy said. He glanced down at the elevators and then added. "You know, he's not a kid anymore. And you are not his teacher." "

"Still... It's wrong. I'm so old." Kaylee pointed a finger at Teddy warningly. "For him."

"And he has held onto his feelings for you for the last six years. And if I remember correctly, has been coming to visit you for the last year or so. Seems like, at the end of the world, love is a rare enough thing," Teddy advised.

Kaylee shook her head and then fixed Teddy with a stern gaze. "And you? You're telling me that. When was the last time you and Janet did anything romantic?"

"I... This isn't about me!" Teddy crossed his arms and twisted away. How dare she. He was just trying to help.

***

An hour later, Janet finished translating the transcript of the latest meeting between Vancouver and another of their trade partners, adding in notes about subtext and cultural topics that might have been missed in the initial talk. All of this was not strictly necessary, but it was useful for the staff for their next meeting. The more they understood, the better.

To her surprise, there was a blinking light in the corner of her vision. She'd muted all the notifications while she was working, but this message had a special alert on it. After all, it was from Teddy.

Dinner?

The message was a single word sentence. Janet's lips twisted, annoyance bubbling up. He could be so verbose in his work, but when it came to personal communication, he'd send these single-line, single word queries. The worse part of it was, she knew what he meant.

She quickly dictated out her answer and sent it back to him. Almost, almost she had decided not to answer him. But that would have been petty.

***

Whatever you want.

The simple declaration looked more like an accusation, a demand that Teddy do a little better than another bowl of Ramen. He stared at it, imagining he could feel the disapproval radiating from the very words themselves. It might be his imagination or it could have been the way that she felt. Sometimes, having lived with one another so long, it was hard to tell where intuition ended and imagination began.

Teddy swayed side to side in his chair as he categorized the latest monster reports, dumping them into their appropriate file with their threat levels while highlighting the latest increase in the number of mutated crows and the anomaly that were the unmutated flock of pigeons. Somehow, unmutated pigeons survived and thrived. Those inane flying rats. There was a research topic there, for someone.

At each sway, each full twist of his chair, he caught a glimpse of the bouquet of flowers that Kaylee had carefully set on her desk, having purchased a vase and filled it with water for the flowers. When he'd asked, she'd just huffed that it would have been rude to throw it aside. But…

What was it that the boy had said? Something about love in the apocalypse?

Teddy stopped, putting both hands on the desk. He stared into space for a time, before he exhaled. Well.

Maybe.

Another command and he pulled up the directory that he had access to. Maybe… A half-hour later, he was done and had composed the short message to his wife.

6pm. Atrium.

***

As Janet arrived downstairs at 6 PM as requested, finding herself alone except for the continual stream of adventurers. She stuck herself in a corner, eyeing the groups that came in. In one corner of the atrium, a beggar sat, casting Cleanse spells at those that needed it for small change. In another, a musician played a jib on a fiddle, giving everyone a Stamina boost with their music. It was a typical evening, except for the occasional loving couples. The one thing that she didn't see was her husband.

Seven minutes later, she saw him hurry scurry down the steps, looking around for her. She waves slightly to get his attention, and then again when he missed her. She was still incredibly grateful that he'd been in the library when the apocalypse arrived. With his sense of awareness, he'd be lucky to not have died within the first day. Like so many of the others.

She frowned, as he walked up to her and said. "Come on, this way."

Rather than lead them out of the atrium, Teddy led them right back into the library. And rather than take the stairs, he went for the elevators. She frowned, when he waved for her to join him.

"Where we going? If you've got more work, we could just eat by ourselves."

"Just be patient."

Janet narrowed her eyes, because something in his tone made her concerned. She watched as he hit the top button, the one that took them straight to the roof. She bit her lip, knowing that whatever was happening, he wasn't going to say. Not after telling her to be patient. He was stubborn that way.

Once they reached the roof, he stepped out immediately, the tension that had tightened his shoulders relaxing. He then led her along the pathway in the rooftop garden they had finally managed to finish. Initially, the library had meant to finish the work in 2018 but a little apocalypse happened. The work had been left abandoned, half-finished until six months ago when Lana dedicated funds to the construction. Ordered rows of grass was interspersed between green stretches, beds of vegetables and maple trees along the edges of the rooftop. Benches and smaller, private offices lined the top of the building in opposing corners, while the edges of the rooftop were planted with grass.

In short order, Teddy brought her to one corner of the roof. A bed of grass demarcated the edges, lush greenery to walk upon. Teddy stopped at the edges and proceeded to take off his shoes, gesturing for her to do the same. Cocking her head to the side, she eyed her husband again but followed suit. The setting, beautiful and unique made her intrigued, just like his lack of communication. Once on the grass, it didn't take long for Teddy to pick a spot and pull out a picnic blanket to lay out. Janet slowed her steps, calling for her husband.

"What is it?" he asked.

"What is this?" Janet couldn't help but let a little of the skepticism escape into her voice. Skepticism and, perhaps, a little hope.

Teddy scratched his head and shifted from foot to foot. "Yeah, sorry. I should know this isn't right. We can just… go." He began to walk back towards the edge of the grass, where their shoes were.

Janet drew a quick breath and stepped to the side, grabbing his arm with her hand. She felt the biceps in his arm, bigger and more defined than before. She looked up, and spotted his eyes focused on the ground. Dark brown eyes, large for a Chinese man, with eyelashes that were to die for.

"Don't. It's fine. No, it's good." Janet said before pulling on his arm, guiding them back towards the picnic blanket.

When they were both seated, she looked about, seeing that the entire section was empty but for the two of them. Also, empty of anything like dinner, which her stomach loudly complained about.

"Oh! One second." Teddy reached sideways, conjuring his purchases from his inventory. One after the other, he pulled sealed containers and set them out beside her. Half a dozen metallic boxes later, he also added a pair of candles and candle holders, which he lit with a flick of his fingers.

"What did you buy?" she said, eyeing the containers hungrily.

"All our favorites. Roast pork, BBQ duck, bok choy, Moroccan lamb stew, chicken fried rice and of course, beef curry." Teddy said, pointing to each.

"Isn't it a bit much?" Janet asked, even as she was busy opening each of the containers. The smells that hit her the moment the containers were open set her salivating. It was a strange mix, but one that she was more than happy to pile into the plate that Teddy offered.

"Well, I… I thought we could have a nice dinner." Teddy coughed and looked around, adding. "I can always pack it up again afterwards. The leftovers, that is."

Janet laughed and shook her head. "It's perfect. But, what brought this on?"

"I can't just be randomly romantic?"

"You?" Janet snorted, and stuffed her mouth full of fried rice and lamb stew. She chewed on the meal, tasting the spices, the hour-long preparation that had gone into the meal. And she let out a little moan of pleasure.

***

Teddy watched as his wife was distracted by the food, as she chewed and swallowed and then took another bite immediately after. He fell silent, enjoying watching her eat as he lightly nibbled on his own meal.

The happiness on her face, the simple joy of eating, the way she had grain of rice stuck to the corner of her lip made Teddy smile. He'd missed this. For a moment, she looked like the woman that he had fallen in love with. Even if she did have purple hair now. When he brushed the rice grain from her face, she didn't flinch away but leaned into it. Their eyes met briefly and he leaned forwards, only to see her retract. Retract and duck down to pop a

---

slice of roast pork into her mouth before gesturing to get on with answering the question.

"Oh. Fine. You know Kaylee right?" At that Janet snorted, he continued. "That boy who's been showing up. He brought a bouquet of flowers. Asked her out." He continued to relate the entire event, in more detail at Kaylee's urging. The initial conversation transitioned into more gossip, one related between bites of Skill-enhanced food.

Teddy soon realized, he'd not talked to her for a bit. She never really mentioned her own colleagues, just the work itself. So, he often had to ask for clarification of the named individuals, and that often elicited even more side stories. Time passed swiftly as they had a couple of years of office gossip to catch up on. They spoke and spoke, just finding time for one another, without System notices, without apocalyptic danger or work filling in the spaces.

Just talking.

Connecting.

At the end of the night, the pair packed away the containers by the simple expedient of tossing it all into their inventory. A Cleanse spell saw the crumbs and food stains disappear, leaving the pair pristine under the moonlight. Teddy took the lead in rolling up and storing the picnic blanket, making a mental note to thank Lana for this favor. And perhaps buying her a thank you gift for letting him use the rooftop. Maybe some wine. Not chocolate. She had a thing against chocolate for some reason.

When he stood, he spotted Janet staring out over the skyline of Vancouver. He spent a moment watching her, the way the wind pushed against her hair, making the light curls twist, the way it outlined her body. And then he finished his turn, to look over the strange mixed alien and human skyline that was their city now. The way the alien buildings reflected the moonlight, glinting in the darkness. The way human buildings were lit and shaded by their occupants moving about. And over to the north, the familiar mountains that dominated the skyline, lit up in one corner by the bioluminescent, mutated pine tree forest.

"It's weird, isn't it? How much it's changed. And hasn't," Janet said.

Teddy stepped closer, wrapping an arm around her waist naturally. She moved into the crook of his arm, squirming down a little to find the best spot, the point where they both fit.

"Definitely weird. But it could be worse."

"Thank you. For tonight." Janet turned, staring up at Teddy. He looked down, meeting her eyes and then leaned in, slowly.

Lips touched, brushing against one another, noses nestled. Her lips parted slightly as he deepened the kiss, one hand clutching her tighter to him. She returned the grip, continuing the kiss before she leaned back, her breathing short and her cheeks flushed.

"You know…"

"We should do this more?" Teddy finished for her. "Maybe start-up date night again?"

"Yes. But no." She kissed him again. "I was thinking we should head home. To our bed."

"Oh. Oh!" Grinning, Teddy released her body and tugged her with him. To their strange alien home. But, in all that strangeness, all the change, some things stayed the same.

Some people.

Some feelings.

You just had to remember to look.

The End of *Valentines in an Apocalypse*

Thirty-Two Months Post-System

This is Harry Prince, reporting from Toledo, Spain. The past few months have been hard. No harder than the first year, but difficult in different, more political ways.

A new form of détente with the alien races has been established. While battles for supremacy rage between cities and among the various alien races, their dominion has also brought safety from the monster hordes.

The increased number of Advanced Classes—both alien and human—has seen losses slow down to a trickle. Fewer outposts and towns disappear from the map every day as we establish new lines of communication and support. New life springs anew. Children brought to maturity during this period or conceived during the start of the System add to the human population.

Our numbers continue to fall, but I believe we can see the end to this stage now. It is possible, just possible, that humanity might survive the System and this Dungeon World designation. Certainly, small enclaves of Serfs and explorers have escaped Earth itself. Europe, America, China, India, portions of South America have all new rulers who watch over them in a bloody steel grip, whether human or alien.

Other locations, like Australia, have been wiped out. Few remnants have survived the unholy mixture of Earth's deadliest continent and System mutations.

This is not the beginning of the end. But it is, perhaps, the end of the beginning.

Separate but Equal

"You want to steal the Declaration of Independence?" Kiloff shouted, brown eyes opened wide, gold tooth flashing as he exclaimed surprise. He waved his hands around as he continued, nearly toppling over as he sat with one foot propped up on the stool. "It's guarded even worse than before the System arrived! It literally has out of this world security."

"And we have paranormal abilities too," Jacopo said, tossing long floppy hair out of the way unconsciously, revealing piercing green eyes over sharp cheekbones and a strong jaw. The movement made the only female in the room stare, a little grin on her lips as she drank in the sight. "I gathered all of you here because you're the best at what you do."

"Bullshit," Trip drawled. For their hacker and general dogsbody with anything electronic, the man was the complete opposite of what you would expect. Over six feet tall, hefty due to pre-System earned muscle mass, kindly gray eyes, and salt and pepper hair cut short. Military style—or just because he was balding a little and hadn't bothered to pay for a fix. "I'm good, but not that good. I'm only Level 42."

"Oh, sure, there are higher Leveled humans out there," Jacopo said with a sniff. "But they're all meatheads. Throwing themselves into the fire, over and over again. I meant the best at what you do for the jobs you have. Not for killing aliens."

"I still don't like the term…" Rosa said, big curly hair bouncing a little as she shifted on her seat. The woman was short, thin, and slim with barely there hips and ass—a complaint she let everyone know of every time she got drunk. Yet, she never got body sculpted to change it, because the lack of hips or buttocks made her job as their thief and cat burglar so much simpler. "Used to be what they called us."

Jacopo—Jac to his friends—grunted. "Well, we didn't invade the country, buy up all the lands, and throw a new System in place."

"What's this 'we'? You're Italian."

"You think they haven't thought me Latin before?" He waved one very tanned arm up and down his body. Even if half the view was Charisma-stat driven, Rosa could not help but look. One reason Jac was their face and brain—where he led, people followed.

It was just a little too bad he was still hurting from earlier this year. Then again, you could say the same thing for all of them—with nearly eighty percent of the DC population killed, enslaved and shipped off as serfs, or just missing, every single person in this room had a sob story of their own.

They coped in different ways, all of them. In Jac's case, it was working out new ways to annoy their alien overlords.

"We're getting off-topic," Trip grated out. "You know the National Archive Museum is now run by the aliens." Then, reluctantly, he added, "As a sort of archive of all that we were. They paid for spatial distortion too, so it's much bigger than ever, with a whole section split off for vehicles, another for our computers and the like."

"Not that they let us low humans in anymore," Rosa sneered.

"Who'd want to go?" Kiloff replied. "All the new stuff is so much better." A slight pause. "Except the food. Our snacks don't taste right anymore."

"That's because they took out all the corn syrup," Trip said. "Made it 'healthier.'"

"Another thing we didn't ask them for," Rosa said. "We'd love to stick it to them, boss, but how are we supposed to do it?"

Jac, clapping his hands together, said, "From their desire to keep adding to their collection, of course."

"You want to get invited in because we're donating something?"

"No, because we're getting paid for fulfilling a quest of theirs." A single gesture and a new notification, clad in blue with white text, bloomed in their eyes.

New Quest: Add to the National Archive Museum of Earth's Collection

Objective: Retrieve a pristine Republic F-105 Thunderchief and deliver it to deputy museum director Morris in 4 days, 3 hours, and eleven seconds.

Rewards: Credits and XP commensurate with condition and historical authenticity of plane

Wonder bloomed in their eyes as they looked at Jac. He clapped his hands together, grinning.

"Alright, people. Time to go steal us a plane."

***

It wasn't that easy, of course. Sure, you could buy a plane from the Shop, drop it right into the National Archive Museum, and call it a day. Problem with that was anyone could do it, but the authenticity of the plane would easily be called into question. The museum did not want a Shop-created artefact but an authentic piece, one worked by human hands and, preferably, with a storied history.

"And you're certain this one will work?" Jac asked, his right leg shaking as he jittered in the modified car, staring at the warehouse they were turning towards in the middle of industrial country. The vehicle was a luxury BMW, since if you were about to modify any car to work post-System, you might as well go with something a little more luxurious.

For a while, vehicles had littered the streets in Washington, abandoned where they had died. Then, of course, the Wreckers and Scavengers and Metal Elementalist had gotten their hands on them and people had decided they needed the roads for other things so they'd started disappearing. Moving a car yourself when your strength was over 50 became a lot easier, and so the sight of a tiny woman putting her shoulder into a vehicle and shoving it into an alleyway or stacking them five high at a time became not uncommon.

Even so, there were still parts of the city—like this one—where vehicles and buildings lay abandoned and untouched, the air of disuse and crumbling infrastructure etched all over the environment. So far from civilization, monsters had taken over many of the environs, lurking in shadows and sleeping in office spaces.

"Look, it's not my fault the records were false!" Trip grumbled. "The websites all said the previous F-105 had flown in the wars."

"The Korean War," Rosa said sarcastically.

"How was I supposed to know they weren't even made before then? It's all ancient history," Trip said. "And I was never that much of a plane guy."

"Just electronics and mechanics and computers, eh?" Kiloff said, stroking the modified BMW. For all that its outer shell—and the luxury seating within—was human-made, near every other part had been modified by the man himself. Made sense, of course, since he was only as good as his vehicle, being a Driver.

A twitch of the vehicle's wheel brought the group rolling up to the front of the still-barred warehouse fences. Without needing to be asked, Kiloff deployed a pair of lasers to cut through the gates before utilizing a simple magnet to remove them from their way. As the clatter of the shorn gates echoed through the surroundings, the vehicle rolled forward nearly silently, the group eyeing the surroundings with trepidation.

"Drones," Jac ordered.

Moments later, a pair of drones was shooting through broken windows, entering the top floor and bottom of the warehouse. Controlled through the simple touchscreen interface of Trip's tablet, the team watched as the drones displayed the inside of the darkened warehouse, showing flashes of chairs, desks, broken vehicles, and, there, under the cover of a tarp still, the unmistakable silhouette of the plane.

"And you're telling me an 'industrial artist' chose to buy a whole plane to make into some performance piece?" Jac said with a sigh. "Maybe we did deserve to get—ow!"

Rosa withdrew her hand, glaring at him. "Don't you dare."

Jac returned her heated stare for a moment before he lowered his head, abashed. "Yeah, sorry. You know how it is. Sometimes my mouth runs without thinking…"

"Then think more," she hissed.

"Maybe you guys can argue later?" Trip said, waving a hand at the sight his drones had caught. Up on the top floor—and the reason the bottom floor and surroundings were untouched—was a nest of insects. A moment later, the automated search came up with the results.

Mutated Carnivorous Elm Zigzag Sawfly Colony (Level 38)
HP: 23/23 (Individual)
MP: 18/18 (Individual)
Quantity: 108

"Not so tough individually," Kiloff muttered. "But a really high level otherwise."

"Must be the colony aspect," Trip muttered, fingers flying over his keyboard. "I wonder…"

"Later," Jac interrupted the man before he could finish his thoughts. "Right. This is just an in-and-out job. Rosa, you have the DS?"

She patted her belt pouch, where the very expensive piece of gear was attached. The dimensional storage trap, when deployed, would swallow the entire plane, allowing for easy transport. No need for a hauler, though the biggest problem was how long it took to set up.

"Then, get to it. Trip will watch your back. I'll get the decoys set up while you're sneaking in." Jac gestured to the perimeter to indicate his intentions. More details were hashed out in quick order, the group having worked together enough by now to not require highly detailed plans. In fact, as Trip was wont to say, best to keep it simple. The last letter went unsaid—mostly.

Sliding through the doorway, anti-rust spray liberally applied to hinges before she swung the door open, Rosa slipped through the office entrance downstairs. She could have tried the main hangar doors but knew they were guaranteed to make noise. If things went well, the entire proceedings would happen without the sawflies ever being alerted.

To help with that, she had four of her major Skills as a cat burglar running: Silent Steps, Hidden Presence, Shadow Friend, and Threat Detection. Together, she was able to avoid the notice of the sawflies until she was by the plane. Carefully, she lifted one end of the tarp, poking her head underneath to verify the contents. It would be rather embarrassing to steal the wrong plane after all.

"Thunderchief confirmed," she whispered over the comms before she began the process of laying out the necessary pieces. The boundary pieces were tiny, barely finger-sized, but each had to be placed in the correct position before the storage device could be activated. Thankfully, there were guidelines that appeared before her gaze once she began the activation process.

For Rosa, this was the most dangerous process. Though her Skills hid her presence, they only hid *her* presence—not those of the dimensional storage pieces. It took her five minutes to complete most of the placements before a sawfly, meandering through its own home in buzzing, random directions, noted something different.

There was no indication if it was the smell, the visual aspect of new items, the inflow of Mana from the activating items, or another, unidentified sense, but the volume and frequency of the beat of the creature's wings increased.

Rosa froze, breath catching in her chest as she stared at the sawfly. It turned in the air in tight circles, one after the other. She watched it for long moments, curious what had changed, and then realized that the volume of sound had increased again as more of the sawflies made their way down.

"Shit! They're on the way," Rosa said.

"Deploying decoys." From outside, the harsh scream and pop-pop-pop of scent markers echoed through the air. The sawfly buzzed, turned sideways, then went back to its circling motion as it waited for reinforcements.

"Didn't work." Given no other choice, she drew and threw a throwing knife from her hip holster. The creature shifted, dodging the attack, only for the knife to turn in mid-air, tracking its motion to strike it. The monster tumbled to the ground moments later, dead.

"Incorrect. We've got the swarm coming," Jac said from outside.

"Must have split," she said, rushing now and giving up on moving quietly. She slammed down the remaining pins for the dimensional storage, triggered the equipment, and stepped back, slipping into nearby shadows. She would have to be within five meters for the dimensional shunt to work, so she could only wait.

"Oh, gods. They're tearing into the decoys like a bandsaw through dry wood," Trip muttered. "Best hurry."

She would have replied, but, unfortunately, the reinforcements had arrived. Thus far, they were only buzzing around the glowing dimensional shunts, the pins that she had embedded in the concrete floor. One flew near her, the palm-sized orange and yellow body of the creature a stark contrast to the shadowed hangar. Most worrying were the creature's 'mouths' where the pincers had grown in size and had a strange, yellowish color around them.

A dozen, no, two dozen of the creatures flew through the air, searching for the intruder. Just as one neared her, a sudden pop of displaced air and a rush of wind occurred as near a third of the creatures disappeared along with the plane and its tarp.

At the same time, the motion and flow of Mana alerted the creatures to Rosa, causing her eyes to widen in terror as the remaining insects honed in on her.

***

"Go, go, go!" Rosa screamed as she ran out of the office door, spinning as she exited to kick it shut. The thump, thump, thump of sawflies striking the impediment was counterpoint to the pair that was buzzing while stuck on her thigh and back.

From ahead of her, Kiloff's car came barreling forwards, a door thrown open. She leaped through the air, a drone sacrificing itself in a display of violence and shrapnel as more of the sawflies emerged from the second floor.

The moment Rosa was within the car, it zoomed away, Jac helping the woman to kill the pair still on her body.

"Did you get it?" he snapped.

"Of course!" Rosa said.

"Kiloff!" Jac cried.

"We're going… we're going…" The Driver triggered his Skills, one after the other. Nitrox accelerated the car at a rapid rate, putting even Formula 1 cars to shame. Smooth Sailing ensured that the rough streets felt like they were in Au-Tenleytown before the System. And Evasive Driving meant that the car automatically shifted course to avoid the buzzing sawflies. A small percentage of them were able to match the speed of the car, though even they were soon lost behind.

"Told you!" Jac crowed. "Now all we got to do is get the plane to our employer and steal the Declaration of Independence."

***

Organizing entry into the National Archives Museum after two failed attempts at selling a plane was actually easier than the first attempt. At this point, their entry—and the scans that accompanied their entrance—was routine. The group—sans Kiloff, who sat outside in his car awaiting the others—entered through the loading dock, through a door beside the massive loading dock doors at the back of the building. Not that the loading dock doors were required to be opened that often anymore, as dimensional storage made transporting goods much simpler.

Especially when the number of shipments arriving at the museum had decreased significantly over the last few months. While the museum continued to add to its needs, it had entered a small period of overall consolidation, as alien attendance to the exhibits had yet to reach the numbers required to justify further expansion.

"Not that attendance, in itself, is what the current owners of the museum seek, you understand," the thin, squirrely human that spoke to them explained after Jac's question about the doors had led to a meandering conversation that had led to attendance and visitors. "The entire museum is, in fact, currently sponsored by a few aliens who believe in the preservation of native culture before System-advent."

"And that's what the current exhibit is for?" Jac said, surveying the half-complete surroundings. Holographic projectors filled in the hellscape that surrounded them, native plants from Vietnam growing all around while smaller drones ran around, trimming and otherwise caring for these plants. "Showing our 'culture'?"

"North American history and an archival recreation of various activities, yes." The Caretaker bobbed his head. "We finished the Korean War already and, of course, are moving on to Vietnam." He let out a long, weary sigh. "My South American compatriots have it easier. There are so much fewer props required. Transporting the necessary buildings for the various assassination attempts and other activities are easier too, because at least many of those are still around!"

"Where do you want us to put the plane?" Trip asked, tapping the box at his hip.

"Over there will do." The Caretaker waited for them to deploy the storage device and let out a little squeak of surprise as the plane, tarp, and sawflies all appeared at once. The sawflies, of course, fell to the ground, dead after being held so long in stasis in another dimension. "Oh, my."

"Sorry, had a little trouble getting them."

"So I see…" Nose wrinkled, he made a few gestures and the cleaning drones swept over. Taking hold of the tarp with Jac's help, he pulled it off the plane and smiled at what was revealed. Holding a visor to his face, he wandered up and down, scanning the plane for long minutes, leaving the pair waiting to shift uneasily on their feet in boredom till he was done.

"So?" Jac said.

"Perfect! It'll need to be modified, of course, but this will do." A slight twitch of his fingers, and their quest notification updated. "Pleasure doing business with you."

"And you!" Jac said, shaking hands before the pair walked out, leaving the plane behind.

***

In the early hours of the morning, in the new exhibit, there was a slight shift of a panel in the plane. In a location that would have been too small for even a contortionist to have hidden within, Rosa popped out, landing on the ground silently in a crouch. She froze under the plane's body, listening to the silent hum of the air circulation and the swish of cleaning drones. All of it, absent the harsh klaxon of alarms. Slowly, she relaxed, straightening and flexing her body.

Smaller Than I Look was a strange Skill, perfect for cases like this. Combined with her other abilities, it allowed her to fit into spaces that were smaller than should have been possible, somehow shunting herself—or perhaps the space she was within—into a different dimension, such that she could squeeze into those spaces.

Perfect for things like ventilation shafts—actual ventilation shafts, not the unrealistic movie-sized ones—and hiding in cramped boxes or hand-sized luggage. The only negative was that as an Active Skill it required a certain amount of Mana, which, when combined with her other Skills needed to keep her hidden, often only left her able to keep it running for a certain amount of time or tradeoff for other Skills. Only in the last few levels had she gained enough Willpower to keep her passive regeneration near equal, with the use of some very expensive Mana potions and Mana Regeneration potions.

Still, she had that queasy feel in her stomach and the tightness in her head from potion sickness. Too much more and she would really be on the ground, throwing up. Still, it had been worth it to get her in, silent and unseen.

Now, all she had to do was get to the Declaration of Independence. To do that, she deployed a series of drones from her inventory. Each of them was no bigger than a hornet, the drones moving with purpose through the air to hunt down the cleaning drones. A few seconds later, she had her first word from outside.

"Drones attached and comms piggy-backing off their signal. I'll send them out to find you the route." Trip's voice buzzed in her ear, and Rosa felt a thread of tension unwind from her back. It would have been bad if he had not been able to sneak into the system.

Now, all she had to do was pick her way through the museum, led by the suborned cleaning drones, and extract the document from its case.

***

"It's a right beauty, that one," Trip muttered, staring at the information flooding into his mind from the drones. Between the Neural Link he had attached to the back of his mind—how cyberpunk!—and his Skill, System Overdrive, he was getting near 100% fidelity from the drones' sensors. Of course, the sensory apparatus of a cleaning drone was strange—lots of visuals, a sonar, and a 'nose' that was focused on breaking apart chemicals and dust levels. No audio required, but his hornets offered that, even as they were attached to the cleaning drones themselves. At a lower fidelity, of course, but that was fine.

Utilizing the cleaning drones had been his idea, a perfect camouflage that none of the systems would notice. A massive opening in the museum's security. That was typical though. The ones in charge never looked far down enough to recognize all the different people—or things—that made their lives easy. All it meant was that it left a million and one gaps in their security that a dedicated, careful man could find if he was looking.

And Trip was looking. In particular, he was looking at the glass case, scanning it with the hornet's own specialized sensors as well as the drones, rattling off the various security measures for Rosa. Not that she wasn't doing her own scan, not trusting him with her life alone. Not that he blamed her at all.

In fact, if she hadn't been doing her own scan, he would have worried.

"Pressure plates. Negative air pressure on the inside, so any breach of the glass itself is going to be informed. Anti-dimensional and teleporting runes on the pedestal itself. Electronic trip wires on the case itself and laser trip wires on the inside. Temperature controls too and the way the light's refracting, I'm assuming there's a stable gas within as well," Trip muttered.

Those were the basics, and not long after, he was adding more specialized protections.

They were, at the least, making sure to take good care of the Declaration. Wouldn't want to lose their most precious document, would they?

It was funny. The real document in the National Archives had actually been hidden, and the concern was whether the aliens had kept the same deception running. If so, stealing it would be harder. However, Jac's research had shown that not only was showcasing fakes considered gauche with the various Skills and abilities available, but doing so often backfired in the System.

So this was the real document, which made their lives simpler.

Watching Rosa work was always a pleasure, though half the tools she used were either things they had purchased from the Shop for this very instance or ones Trip himself had modified. In less than ten minutes, she had bypassed the various systems, attached a simple device that re-routed the anti-teleportation matrix into a teleportation matrix, and replaced the document with an exact replica. Of course it would not hold up to any actual scrutiny, but it fooled the pressure plates.

After that, it was just a matter of guiding Rosa to the loading docks once again, where the team was waiting to pick her up.

***

Jac watched as Rosa slipped out of the backdoor, waited a few moments for the video of the security cameras to loop, and then loped across the distance. Since there were no physical fences in place, she just had to cross the ground between her and the road where the group idled. After that, they would have to leave DC itself. He had the entire cross-country trip planned out, including the Explorer and team that would be taking them along as well as a few spots they would hit on the way.

After all, there was no way staying in the same city would be a good idea. As it stood, he expected the bounty on their head to be significant—but thankfully, he figured most human hunters would ignore them. Most of the non-human ones were asses anyway and often chasing down other aliens or serfs.

Hands slapped lightly against the car door as Rosa finally reached him, a little out of breath, a big grin on her face. Slung across her back was the specialized carrier they had purchased to hide the document from all scanning. The woman's eyes were bright.

Everything was going perfectly as she swung the door open.

Which was, of course, when the force shields slammed down around the car, blocking it in and trapping them.

"I could break out," Kiloff growled, tapping a series of buttons on his dashboard, foot hovering over the accelerator.

"Do not attempt to escape or additional measures will be taken!" the voice that came barked out—quite literally. Jac turned his head to see one of those half-jackal aliens wandering over, a whip by his side that cackled with electricity and a wide, savage grin on his face.

"Don't," Jac ordered. "Wait…"

"Exit the vehicle slowly. Any sudden movements will be faced with extreme force." Now the speaker was bored. Not that Jac doubted Haruff's words. The museum's head of security was well known for his penchant for violence.

"Let me go first," Jac muttered. "I'll try to talk us out of this."

Swinging the door open, Jac moved slowly, making sure that his Skills were in full play. Charming Smile, Butter Couldn't Melt, and Your Best

Friend were all running at full speed, though the last was a passive that just added to his base Charisma bonus—his highest stat by far.

More importantly, he made sure Calming Voice was active as he spoke. "Now, Haruff, my good man. No need to be like that. We're just taking in the sights."

"Hah! Don't bother. You don't think we were watching you all through your little escapade?" Haruff snorted. "We just needed someone to test our security after our latest upgrades. Looks like you missed about half of them…"

Laughter echoed from all around and Jac blinked. He turned his head sideways, taking in shadowy figures in sudden stark relief, figures that none of the team had noticed at all. There was even a full-fledged APC there, the massive main weapon on the top of the vehicle leveled at Kiloff's. A single shot from the plasma cannon would have been enough to destroy the vehicle and everyone in it.

Definitely not the time to be shooting.

"Now, quit stalling and hand over what you stole."

"And what would that be?" Jac opened his hands. "We are scavengers and sellers, Haruff. Salesmen."

A flick of the man's hand and the whip sped through the air so fast that Jac never saw it before it struck his face. He reeled backwards, head throbbing, a deep cut down one side that had bisected his—now missing—eye and left his eye socket bloody. The pain hit a moment later and he stifled a scream, only managing to hold it off by leaning heavily on Butter Couldn't Melt, which kept him calm at all times.

"Do not lie to me." Haruff's voice was filled with a touch of glee. "Or do. I don't like it when my victims don't scream…"

Head down, still holding on to his wound and feeling the blood clot as the accelerated healing of the System kicked in, Jac bought time. His mind was spinning through options, contingencies—so many of them that he had not mentioned to the others—and finding many of them blocked off already.

No communication, everything jammed. So calling in extra help was out.

Kiloff's car was blocked off and targeted. He might be able to throw them for a loop for a few moments, but the shield around the vehicle—except for where it had opened to let Haruff attack him—was blocking easy escape.

The timed triggers to blow up the plane and cause a secondary diversion should have gone off just about… now? He strained his hearing, hoping to catch a hint of… something.

"Don't bother. We scanned your plane and removed the explosives in the fuel tanks," Haruff said, bored. "Already rounded up your backups. Disabled the extra drones and cut your connection to the security feed. We have you, boy."

"Flattered you did so much work…" Jac said, pushing himself to his feet and waving the others with his free hand to stay in, since Haruff was willing to gloat. "What will happen to us?"

"The usual." Haruff sniffed. "We'll bring you before a Galactic Judge, have the case reviewed, a Serf bond emplaced for the value of what you stole. You'll serve your new masters till it's paid off and then you're free. We're not savages."

That would depend on your definition…

"And what if what we stole was incalculable?" Jac asked, raising his head so that his remaining eye could fix Haruff in place. He could hear it, that drumming noise.

"Nothing is incalculable."

"And that, my dear wolf, is where you're wrong."

Haruff frowned, head turning. He heard it now, spotted the incoming moments too late. Jac was throwing himself back into the open door, screaming for them to get moving. Chaos descended as a swarm of sawflies, lured over by the smell and corpses of their swarm members, arrived.

They were much depleted after their long journey but dragged with them, across the entirety of the city, other monsters they had enraged. The screams, snorts, shouts, and squeals of descending bedlam filled the air, accompanied by the musk and smell of firing ozone, burnt tar, and melting metal.

Chaos was here, and Jac could only hope Plan G would work.

***

Kiloff gunned the car, the vehicle shooting out sideways as hidden maneuvering thrusters deployed underneath it shot it out into the only open area. Right towards the surprised Haruff, scooping up Jac as he threw himself in and cracked an ankle rather soundly.

Not that Kiloff was paying attention as he shifted gears and accelerated, desperately controlling the wheel and vehicle as it was thrown sideways due to the massive APC's plasma cannon unloading into their previously held spot.

Flames spat out of exhaust fumes as the vehicle accelerated, tires screaming across the ground as Nitrox and Pinpoint Handling took effect, allowing the wheels to grip the ground in a way that would have been impossible before the System. He accelerated through a fast-closing gap, the world passing by in a blur of motion and half-noticed events.

Stasis nets deployed, trying to slow his vehicle down. A touch of a button and a dimensional shunt displaced the vehicle half a step to the side so that the stasis field could not grip. However, that took out the grip on his wheels, which meant the vehicle started sliding a little to the right.

That required another touch of a button, which deployed wheel spikes. They broke through the tar, punching hundreds of tiny holes into the asphalt in seconds as he tore through the road. All along the sides of the car, through the still-open door, additional attacks began to land, burning off paint and leather alike.

"Shut the door!" Kiloff roared as the first of the beasts, the sawfly swarm that had been led all the way here via the dead bodies that Rosa had brought, arrived. Rather than dispose of the bodies properly, the idiots had dumped the corpses on the top of the museum's 'green' roof as compost, which meant that there was a direct line of sight and smell for the creatures.

The sawflies mostly ignored them, of course, their destination the killer of their nestmates. On the other hand, the other monsters dragged forth, the humans who were fleeing the rampage, and the ones hunting down monsters on the edges in a bid for more experience all crashed over the group like a crazed wave.

Amidst the chaos of flying bodies and vehicles, monsters and aliens, explosions and spells, Kiloff wove through the throng, Skills triggering, vehicle smashed, bashed, and blasted in turns. Moving perpendicular to the battle, turning up the main road and away from the automated defenses around the museum as they came to life, the team fled.

Cackling.

***

Hours later, the vehicle ditched and the group piled into a non-descript minivan—with rollbars, weapons, and reinforced windows because it was still the apocalypse—they finally pulled into a local fort on the outskirts of DC.

A single man with dark eyes stood, hands crossed before him, ramrod straight. Shifting shadows spoke of more than a single man as Jac climbed out of the vehicle with his team. Trip and Kiloff stayed behind, tiny drones deployed and vehicle still running in case they had to run.

Again.

"Rosa, meet our employer: General Ross," Jac said, grinning as the man led them over to a worn and half-broken park table. A small gesture had a simple tarp appear on top of it, onto which Rosa placed the Declaration on their urging. "Thanks, by the way, for the distraction."

"Corralling all those beasts was not easy," General Ross rumbled, white teeth flashing under umber skin as he added, "Was fun seeing the aliens run though. Too bad that head of security was too smart. My sniper couldn't get a good shot on him."

"Sniper?" Rosa said.

"What? You think this was the only objective?" The man shook his head. "Testing their defenses, whittling down their Advanced Classers, and reminding people that even a 'safe zone' is not that safe, no matter what the aliens say, were all part of the plan."

"Never one to take aim at a single target, because you might miss," Jac said. "Whereas we just make sure we hit it the first time."

"And you're sure this is it?" General Ross asked, leaning forwards to stare at the Declaration. There was a touch of reverence in his eyes as he stared at it, the document that had created their nation. Not that there was much of it left, not with numerous petty tyrants—all of them of the megarich or aristocratic variety—running around.

"A hundred percent. You can check if you wish."

There was a slight shift of his head as Ross read something in his notifications, a small smile as he touched the document in its glass case before he gestured for Rosa to wrap it back up. Once he had the document in hand, he stuck his hand out.

"Payment has been sent."

"And confirmed."

"Thank you. What you've done for this nation…" General Ross faded off, seeming to choke up.

"The Credits are more than enough thanks," Rosa said.

"Speak for yourself." Jac grinned as he received the notification he had been waiting for: a Quest completion, experience, and a Title.

"Oy!" Trip called out, sticking his head out. "My drones are getting chatter of bounty hunters closing in."

"That's our cue," Jac said, shaking the General's hand again. "Give us a call if you need something else stolen."

Not releasing the hand, General Ross asked, "How about a nation?"

"Can't fit that into a pocket," Rosa said, already walking off. "Try again later when the heat's dropped."

"What she said," Jac said, joining his thief.

Moments later, the van was peeling out onto the battered interstate, camouflage panels deploying so the entire vehicle disappeared as they ran. They'd have to keep running for a bit until the heat would die down, but it had been worth it.

"Tea Partier?" Rosa's voice rose, incredulous, as she stared at the Title. "Really? The System really has a terrible sense of humor."

"Or maybe it thinks we actually did start something," Kiloff said thoughtfully.

"Start what? Not as though we've stopped fighting," Rosa scoffed.

"The System, maybe. The aliens, sometimes. I hear out west, they've been pushing real hard. Over here though…" Jac shrugged. "That document, it was a declaration of intent for something that had been brewing already. Maybe it means nothing to you, but for some it might be the sign they needed to fight back."

"Maybe." Rosa crossed her arms, added, "Maybe this time, we can try to do it better."

"Maybe," Trip muttered and then added, "So, what's the plan now, boss?"

"Well, we've got to run for a bit, but I might have a lead on another job."

"You don't say…" Trip said sarcastically.

"Yeah, see, there's this ball of yarn…"

###

The End of *Separate but Equal*

Year 7 Post-System

This is Harry Prince, reporting from Medea outside of Algiers. I will be stitching together additional footage shot earlier today of the remnants of Algiers. Remnants, I say, for the city is a crumpled ruin, having transformed into a massive dungeon that spans tens of kilometers and which creatures Leveled in the 80s and 90s call home.

The Crezar who resided in the city, the aliens who believed themselves equal to the Dungeon World, have fallen to a biped. They kept the Dungeon from expanding for four long years but can no longer do so. Monsters emerge from the remnant city on the regular, harassing nearby settlements.

Around me, you can see intrepid Adventurers gathering from all across the globe. Humans and aliens, together they will be entering the dungeon in an attempt to destroy its core. If they succeed, they will return the surroundings to normalcy.

If they fail, we might lose Spain entirely.

There are familiar figures here, including the Spear of Humanity, Mikito Sato, Cheng Shao, the Chinese Metal Mage, and Rae the Silver Cyborg. The luminaries of our world, the Champions of Humanity. We hope they are sufficient.

If not, there are rumors of another that could be called in. A man bearing an alien Master Class. The Redeemer of the Dead, whose coming brings with it chaos and relief in equal order.

The Redeemer Returns

"Remind me again why we didn't just take the teleporter," Lyrra muttered.

You'd think being a bounty hunter on a dungeon world would mean constantly running down marks, but the truth was we spent even more time as mercenaries and run-of-the-mill Adventurers. Seven years after System advent, there was no shortage of monsters, and the number of worthwhile bounties that required a Master Class to chase down was low, which explained why we were packed into the converted military transport truck like sardines. The smell of unwashed bodies sweltering in armor filled the compartment and made it clear that few humans bothered investing in a Cleanse spell.

The Movana jostled against my shoulder as the truck rocked over yet another rut. The poor condition of the road was typical outside of settlements and safe zones, even with borders between the territories largely settled these days.

I shrugged, pushing the pale-skinned elf back upright with a slight nudge. "The contract specified keeping a low profile as much as possible. It's just a Field Boss battle. We're not even here for the monsters, just keeping the Galactics in line."

Left unsaid was the other half of the job—and the real reason the organized alliance of human military forces dared bring in an outsider like me. An Oracle's prediction had calculated that an infiltrator aimed to cause trouble during today's fight. The wording of the augury and subsequent Shop inquiries hinted that the target could be found among the snipers and other long-range damage specialists, so that's where my assignment started.

"We don't need a babysitter." The interjection came from a slightly pudgy and balding middle-aged man sitting opposite me in the troop bay.

I raised an eyebrow in response. "Good, because I hate babysitting."

"Elf lover." The man spat at my feet and leaned back, crossing his arms and wrinkling his nose in disgust. It seemed plenty of folks still weren't happy to see aliens on Earth, regardless of the political reality where they were allies as often as enemies.

Annoyed, I drummed my fingers over the holsters that rested on either side of my hips. Then a snort of laughter came from the Movana beside me as she looked the man up and down dismissively. "You're lucky Hal's girlfriend is busy shopping. I think you're just jealous."

The man looked between Lyrra and me with confusion until I finally realized that he thought we were together. Sliding my hands away from my weapons, I just chuckled with a shake of my head.

The woman beside the man jabbed an elbow into his side and whispered in his ear. Even with Keen Senses boosting my hearing, I failed to catch the muffled conversation over the hum of the transport's engines, but I could guess the subject from the way his head jerked back around to stare at me wide-eyed.

Beside me, Lyrra shifted just enough to glare in my direction, though her gaze lacked any real animosity. Unlike the other half-dozen eclectic humans stuffed back here, who stared at me with emotions ranging from suspicion to fear. Humans with a Master Class were still rare enough that rumors still spread despite my efforts to remain in the shadows. My reputation had grown and I still hadn't figured out how I felt about that.

Silence fell over the compartment, with only the hum of the engines echoing through the vehicle's interior. Several people fidgeted or spent the time checking over their weapons yet again. It reminded me of my time in the Marines, but the lack of uniforms and the sci-fi glow across most of the weaponry highlighted just how much things had changed in the last seven years.

A sudden jerk signaled that we'd reached our destination a moment before the rear door dropped open. Sunlight and heat blasted into the now-open compartment and several of the other occupants hissed at the sudden change. Between my resistances and the protection of my armor, I barely noted the difference in temperature as I hopped from my seat before vaulting out of the transport. Sand crunched beneath my armored boots as I stepped off the ramp and into the milling chaos of a staging area.

Hundreds of people rushed around the field camp, carrying crates of supplies or erecting fortifications, and those were just the ones I could see from here. Over the din of voices and the sounds of construction, distant gunfire echoed across the desert. I picked out the firing of individual shots, even this far away, and that told me that the fighting had yet to begin in earnest.

The local tactical network finally connected, and waypoints lit up across my helmet's heads-up display, directing me toward the slope of a massive dune and closer to those distant sounds of combat. I shot a wordless glance over my shoulder at Lyrra and started off. Behind us, the rest of the transport's occupants shuffled down the ramp and headed off in response to their own orders.

Somewhere in the sprawling camp, officers and intelligence specialists used Skills, spells, and technology to direct traffic around the base, providing the orders that would see the battle through. The bonuses they provided to the combatants would offer us an edge in the coming fight.

The two of us joined the flow of combatants heading toward the battle at a jog and the distant sounds of combat intensified. Several of the fighters looked nervous, despite the numbers being devoted to this engagement. A crude joke or the occasional curse were the only words spoken as we drew closer to the fighting.

Following the waypoints, I split off from the main force to ascend the massive dune with Lyrra beside me. While most of the fighters continued directly toward the battle, our assignment today wasn't to fight—at least, not directly.

Atop the dune, Lyrra joined a growing group of snipers and heavy weapons specialists as they set up firing positions along the crest. A few had drones that dug foxholes into the dune while deploying some kind of quick-setting adhesive to keep the sand from collapsing in on itself. Others deployed mobile shields or armored barriers directly from their Inventory.

I took special note of the two positions where the owners took extra effort to hide their occupants from observation. A few subtle hand gestures to Lyrra brought the pair to her attention, but we left them alone for now.

While they worked, I scanned the battleground forming on the desert plain below the dune. Directly below, ranks of heavily-armored melee fighters formed a bulwark of armor and shields. Just behind those front rankers, close-ranged fire supporters packed tightly, while mages and supports held to the rear of the lines. In the rear, medics set up triage stations and non-Combat supports pre-positioned stockpiles of ammunition and other supplies. The highest Leveled of our forces held the center of our line in preparation to bear the brunt of the approaching fight. It even looked like one or two of the Champions of Earth had made an appearance.

Beyond the forming army's front line, thousands of monsters swirled across the terrain as groups of skirmishers and scouts harried the edges of the massive mob to direct the swarm into favorable positioning for the fight to come. And not all of the advanced forces were working together.

Several of the groups consisted of Galactic forces who worked to their own ends while attempting to position the monster horde favorably for their own army, which was forming up at an angle to our own forces. The two armies formed a V-shape, with the skirmishers pulling the monster horde into the triangle's open side. Intermittent fire flashed between the two groups at the point of the V, more harassment than any serious attempt to cause harm, but those hit by the barrages probably disagreed.

From my elevated position, I spotted a disruption in the Galactic lines where a troop of heavily armored aliens pushed through their own ranks as they angled toward our flank. My HUD refused to lock onto the squad, blocked by jamming fields and conflicting Skills, but my analysis with Greater Observation overpowered the disruption to reveal the truth. High Leveled Advanced Classes were pushing through their assembly to hit our flank.

Sand flew into the air from each of my steps as I took off in a sprint down the side of the dune, tagging the Galactic heavies in my HUD with a priority update to command. My armor automatically mirrored the update to Lyrra, and her voice echoed in my ears. "You know, we're just supposed to be overwatch for this operation."

I grunted in acknowledgement, already at the bottom of the dune and leaping twelve feet into the air to clear a gaggle of medics setting up a triage station. "By the time anyone responds, those elites will already be in our lines."

The medics stared up at me as I passed overhead, and the elf sighed over my helmet speakers. I hit the ground, barely missing a wide-eyed porter with an armload of medical supplies, and bounded upward again as I jumped over the fighters blocking my path, gravity and friction mere suggestions that did little to slow my advance. I may not have spent much time studying how the System interacted with the once-immutable laws of physics, but the better part of a decade of fighting and killing had provided more than enough first-hand experience of how to manipulate things to my benefit.

A circular ripple of sand blasted out from my landing as I slammed into the ground at the army's flank with pistols clenched in both hands. My knees barely flexed and both of my weapons roared at the first of the alien elites to emerge from their lines. Individually-enchanted projectiles, further enhanced by my Skills, caught the lead Galactic by surprise.

My initial barrage tore through that first elite's defenses as if they were no stronger than a soggy paper towel. The corpse face-planted, its momentum digging a furrow until it stopped partially buried in the sand. The dozen or so Galactic elites faltered as they emerged from the cover of their army, but their hesitation only lasted for a fraction of an instant at the sudden escalation of violence before their momentum carried them onward and they started charging.

I raced to meet them, ducking and dodging a barrage of attacks that raked the flanks of the human forces behind me despite my attempt to draw the fire away. Updates flashed within my HUD, but I ignored them to focus on the elites. Fire belched from my pistols in a steady stream as my attacks swept across the advancing aliens. My shots punched through shields and shattered weak points. The punishing fire raked across the front ranks of the advancing aliens, slowing and hindering them, but not enough. The distance between us closed.

Return fire ate through my shields and melted through the outer layers of Ice Armor, burning and chipping away at the solid plating beneath. The wireframe outline in my HUD flashed with yellow splotches, highlighting the damage as it penetrated through my defenses, but the firefight wasn't entirely one-sided. Several of the aliens dropped, injured or out of the fight. Only ten elites remained.

We closed in on each other at the midway point in the no-man's-land between the two armies. The Galactics converged in an arc and I swept my gaze across their line, classifying their threats and simplifying their Advanced Classes down to general categories. Rifleman, brawler, fire mage, heavy gunner, pistoleer, and more. All direct combatants. And all of them had their focus fixed firmly on me. They've realized now, as the intensity of the plasma weaponry and spellfire scorched and melted the sand around me to glass, that I'm not just another soldier.

The brawler blinked forward, its broad-shouldered, stone-skinned bulk streaking across the space between us with the activation of a charge ability. I launched myself sideways, despite the knowledge that it was far too late to avoid the Skill. Hidden beneath the mirrored visor of my helmet, a grin crossed my face despite the punishment headed my way. Desperate to counter my threat to their flanking maneuver, the Galactics had forgotten that I'm just one element from a much larger army.

A human figure slipped between us in a smooth maneuver, which brought the charging Galactic up short. Ghostly samurai armor shrouded the new arrival before blurring under the effects of haste Skills as the blade of a slightly curved polearm deftly deflected the blocky alien's devastating strike. Shards of stone shattered under the blow and rained across the desert sands.

Before the Galactics could react to the new arrival, a stooping gryphon dropped out of the sky and flattened the rifleman at one end of their formation. The gryphon's sharp beak snapped out to catch the fire mage, flinging the alien through the air while the busty redhead mounted on its back blasted shotgun fire across the Galactics. A pair of oversized dogs and a tiger suddenly erupted from the ground, sending up a cloud of sand that obscured them from view as they tore into the remaining elites.

With allies on the field, I held my ground and lent supporting fire to the beasts when offered a clear shot but conserved my Mana in case the

Galactics hid any more surprises up their sleeves. The blocky alien fell to the ground in shattered chunks and only a couple of the Galactics survived the onslaught long enough to retreat to their own lines.

Pounding footsteps echoed across the sand from behind, and I turned to look. A platoon of Hakarta marched along our army's flank, weathering the Galactic fire until they activated a series of energy shields that prevented the worst of the harassing fire. The plasma spears of the orc front-liners should deter even the most adventurous of the Galactics from drawing too near the impromptu defenses.

"You need to pull back. We don't need to give the Galactics an excuse to deploy their Master Classers."

I glanced over at the armored samurai, trying in vain to read her expression through her visor. "You think they figured out my Class?"

"You stood against a dozen Advanced Classsers and dropped four of them in less than thirty seconds without using an active Skill. Their commanders aren't that dumb." The steel in the samurai's tone cut off any argument. Few argued with the Spear of Humanity, after all. Not to mention the fact that she held today's contract for me and Lyrra.

Mikito was right. While I could justify stepping out of the human lines in defense at the sudden Galactic offensive, a full pursuit of the vanquished Advanced Classes back into their own Basic Classers would just let them unleash their Master Classes in return. That sort of escalation defeated the purpose of forming the raid armies in the first place.

Instead, I nodded to acknowledge her point and in gratitude for her timely aid. Her arrival, and that of her companions, had kept me from unveiling the Skills that would have given away my presence and forced an escalation from the Galactics.

Dropping my pistols back into the holsters, I turned and jogged toward the distant dune. The woman stayed behind, standing fast in the middle of the glassy patch of sand as the redheaded beast tamer and her pets harried the Galactic lines.

By the time I returned to the crest of the dune, the snipers and other long-range specialists had nearly finished their preparations. Most were now nestled securely into their assorted fighting positions with weapons pointed at the milling pool of monsters funneling into the gap between the armies.

Lyrra crouched behind the line, a sniper rifle held across her chest as she scanned for threats, and I dropped to one knee beside her.

She raised an eyebrow as she glanced over my charred and blackened armor. "Have fun?"

Beneath my helmet, I grinned without responding.

A moment later, a pair of images appeared on my visor's display, each of which showed a live feed. The Movana had used my flashy antics to slip micro drones with a video relay in range of the foxholes that I'd pointed out to her.

Before our conversation got any further, a murmur ran through the ranged fighters around us. A ping across the network from command announced the day's primary target had finally drawn into range.

"That's one ugly son of a bitch," muttered one sniper.

A nightmarish amalgamation skittered in the midst of the monster horde. The ten-limbed scorpion appeared like a typical giant insectoid monster from the front, with a couple of notable differences. Its front-most arms ended in thin hand-tentacles instead of pincers and a humanoid torso rose from the back end in place of the scorpion's tail. The gangly humanoid portion gestured, twisting its hands through intricate spells as it used magic to bolster the ranks of the surrounding monsters.

Aqrabuamelu Alpha (Field Boss Level 129)

HP: 15310/15380

MP: 10180/10230

Status: Greater Regeneration (IV), Field Advantage

The monster's health bar barely flickered despite a steady stream of hits landing across its body from the skirmishers luring it into position. With regeneration that powerful, it would take quite a bit more firepower to breach the alien's defenses.

More attacks reached out toward the boss from the battle lines, growing in fury and fervor until command ordered our heavy hitters to join the fray. A cloud of dust enveloped the top of the dune as the snipers and heavy gunners finally opened fire. A deafening cacophony filled the air as the scream of beam weaponry competed with the thunder of projectile fire to overwhelm the senses.

As they focused on the boss, I turned away from the fight and scanned the backside of the dune. I wasn't getting paid to watch the boss fight.

After several scans over the empty sands, I spotted a trio of barely perceptible traces as something burrowed beneath the surface. My HUD identified no friendly forces in the area around the snaking trails, so I drew out my pistols and opened up on the approaching traces.

The burrowing objects burst upward and sent a cloud of sand in all directions as they raced closer. Despite the obstructed view, I stayed locked onto the targets thanks to the combination of Greater Observation, Keen Senses, and high Perception. My shots drilled through the moving clouds, sparking against the energy shields that protected the trio of shoebox-sized drones as they belched fire at me in return from the weapons ports that lined their sides.

Rather than dodge and let the attacks hit the firing line behind us, I took the hits on my shields and armor. Explosions blossomed around me, but they barely registered when compared to the earlier damage from the Galactic elites. Though I held against the storm, I doubted all the Basic and Advanced Class shooters on the crest of the dune could have survived the barrage.

Now airborne, the trio of drones broke into evasive maneuvering to avoid my attacks. I picked out one as my primary target and my rounds tracked it through the air. The first few shots flashed off its shields before penetrating and tracing a line of sparks across the armor. Each impact shook the boxy frame until a round punched through the armor and the drone exploded in a flash before tumbling to the ground.

Lyrra's rifle barked as she joined her attacks to mine, and together, we quickly dropped the last pair of drones.

As we fought, I kept a portion of my attention on my visor displays. Though one foxhole kept up a steady rate of fire, the other slowed and the oversized rifle barrel shifted away from its assigned field of fire as the last drone crashed to the sand.

Sand geysered away from my feet as I launched myself across the top of the dune, crashing through the thin camouflage covering over the foxhole. The startled sniper barely started to turn before I batted the rifle from his grip and pinned him against the foxhole's wall. He grew still instantly when the hot barrel of Last Word pressed against his temple.

"Can I help you?" The question was far too calm for a man with a gun to his head.

I nodded toward the drone control unit in the corner of the foxhole. "You can tell me why you were calling in strike drones for an attack on our lines."

The man blinked. "I don't know what you're talking about."

"Who was your target? One of the Champions? The Spear?"

Silence.

"Who hired you?"

He just blinked.

Answers would have been nice, but I'd done the job and stopped the threat before he could attack. I sighed and summoned a pair of Skill-disabling restraints from my Inventory.

Before I could attach the manacles to his wrists, the sniper's body shifted. The arms that had been pinned in place suddenly switched their orientation and swung at me with bladed weapons.

"Shapeshifters," I snarled as I pulled the trigger. Kill Shot activated and the echo of Last Word roared in the enclosed space as brainmatter splattered across the wall. The knives clattered to the hardened floor an instant before the body slumped down on top of them.

I dumped the corpse into Meat Locker and stored the weapons before crawling out of the now-empty foxhole.

Lyrra watched me with a raised eyebrow and I answered her wordless question with a nod before dropping a grenade into the abandoned foxhole. The job was done.

The battle continued and I looked around for any additional threats. Muttering drifted from the line of marksmen, but it had nothing to do with us. "What the hell is that?"

Turning back to the main battle, I found it wasn't the fighting against the Field Boss or the Galactic forces that had drawn the muttered concern.

A black vortex flickered above the fighting, barely a hundred feet above the Field Boss. For a moment, the portal hung ominously in the air before fire erupted from its center. A single human figure emerged at the heart of the flames, diving amidst a blazing inferno that spread out to cover the monster army. The swirling firestorm rained down on the horde in an apocalyptic meteor shower.

Shrouded in fire, the falling figure burned at the center of the blazing storm as he dropped toward the boss, drawing the attention of both armies.

John Lee (Erethran Paladin Level 14) (M)

Redeemer of the Dead, Monster's Bane, Duelist, Explorer

HP: 2933/3020

MP: 2104/2340

Status: Soul Shield, Aura of Chivalry

My eyes narrowed at the details exposed by my Skill. Master Class individuals remained extremely rare on Earth, and I'd thought that I'd kept up my intel on all of them. Clearly, I'd missed one, which felt surprising given his number of titles.

His armor appeared battered and worn. Numerous patches covered the material, as if stitched together from multiple suits at various degrees of repair. Despite that ragged appearance, it spoke to a degree of resourcefulness and determination that reminded me of scraping by in the early days after the System's arrival on Earth.

After a crash landing, the Paladin bounded back to his feet amidst the falling spells and artillery fire that continued to cascade onto the horde. He charged the Field Boss, dodging a rainbow stream of the monster's magic and blinking onto the monster's back with a short-range teleport Skill. His first attack scraped across one of the monster's arms, followed by a series of after-images that repeated the sword strike and slashed deeper into the Field Boss with each repetition.

Monsters swarmed the Paladin, with a golden-furred leonid monster pouncing first. The man caught its throat one-handed and slammed the creature into the ground without releasing it. Another monster launched itself at the Paladin's exposed rear, but a back kick sent the ambusher tumbling away. In a smooth movement, he launched the leonid into another group of monsters and toppled them like a bowler throwing a perfect strike.

In a feat that highlighted the value of Agility, the Paladin flipped off the Field Boss and grabbed hold of an arm. At that range, the monster's spells pummeled the much smaller human, but he ignored Mana bolts powerful enough to annihilate anyone with a Basic Class. A single kick from the Paladin lifted the Field Boss from the ground and then he spun, swinging the massive monster around like little more than a toy.

While the Paladin played, the surprise faded from the command elements and new orders flowed across the network. The snipers along the dune shifted fire to the supporting Elite and Alpha monsters throughout the horde. One by one, monsters fell, but the horde remained numerous despite the losses.

Interestingly, one update marked the Paladin as a friendly unit within my helmet's HUD.

Though I remained skeptical of the new arrival, my own duties took precedence. I half expected the Galactics to launch another sneak attack now that our fire support elements were heavily engaged, so I pushed Greater Observation out along the backside of the dune. That I found nothing failed to reassure me and I kept my pistols in hand. A portion of my focus continued watching our backs as I glanced over my shoulder to check on the progress of the larger battle.

The Field Boss had freed itself from the Paladin's grip, but that hadn't helped it much. The man now used the creature like it had the earlier leonid, launching it into one group of monsters after another. Instead of a consolidated horde, the monsters grew increasingly disrupted as the Field Boss kept landing on any creatures that seemed close to getting organized.

It was an impressive display of raw power and battlefield control. The man was clearly making a point, though I wasn't sure where the lesson was aimed since he continued to show as friendly to our raid forces.

The Paladin jumped high into the air, floating for a moment as he pointed his sword at the Field Boss. The longsword lacked any ornamentation, but that only emphasized the deadly nature of the weapon and its wielder.

A dozen replicas of that sleek sword appeared around the hovering Paladin, glowing with increasing brightness while pointing at the Field Boss. Brilliant beams of concentrated energy stabbed from each of the blades, tearing through a few smaller monsters below and shredding the Field Boss as thousands of points of damage descended in an instant. The Field Boss dropped, collapsing under the overwhelming assault, most of its health bar spent and its regeneration largely negated by the sheer severity of its wounds.

Across the field, humans and Galactics blinked away the afterimages of the blindingly bright strike. There was no questioning that demonstration on either side. A Master Skill just took down that monster.

The Paladin landed on the blasted and cratered ground in front of the Field Boss, crossing to the creature as it struggled to pull itself upright. A single stab, delivered almost casually, finished the beast, sending a tangible ripple washing out from the sagging carcass of the Field Boss and sweeping across the horde as all semblance of cohesion evaporated from the monsters.

I breathed a sigh of relief as the Galactic army also pulled back, only leaving a token force to gather their fallen. There was little else to gain now that the Field Boss was down and an informal truce held for situations like this. Still, I kept watch from atop the dune in case any of the Galactics held a grudge.

Commands streamed through the network, directing fire at remaining targets of opportunity, but the true battle had ended with the death of the Field Boss. Now it was just mopping up. With the fighting winding down, I doubted the Galactics would risk any further direct conflict. That brought my contract to its end, but I still kept an eye on the man who'd brought an early end to the day's conflict.

The gryphon rider from earlier landed her mount beside the Paladin and leaped to launch herself at the man. They remained locked in that embrace as others gathered around them. Mikito, still clad in her ghostly samurai armor, pushed into the heart of the crowd as the Paladin and redhead finally let go of each other. Questions mounted as the impromptu reunion continued amidst the diminishing conflict as the last of the monsters fled beyond the range of our forces.

The dune emptied as the snipers and artillery specialists packed up their gear, though most stopped by to thank me and Lyrra for keeping the Galactics off them during the fight.

"You heading back to camp now?" Lyrra asked.

I shook my head. "You go on and get some food. I'll wait until the harvesters finish."

The elf nodded and followed the line of ranged combatants making their way back to camp.

With the threat of the monsters eliminated, a swarm of skinners, butchers, and other gathering Classes arrived from the field base. They descended on the carcasses that covered the battlefield and spent the afternoon looting the dead monsters before hauling the take back to the camp.

I finally left the dune as dusk fell over the sands and reached the camp to find the victory celebration in full swing. Cooks barbecued the freshly cut monster meats and mouthwatering scents filled the air, thanks to the usual competitions to craft the best foods with the highest bonuses.

As the evening grew late, a constant crowd surrounded the Paladin. It seemed that most of the human forces knew the man, especially those who'd fought the Coast on Fire campaign that had seen the western edge of the North American continent largely freed from Galactic control.

That seemed odd, since I'd fought alongside a good portion of those forces in the battles for Denver. That was where I'd met Mikito, after all.

When the Paladin slipped away from the crowd, accompanied only by the angry-looking gryphon rider, I sought the samurai. The diminutive woman stood alone beside one of the empty cook fires, staring into the dancing flames. Though part of me wanted to just report on my completed job and move on, I found myself asking another question instead.

"Why isn't he one of the Champions?"

Mikito showed no reaction to my question. Her face remained blank and only the flicker of light reflecting from her dark eyes offered any sense of life. The unsettling quiet dragged on, and I wondered if she'd even heard the question.

"He wasn't here."

I turned my head to stare down at the woman with a raised eyebrow. Silence continued for several long moments before the samurai spoke again.

Her halting sentences briefly explained that the man was the true owner of Vancouver, the major west coast hub of human habitation on the continent, not the redhead who had been running things for the last several years. He'd fought in the vanguard of human forces until after the battle of LA, where he was taken away by an Erethran Champion.

"That was four years ago," she said, then fell silent once more.

"Where was he?" I finally asked, but Mikito just shrugged without speaking, her eyes locked on the slowly dying coals in the fire pit.

She might not know where he'd been, but I knew where he was now. I didn't even need Greater Observation to feel the turmoil of the Master Class aura that stood just beyond the camp's perimeter. "Well, you might want to check on him. I think he's got the camp guards so spooked that they're focused on him and nothing else. It's a good thing the Galactics all went home or they could sneak an entire army in here."

Mikito finally turned away from the fire to roll her eyes. Then she turned toward the distant Paladin, muttering under her breath. "Baka."

The samurai sighed and then looked back long enough to nod farewell before stalking off toward the solitary Master Classer. When Mikito reached him, she barely spoke before dragging the Paladin over to the teleport pad set up in the middle of camp.

"What a story," Lyrra said, stepping out of the shadows to join me as the two figures disappeared in a flash of light. "Another Master Class isn't that big of a deal."

I snorted, folding my arms over my chest. "We don't exactly grow on trees."

The elf just shrugged. Maybe she saw things differently as a non-native.

Still, I continued to stare at the empty pad and then shook myself back into motion. It was time to get back to work, and I had another job lined up. "We're done here. Let's go."

The rumble of engines greeted us when we reached the camp's motor pool. Climbing into the back of an outbound truck, I took one last glance back at the distant teleportation pad as I offered Lyrra a hand up. "Something tells me that things are going to get even more interesting around here."

The elf slipped into a jump seat and folded her arms as the truck rumbled into motion. "Are you sure we can't take the teleporter?"

\#\#\#

The End of *The Redeemer Returns*

Year 7.5 Post-System

This is Harry Prince, reporting from space, just outside of the International Space Station on an alien spaceship. We prepare to leave Earth and journey to Irvina, capital of the Galactic Republic. The battle over Earth, over control of our destiny, has finished, though not without loss.

I am standing on a spaceship crewed by an alien race and staring at the sight of the Earth beneath me, a too small globe wracked with so much pain and death.

It might be the last time I see our home world. I have met the Redeemer of the Dead, and he is everything and more than what you might have heard. Unrelenting, vicious, and deadly in equal measures, a rage burns in him that makes even our alien guests quail.

He has a mission and a grudge, and he is taking it with him to the heart of the Galactic Empire.

I know not what he plans. I do not think even he knows. But where he goes, chaos follows. As a Reporter, it is my job to follow the story, so I will journey with him.

Nor can I not help but think, it is about time the Galactics have a taste of their own medicine.

Questing for Titles

Golden arches on an elevated billboard glowed in the dark of the night, illuminated internally by Mana lamps and offering the surroundings its only source of illumination. The lights glowed brighter than they ever did before, which allowed the words beneath the sign to stand out even more starkly. Both words and viscera decorated the billboard.

Over a million served at this location!

Dried blood, poisoned spittle, and globules of torn flesh covered one portion of the sign, much of it originating from the ground beneath the sign and leading all the way to the sole standing building in its expansive parking lot. To the right of the group that stared at the billboard stood their goal, little concrete barriers helping to designate the drive-through windows. Knee high, clear glass windows offered a view of the inside where overpowered-florescent lights powered by Mana illuminated the familiar red and yellow upholstery and white plastic tables. In the corners, where light failed to penetrate, shadowy figures moved within.

Of course, only one of the parties would recognize what was normal for florescent lights. Of the three that stood before the building, one was native human, barely breaking five feet in height, clad in a simple white blouse and black slacks that gave her a business casual demeanor. As she stood, she fiddled with the glasses that she still wore, frames adjusted to remove any magnification or light refraction and offered additional data on the System world.

For most though, it was the other two who would have brought an exclamation of surprise, at least five years back unless you were at a cosplay convention. Before the System Apocalypse, before the changing of everything. One of the figures was over six and a half feet tall, muscled like a steroid-ridden bodybuilder with a simple orange mohawk. More importantly, his green skin and tusks gave a clear indication of the Hakarta's origins. The space orc wore an eccentric combination of modern tactical wear and silver medieval armor over his body, tactivest holding the double-bladed axe and the pair of belted beam pistols.

The third figure was a menuhene, a three-foot-tall, chubby and happy pink figure who carried a bow slung over his shoulder and a quiver of arrows by his hip. Mostly though, the menuhene watched the surroundings, fingers twitching by his side, Mana flowing from his eyes and body.

"The System has a sense of humor it seems. This is the nine hundred ninety-eighth such establishment and there are hundreds more turned into dungeons?" The Hakarta said. "It doesn't normally highlight individual establishments when they are of great cultural importance."

"Well, they did serve over a million humans," the menuhene said.

An errant gust of wind brought the stench of rotting corpses to the group. It was strange, but even the smell of rotting flesh had changed since the System, as monsters and aliens whose body compositions were entirely different from the carbon-based life forms of Earth made their way over. This one, mixed with the usual breakdown of human and animal flesh, also consisted of a slight, almost sweet smell, reminiscent of smoked paprika. Smoked paprika, cinnamon and of course, rotten eggs.

"We told you before, if you wish to speak, speak up!" the menuhene shouted.

The youngster flinched, tucking her head low. But at the urgings of the menuhene she looked up and saw his Status once more.

Kyaz Zeal, Brotherhood of Title Guides – Yellow Initiate, Slayer of Goblins, Partaker of Feasts, the Variable Discipline of Moya, Appreciator of the Music of qWaz, more… (Level 18 Kismarnos Guide – Av14)

Con Variable-9xmil43: 254/254

ManaAbsorp-xneg-Regen-Overflow-W-minusgras: 540/540

As always, it took her a few seconds to put together the information that had been showcased to her, comparing it to the same information that she had on her sheet.

Xi Ping, Wen (Earth Food Guide Level 2 – A-m)

Health (ConVar): 160/160

Mana (AbsorpoReg): 180/180

The Status Screen alteration that she had paid for eleven restaurants back had made understanding other people's Status information so much easier. She knew that there were actual Classes and Skills that would fix her view of the System completely, but the cost of doing that was too high. At least, until such time as she made enough for a goal. She was going to earn enough to buy the Ares armored food truck - Fireball v2.3 no matter what.

In the meantime, penny-pinching on things that she absolutely did not require like new Skills to read the System was definitely something she could do. It wasn't as if she hadn't done it before, when she'd scrimped and saved to put herself through chef school, all the while working late into the evenings at her father's restaurant serving fried noodles.

That she still hadn't received a Chef Class from the System on integration, but a Foodie Class from the random blogs that she had posted on the

Internet rankled. Sure, she had a decent following, but it hadn't been her passion. Cooking had been.

Then again, she wasn't exactly sure if she would accept a Chef class now. After all, it still felt a little like cheating. Using System skills to make food taste better, make your ingredients stretch a little, give buffs. It didn't feel like proper cooking, not the way she had learnt from her father, from Chef Ward. It was also why so many of the 'Chefs' she ran into couldn't cook any better than a first-year student. They were so focused on their Skills they'd forgotten their skills.

Still, a portion of the savings was being set aside for a Class reset, just in case she changed her mind. There definitely was something to be said about being able to give full buffs to a party for eating your food. It certainly made for good money. And a Chef or not, she was her father's daughter, and Yi Ping knew that money mattered if you wanted to keep cooking.

"Well?" Kyaz asked.

"The company was innovative for its ability to serve food quickly and cheaply and with good quality. At first. And then, it became quick and cheap," Xi Ping said. "along with being a sign of American cultural dominance."

"You speak, but so often, your words make no sense," Chogfal rumbled. Xi Ping looked over at the Hakarta, who shook his head. "Dominance is a matter of strength, not... culture."

Chogfal Barellyz, Wearer of the Indigo Sash, Partaker of Feasts – Flowers Division, Landslide Architect, Master of the Sixth and Eleventh Form of Opdeff Puzzles, Famed Hunter of vaxX, Asteroid Bounty Hunter, Pilgrim of the Jungle, ... (Level 9 Weekly Disaster – Mpv-14.v3)

Con Variable-13xmil678: 3780/3780

ManaAbsorp-xneg-Regen-Overflow-W-minusflaxfor+endvar82_ks: 1270/1270

"Oh, America had strength," Xi Ping said. "They had the fastest planes, the most modern technological pieces, aircraft carriers and ICBMs and, of course, nukes."

"Much good it did when the System came. It fared worse because it had too few people of worthiness!" Chogfal said, pounding his chest. "Strength from Skills and Classes, from warriors is all that matters."

"And Titles." Kyaz said.

"And Titles."

Xi Ping lowered her head again and fell silent rather than argue as it would get her nowhere. In truth, there was little to be argued with. The countries which had been packed with people had been both fortunate and tragic at the same time. They'd been targeted with higher-level creatures, some of which had rampaged and massacred populations, and others which had just found new lairs after their initial surprise, coming out only to snack. Due to the higher volume and higher level of their monsters, they'd lost more people as a percentage of population than other, less dense countries and cities. But dense as many of their cities had been, it had also meant that they had more people.

With danger came opportunity. Opportunity to Level, to kill and keep killing. Those who managed to survive the initial days and to increase their Levels managed to pile advantage on advantage, working the hard way to climb higher and higher in Levels. Of course, more died than survived, but the uncaring mathematics of numbers meant that heroic survivors began to shine.

A few, a very few, even managed to kill the titanic monsters that had been portalled into their cities, working in small groups or alone. Titles, Levels and prestige followed those victories. As for other cities, the sheer volume and numbers finished them off. At least, where the cities had not been destroyed entirely.

All of which lent itself to the argument that individuals and Levels were more important than technology. For cities that tried the same with Shop-bought equipment often found themselves unable to wield the equipment or unable to secure their victories.

Chogfal sniffed. "Now, come. Let us clear this dungeon."

Xi Ping bobbed her head and fell in behind the hulking Hakarta as he strolled toward the doors. Behind the human female, Kyaz hopped along, his bow unslung from his back. He kept a little farther back than Xi Ping, the human having activated a simple Shield enchantment to keep herself protected.

Halfway across the empty parking lot, cracked asphalt filled with fallen leaves and plastic bags, the first trap sprung. From the ground, weeds that had forced themselves through gaps exploded into motion, tearing at Chogfal's legs as they attempted to slide through his armored jumpsuit and drain his blood.

The weeds slithered and twisted, striking at the Master Classer's feet and armored jumpsuit. They thrashed, desperate to find purchase, but failed as his high Constitution and defenses refused to give way to the stabbing tendrils of the vegetation. He lifted his foot just once and it tore the vegetation away. Another step, and he stomped down and a Skill-made fire rushed through the cracks, catching upon each of the biotraps hidden beneath. A high, keening whine rose from the ground as the weeds died, burning away.

"Come. Let us be done with this," Chogfal said, his pace never changing even as new traps rose to strike at him.

Muttering quiet agreement, the pair followed.

***

Forty minutes later, the trio stood in the blasted, torn remnants of the kitchen. The dungeon had warped the structure of the building on the inside, making the dining room multiple sizes larger. The corridor to the bathrooms and the bathrooms themselves teemed with monsters and, finally, the kitchen where they found the Alpha.

The battles had been quick, bloody affairs. Using his axe to carve his way through the animated, virus-ridden Mana-created corpses, Chogfal had led the way. None of the creatures could touch him, and the occasional one that he missed, Kyaz shot down. Xi Ping took little part in the fight, firing the beam pistol in her hand occasionally but mostly, spending the time cowering.

At the feet of Chogfal lay the Alpha, an overweight Middle Eastern man whose torn uniform did nothing to hide his bulging belly or the pustulant sores that covered his lower body. Every so often, the body twitched, as one of the many controlling parasites that made the zombie creatures escaped, only to be crushed under foot. Without the controlling parasite, the rest were on a long journey to final death.

"Level 40 dungeon. Pitiful." Chogfal spat to the side. He glared at the monsters within, before gesturing everyone outwards. As he left, he triggered the numerous explosives he'd left behind, the incendiary devices burning the dungeon to the ground behind him. Only when the structural integrity of the dungeon failed did the Hakarta nod to himself in satisfaction.

Dungeon Destroyed

+1982 Experience

"One more, yes?" He said and glared at Kyaz as he dismissed the notification.

"Yes." Kyaz nodded his head quickly at his employer.

"And I'll be satisfied with this Title?" Chogfal snarled.

"It'll be a Title for certain," Kyaz said. He pointed to the burning remnants of the dungeon. "But you have to acquire the loot from within for destroying the dungeon."

"I know," Chogfal said. "Why do you think we wait here?" He shook his head. "This Title better be worth it, Guide."

"I only promised that it would be a rare Title. I'm certain of that much, but more details are uncertain. As you were informed," Kyaz said, straightening a little. "You know that Title guiding is a difficult matter. Especially on new Dungeon Worlds."

Chogfal grunted. Looking around, the Hakarta gestured for the group to leave. They had a long way to go before they made it to the next Dungeon.

***

The creak of metal echoed throughout the machine, the hiss of hydraulics shifting the numerous legs a dull and unending accompaniment to the evening's ride. The vehicle that traversed the sloped, majestic heights of the Nepalese alps walked on accordion-like hydraulically powered feet, bearing the large, bullet-shaped body across the rough terrain. The cavernous insides of the walking behemoth had been divided into multiple cabins for rest, while Riggers, Mechanics and Gunmen ran around on the curved railing outside. Occasional blasts emanated from the vehicle to destroy incoming monsters, lighting up the surroundings with their fire.

The *Ugdam* had been pieced together from the hull of a cruise ship. It had been reshaped and modified with multiple legs and layers of mobile tank armor which had been reworked by Machinists, Mechanics and Blacksmiths as necessary to provide additional protection. Slapped-on Shop purchased beam weaponry had been added to the vehicle, with cabling run against the empty interior bulkheads to the Mana engine which replaced the engine of yore. Of course, the Mana engine was a tenth the size of the old oil burner, along with being significantly stronger.

All of which meant that much of the internal drivers had been ripped out to give even more space for the backup Mana batteries and the hydraulics that moved the legs. With a total of twelve different limbs, the *Ugdam* had significant backups and flexibility in movement. Unfortunately, that came with the necessary drawback of drawing monsters on the regular. Luckily, between the Captain, Vice-Captains and Ship Owner's combined Skills along with the unceasing watch of the Gunmen, most monsters on their path were easily dealt with.

"I can't wait for the teleportation networks to be finished like a civilized world," Chogfal said, not for the first or fifteenth time to Xi Ping.

The young lady ducked her head, lips pressed together in irritation.

Chogfal snorted.

Kyaz spoke up, offering a placating smile. "Even if they did have one, the Dungeons we go to are unlikely to be on it."

"Bah. It's because these Dungeons are so scattered..." Chogfal trailed off as the door to the shared dining room creaked open.

Pushing against the heavy metal obstruction, a Jarack strode in, glancing around. Her eyes fell upon Chogfal, widening into a wide grin that showcased her jackal-like features even further as she strolled over. Behind her, a Grimsar followed, who spotted Kyaz and offered a short nod in acknowledgement.

"Chogfal… so good to see you." The female Jarack looked up purposely at Chogfal's Status, then let her gaze fall as she continued. "Still no luck acquiring a new Title?"

"Edval," Chogfal greeted her curtly, ignoring her barb. At her next sentence, he looked up automatically.

Edval Lurra, Zeus's Chosen, Betrothed of the Lodre Clan, Tushai Varz, Valedictory of the Eleven Lakes, Mistress of the Six Scarves and Fourteen Spotted Lilies, … (Rolling Thunder Level 9) (M)
HP: 2984/2984
MP: 3214/3214

"You…"

"Yes, just got it on our last run," Edval said, preening. "Bateqa was right. We managed to finish the labors of this Hercules and acquire a Title."

"Hercules?" Chogfal said.

"Some mythical human, supposedly with great Strength. Couldn't be more than a few hundred though," Edval said, sniffing. "And it was a bit of a cheat, using what we know. The last task was a bit difficult, having to lift an Earth Elemental for an evening."

"You lifted it yourself?" Xi Ping said, surprised.

"Well, no. We used a series of gravitic beams to hold it off the ground and when the night was over, we blasted it to bits. But setting it up took forever," Edval said. "Still, it was worth the Title." Again she grinned, her mouth lolling open and tongue sticking out as she looked at Chogfal. "Human Titles really are worth it."

Taunted again, Chogfal leaned forward. His curiosity finally gave way to his irritation and jealousy and he asked to see it.

Title: Zeus's Chosen (Semi-Unique)

As one of the prolific god's favorite children, Hercules laboured mightily before he gained his father's respect and achieved godhood. Like him, you have completed the seven labors, and with it, you have received the god's blessing as well.

Effect: +50 Strength, +25 Endurance, +20% Lightning Resistance (stackable)

"That is a good Title," Chogfal said finally, his face twisting in bitterness as he was forced to admit it.

"Yes. Made all the harder because we had to find Alphas for them all," Edval replied. "We didn't know that until we had completed it all the way through once. Could have saved a lot of time if we had known, right Bateqa?"

"It's a Semi-Unique Title. You know what that means," Bateqa said, crossing his arms under his barrel-like chest.

"I don't," Xi Ping said.

Bateqa turned to stare at Xi Ping, his lips turning up into a sneer when he noticed her race. Before he could retort, Kyaz cut in. "Semi-Unique Titles are a term we Title Seekers came up with ourselves. It's to denote Titles that are likely impossible to replicate, but we're uncertain."

"Why uncertain?"

"Because the System can – and has – changed its mind. But for the time being, we'd assume it's unique," Kyaz said.

Xi Ping opened her mouth to ask further but was silenced by Edval talking over her as she spoke to Chogfal. "You still on your original hunt?"

"Yes."

"Must be close to finishing it, I would think."

"Maybe."

"Oh, come on now. You know I would have shared mine with you. I have before…"

"Not shareable," Chogfal said, eyes narrowing. "But what about your next one?"

Edval looked uncomfortable, turning away, and Chogfal smirked. "I thought so. Not that into sharing, are we?"

"They're all new. There's a chance they might even be Unique…." Edval said.

"Exactly."

An awkward silence fell between the group before Edval stood up. "Well, I guess another time then." She strode out, followed soon after by Bateqa.

Silence grew between the remaining trio before Kyaz asked what everyone had been thinking. "What is she doing here?"

Sadly, none of the group had an answer to that question. Just suspicions.

***

It was early the next morning when they were finally alighted from their transportation, the *Ugdam's* multi-faceted legs rising and falling, carrying the crew and the remaining passengers away with deceptive speed. Skills and a mixture of Earth and System-tech powered the moving craft, leaving the trio alone in the vast wilderness of the southern alps. Like its state pre-System, the alps continued to be missing towering trees and dense vegetation, sticking to low-level alpine brush.

A long hike later, the group came across the abandoned town. In four years since its abandonment, the wilderness had taken over the outpost of civilization, buildings lying crumbled, walls torn, roads cracked. Without a System Shop or anyone fighting for it, the town had reverted to its base level, becoming pristine wilderness.

All but their target.

Eyes set- upon the sullied and familiar golden symbol, the group ran down the reclaimed street, its different and raised texture marking its difference from the normal wilderness they'd journeyed through. Eyes flicked from side to side, checking out climbing vines and crumbled walls as they searched for monsters. To their surprise, they encountered no monsters at all, even the occasional maddened attacker missing. The lack of danger only heightened the tension, Chogfal speeding up to such an extent Xi Ping was panting as she expended more energy than even the System could regenerate.

For all their haste, they were too late.

As they arrived at the dungeon, they were surprised to see a familiar duo exit the building covered in gore.

"What are you doing here?" Chogfal snarled.

"Nothing." Edval smirked, and then tapped her wrist. The signal set off the high-explosive grenades left within, causing the building to collapse as the dungeon was destroyed. The rush of Mana as the System dealt with the destruction drew a hissed breath from the surprised group while Chogfal unslung his double-bladed axe.

"You!" Chogfal took three threatening steps forward, raising his axe which burst into flame. "You thieving Title thief!"

"Really, is that the best you can do?" Edval said. "There's no rule against running a dungeon." Her eyes glazed for a second, then she frowned as she did not see what she sought. "Though, this one seems to be a failure as well."

"I should carve you up and send you back to your pack in pieces!" Chogfal threatened. In the back, the pair of Title guides had slunk away, followed closely by Xi Ping as the Title Seekers snarled at one another.

"Go ahead. I dare you. See what my pack does to you and your family," Edval said, jutting her jaw forward. In one hand, held low, dancing pinpoints of light formed and swirled around her fingers.

Chogfal cursed at her, switching to Galactic. His hands trembled as he cursed her, but he made no move to act, cognizant of the greater implication of an attack. As representatives of their clan and family, conflicts could spiral faster than he cared for. And while certain leeway for such conflict could be expected in a Dungeon World, he was certain that Edval had taken steps to ensure this incident would become highly inflammatory.

"Fine," Chogfal said eventually. "But don't expect me to be quiet about this insult."

Edval let out a yowling snigger, her head thrown back. "Go ahead. If you think any Title Seeker cares. Those who can't safeguard their goals do not deserve their Titles."

Chogfal refused to turn back as he slung his axe onto his back, stalking over to Xi Ping and Kyaz. "Come. Let us go. The air stinks around here."

His words only elicited even more laughter, one that followed them as they trudged away. As they walked, Xi Ping watched Chogfal communicate with the local transportation companies, seeking an emergency pickup. It seemed his irritation had burnt away his parsimonious nature.

It was when they were well away, standing on an empty hillside awaiting their pickup, that Chogfal strove to break the silence.

"They can't learn of the Title, can they?" He said.

Kyaz shrugged. "Not unless Bateqa's purchased more Skills. You've seen the notifications we get."

Chogfal snorted. "I've seen what I see. But you Title Guides are always so secretive about your Skills…"

Kyaz smiled at this while Xi Ping rolled her eyes. She stopped when Chogfal fixed her with a heated gaze.

"Find me another dungeon, woman." He paused, then leaned forward. "And if I find out that you were the one who told them about our objective…"

Xi Ping quailed as she shook her head from side to side in mute denial.

"It was probably a matter of simple deduction," Kyaz said. "It's not as if there's much else out here worth doing." He waved his hand around the barren, low-Leveled zone they stood within. "Especially since we didn't try to hide our pickup point, like I recommended."

Chogfal let out a low growl at the implied criticism. He turned away, searching the sky for their transportation, even if there was no way it would have arrived already. Behind him, Xi Ping bobbed a head in thanks as Kyaz rolled his eyes and mouthed the words 'sorry' to the female guide.

***

Two days later, the group stared down at the blasted remains of the city of Malacca. The coastal city that had been colonized by the Portuguese, Dutch and the British before returning to the Malay people – and the various other cultures that had assimilated into the city over its six centuries of occupation – had once again been conquered by another invading force.

Long known for its ability to assimilate new immigrants, the local population was still struggling to handle their new conquerors. It did not help that the invaders had a close resemblance to local legends of south east Asian vampires – the pengallan – with their floating heads and exposed lungs and intestines. That the aliens were a jellyfish-like flying creatures, whose internal organs were thus exposed to sight but not free hanging did little to appease the locals. Especially since the shape-shifting jellyfish-aliens had sought to integrate by changing their faces to look like the local humans.

"Wearer of the Indigo Sash Chogfal Barellyz, it is a pleasure to have you here!" the Junior Administrator said as it floated up. It bobbed low, the boneless body flopping forward, lungs and intestines squishing together and then uncompressing. That Xi Ping could see partly into the lungs and the intestines, where the aliens partially digested food lay made her turn green.

"Administrator," Chogfal said. "I understand my requests have been approved?" Arms crossed, he glowered at the man.

"Yes, completely. We've even blocked a pair of additional requests for the same matter," the Administrator bobbed again. "We were surprised since the dungeon itself is so low-level. We had the local sapients running it for food."

Xi Ping made a face at the mention. The local surroundings were quite high Level due to its proximity to various nautical dungeons and a few plantations, forcing the human populace to find alternate forms of food. If they destroyed it, it would compress the options for cheap food.

Then again, it was five years in. And while there were still children growing up and assimilating into the System, most survivors should have Leveled by now. Or had chosen not to. And to those, Xi Ping could only look upon with disdain.

"I see." Chogfal glowered, making the poor Administrator compress its body in fear. A few more murmured words and the entire group followed the gloop-sweating alien down the streets. As they walked, Xi Ping could not help but look around.

Malacca itself had changed significantly. The colonial era buildings that had lined the streets in downtown Malacca now stood beside towering, alien edifices. A crystal spiral, a lump-sized hillock with numerous doors of stone, a twisting trio of trees that connected over the street via wooden walkways, were the most uncommon. Skyscrapers of metal and glass, twisting high into the sky in defiance of physics beside stone, yellow-washed peranakan houses were a painful contrast. One that, Xi Ping noted, was being protested against by a small but determined trio of old ladies of Chinese and Malay descent, each holding signs and walking up and down the streets.

Xi Ping's lips twisted up, as she bowed to the first lady to cross her path and twisted even further in amusement as she received the donation notification.

Donate to the Restoration of Traditional Malacca Fund!
Help us buy Earth-owned plots of lands and restore traditional Malacca.
Donate? (Y/N)

A moment's hesitation and then Xi Ping sent them a hundred Credits. She dismissed the automated thank you, while hurrying after the trio of aliens. Not that she was the only one following along behind the 'invaders.' In the middle of the day, the sun-baked streets of the city were filled with humans and aliens, all concentrated in the safe zone as they went about their daily business.

As a group, they came to the familiar sight of the golden arches, the building connected to others in the traditional rowhouse format of this particular street. Standing outside the dungeon, barred from entry by a pair of nervous looking human *Polis* and another Junior Administrator was Edval and her guide.

"You. What are you trying to do?" Chogfal snarled. "Do you not have better Titles to acquire?"

"Me? I'm just here to cheer you on," Edval said, all innocent like. "After all, you've worked so hard – and paid so much –" that last elicited another growl from Chogfal, "that we wanted to make sure we were here to applaud your acquisition."

"You…"

"We're thankful to the Wearer of the Indigo Sash for his purchase of the dungeon rights," the original Junior Administrator said, speaking up quickly. "Its presence has caused some issues with the local population."

"Really?" Xi Ping said. That seemed strange considering what he had said earlier.

"Yes, the meat acquired has been very controversial. Something to do with local customs. It's too complicated for us to understand, especially since multiple ummm…"

"Imans," the other Administrator supplied.

"inImans have different interpretations."

Xi Ping frowned, but rather than wait for her to inquire further, Chogfal strode right to the glass doors that separated the dungeon from the street. He did not turn around as he entered the building, disappearing from view as the dungeon warped him away into its own instance. Rather than let themselves be left behind, Kyaz grabbed Xi Ping and dragged the human in after the impatient Hakarta.

***

Kyaz prodded the burnt and crisped body on the ground, flipping it over. The hallways of the building were a pale-grey of faded concrete mixed with the occasional splash of yellowed paint and the dark ombre of clay. As he moved the corpse, its smell assaulted Kyaz, dispersing motes of crisped fat and skin.

"These look familiar," Kyaz said.

"Boar. Humanoid, wild boar," Xi Ping said. She crouched down, touching the corpse to loot it before pulling the corpse into her inventory. Pig – could you call it a pig if it was Mana-warped – flesh was anathema to the Muslim population that inhabited the city. Of course, the Chinese and Nyonya members had no issue with it, unless one considered eating semi-sapient creatures an issue. Which, some might. "I get why they'd be upset now."

Kyaz cocked his head to the side to ask but was interrupted by the resounding crash and the shrieks of dying monsters ahead of them. He sighed, gesturing for Xi Ping to hurry up as they looted and stored bodies. Chogfal had not waited for either of them, tearing through the dungeon with a vengeance. Even the hardened stone of the dungeon had seen numerous cracks, in one case, being broken open entirely to reveal another room.

Not that any of it mattered to Chogfal. He so out-Leveled the Zone 10-19 dungeon that he wasn't even getting any experience. Even Xi Ping and Kyaz were receiving but a trickle and that was mostly because the System was taking pity on them. Certainly, they were barely helping with the actual fight.

Normally, they'd have complained – being carried through dungeons and gaining some experience for it had been part of their contracts – but considering how Chogfal was acting, and the numerous delays they'd faced, neither felt inclined to protest.

In the end, by the time they made it to the final Boss, Chogfal was standing over the gross, minibus sized mother sow, its body split into two by a single strike. The Hakarta was breathing hard, more from suppressed fury than exertion it seemed, forcing calm upon himself.

"Boss? We good here?" Kyaz asked. Chogfal's Class might be powerful in short bursts, but it also had the tendency to overstimulate the Disaster's emotions at times.

"Yes. Plant the bombs," Chogfal said.

"Already done."

Chogfal nodded, striding over to the newly revealed dungeon core. He slapped his hand down on it, leaving a clay-formed mine around the edge before he gestured for the team to leave. Together, the trio scrambled out, stopping only long enough for Xi Ping to finish looting the Boss Pig and adjust her inventory to take it in.

Outside, Chogfal triggered the explosives the moment Xi Ping scrambled out. The rumble of contained explosions covered by the hastily thrown up, temporary shielding by the Administrators contained the explosions. The building the fast-food restaurant dungeon had once been in shuddered and twisted before it finally collapsed in on itself as the furious explosions were reflected back.

Once it was finished, Chogfal dove right into the building once more, ignoring the burning remnants and tossing concrete walls and rebar aside with careless abandon. The team moved back, allowing the Master Classer to work in silence. Finally, the Hakarta walked out, holding a yellow wrapped food substance in hand, ash and dust streaming from his form.

"Done?" Kyaz asked, staring at Chogfal as he reached the waiting group. There had been no talk while they waited for Chogfal.

The Hakarta pursed his lips, glaring into empty space. Long seconds passed after he put the loot away. And then, finally, a familiar blue notification formed.

Congratulations! Title Acquired: Looter of the Hamburgers

You have shown a spirited and dedicated passion for hamburgers and their most famous dispenser. You have destroyed a thousand such dungeon dispensaries and looted them all.

Effect: +10% damage in dungeons, +25% chance of acquiring food related loot (in addition to normal looting opportunities), +5% experience gain when combatting traditional hamburger related monsters.

Lips pursed, Chogfal stared at the Title. It was a good Title with decent effects. The addition of food loot opportunities could make a big difference in certain biomes. It could make or break certain kinds of expeditions, in both revenue levels and survivability. The experience gain was disappointing though, restricted as it was, though the dungeon damage increase could be useful. Overall, as a Title that had taken long Earth months, it was decent.

But was it worth it? There was only one way to tell.

"What did you get?" Edval leaned forward, almost as if she wanted to see the hidden notification. There were, of course, Skills that could allow her to do that. But like any good Title hunter, Chogfal had Skills to block such Title acquisition.

"Let us see." Chogfal's hand raised, and he tapped into the Title Hunting Registry. A few quick swipes, a simple authentication and he finished registering the Title. Long moments passed, while Edval and the guides waited impatiently.

When the notification arrived, it startled even Chogfal who had been waiting for it. Tusks pushed against his lips, before the lips parted into a savage grin.

Title: Looter of the Hamburgers Registered with Title Hunting Registry
Rarity: Unique
Registration Bonus for Unique Title: +5,000 Contribution Points

Acquisition records and Title hunt records received.
Would you like to register acquisition method with the Title Registry of the Azuma-Kiro Order of Title Hunters?
Expected Payout: +25,000 Contribution Points
Quarterly Bonus Payout: Eligible
_(Y/N)_

"Well?" Edval said.

"Look at it yourself," Chogfal said. He showed her the first notification, the marking of its rarity. He debated, briefly, keeping how to acquire the Title to himself. But with these buildings slowly disappearing, he doubted more than a couple others would ever acquire the Title. And the contribution points were well worth it.

"UNIQUE!" Edval shouted. "That's so unfair. Mine was only a semi-unique!"

"I told you, quality is more important than quantity," Chogfal said, smirking. So saying, he rearranged his Titles on his Status bar.

Xi Ping, seeing it for the first time, coughed and hid her grin behind her hand. Chogfal turned, glaring at the human who waved a hand.

"Dust. Just need some water."

Chogfal snorted in answer, muttering something about lacking Constitution.

"Well, we best get started on the next Title," he said. Grabbing Xi Ping and Kyaz, he hauled them away from Edval who had turned around and was shouting at her own guide. A feeling of deep tranquility rose within him as he dragged the pair away.

Triggering a Skill to keep their conversations to themselves, he leaned down and lowered his voice. "So, human. Do you know of any other good Titles? Maybe another one of these... fast food restaurants?"

Xi Ping paused, eyeing the Hakarta. She'd done well and once she got rid of her loot she'd be even better off. Of course, his Title was a little absurd if you knew human pop-culture, but Chogfal seemed more focused on its rarity.

Chogfal gestured, obviously wanting her to hurry up and speak.

"Well, there's a few other fast-food chains. There's the Colonel — a military designation — and then there's the king of burgers. And well,..."

With each word, the Hakarta's grin widened as the trio headed off to the nearby Shop orb. Kyaz fingers were dancing, his eyes glazed as he triggered his own Skills as he attempted to divine potential Titles for his employer.

Grins plastered on their faces, the trio ignored their surroundings as they discussed new options.

Opportunities abounded on a Dungeon Planet. If you knew where to look.

And didn't mind the odd Title or two.

The End of *Questing for Titles*

Year 8 Post-System

This is Harry Prince, reporting from the capital of Irvina in the heart of the Galactic Empire. Behind me, you can see the remnants of the battle between the Redeemer of the Dead and the Master Classes sent to kill him. His actions to free low-Level alien Combat Classers from the unending exploitation by those above have seen him targeted by the entrenched interests of the Galactics.

We have opened Earth to new immigrants, these same low-Level Combat Classers who are willing to fight alongside us, to trim back the never-ending monster hordes and ensure the safety and security of human habitats.

In retaliation, the Galactics have targeted humanity's brightest lights.

Not just the Redeemer but the Champions, our elected representatives, and the governments that support them or that they rule over.

Rumblings from within the corridors of power indicate that humanity will strike back as well, to teach these self-important individuals and organizations that humanity has fangs. That when struck, we strike back.

We will not fade into the dark quietly.

Blue Screens of Death

A snort, a twist of his head. Skin, stuck to damp and sticky plastic, pulled at his cheeks before finally, he managed to pull his head away. A hand came up to touch his face, to trace the ridgelines that sleeping on the keyboard all night long had created. Brown eyes, gummy with sleep, cranked open, and John Lee managed a low groan.

Where? … How? … John's muddled thoughts struggled to catch up to his waking mind. It had been decades. Not since the System had appeared had he woken up like this. Turning his aching head, John took in his surroundings.

His home. The basement apartment suite that he had rented out and stayed in with Anne – *no, she called herself something else. Some stupid elf name. What was it again? Luthien*– before they had broken up. When he caught her cheating on him with Kevin. Except… did he catch her cheating? Or was that part of the dream and this the reality. The thought was distant, more a recollection of an event that he should know than the vivid memory that it should be.

His dual monitor set-up was right there. On one, a game ran on it — one of the latest versions of that fantasy book, the *Heretic III*, with all its scary monsters and intricate storylines. On the other, the code he had been working on as a favour to a friend.

This isn't right. I should be… somewhere. Dornalor… the ship. I can't be here…

Muddled thoughts bounced around in a frenzy. It had been ages since his mind did that ping-pong ball thing, where it refused to focus. Ever since the Apocalypse, ever since that gene update, he had been fine. He didn't ache from sleeping in a weird position; he didn't have blurry eyes from not enough sleep or a pounding headache because he hadn't had coffee yet.

His hand shook as he pulled a bar of chocolate towards him. Cheap, store-brand chocolate, but it gave calories and sugar and a little dopamine rush. Except his wrist ached, and he had to try twice to peel it open because the tendinitis was back, along with the weakness in his grip and slight numbness in his fingers.

"This isn't real…" John said, drawing a breath. *Or was it just a dream? A vivid daydream of a better world, one where I was a… well, not a hero. At least someone who mattered. Where I didn't hurt every single day; where I wasn't betrayed because I did the betraying. Where…*

"You awake, John?" A voice. Too familiar, too female.

John jolted to his feet, wincing as pins and needles made him limp out the door of his bedroom-cum-office towards the living room. Too late. He forgot to lock the door – or maybe she just used her key that she hadn't given back – because she was here.

She was tall — taller than his five-foot-seven frame. Because, of course, he dreamed of being taller. Who didn't? Though… why he wanted to look like Keanu Reeves, he couldn't understand. He kind of liked being who he was, even if it was a generic, big-nosed, heart-shaped, brown-haired, brown-eyed Chinese man. Nothing wrong with that…

"Here, I brought breakfast!" Her hands were filled with brown paper bags from his favorite fast-food place. Not the Tim Hortons but the A&W here. Because Canadians had made the brand right and made the food actually good. It amused him that the food was so different. But…

"Breakfast?" Puzzled, his mind tried to reconcile the dream — her death, their breakup. He never did see her corpse. Never tried to find it.

Just like he never tried to find his father's or his sister's.

Except, that wasn't…

"Yeah. I thought you might want it. I'm kind of beat myself…" She hid a yawn behind a hand, walking over to their small dining table. Over her shoulder, she called out, "You really shouldn't fall asleep on your computer. You know you shouldn't."

"Where were you?" John said, trying to remember. She had done this… a lot. When they were dating before. Disappearing for ages. In fact, she would say…

"We had a long game night. So I just kind of slept over."

John jerked back, remembering now. Of course. But she had never bought breakfast for him, never walked over and kissed him hungrily, mouth still a little raw from waking up. Never held him tight, pushing her body against his in obvious need. Instead, she'd head to bed, not speaking with him, not…

"What's wrong?" Anne said, pulling away as he did not kiss her back.

"I'm just… uhh… morning breath," John said, lamely. Then he cursed himself because he should be more assertive. He would be if he could figure out what the hell was going on. "Just… give me a second."

"Of course. I'll be out here." And then she winked as he stumbled off to the bathroom, leaving him to clean up. To wash away some of the confusion.

***

It didn't help. The shower, the brushing of the teeth, all of it. Everything felt so normal, so real. The memories of his dream were real too — the time in the Apocalypse and the System. It was all so real, but also, it was fading. Like it was a bad dream, fractured and disappearing.

"Snap out of it. It was just a dream, right?" he questioned, staring back at himself in the bathroom mirror. Hands clenched around the sink, pain shooting through his wrists and fingers. This was reality. A girlfriend who loved him, a life as a code monkey freelancing when he could, and a beautiful territory to live and explore within.

Not memories of desperate battles where pain and blood and lives were at stake. No female Samurai by his side, and no male alien lover or mecha at his fingertips. He was no hero, no settlement lord or Paladin.

Another shake of his head, of lips pressed against his, of a blade sunk deep in his chest. John straightened, touching his unmarked, rather sallow chest. Perhaps he should go to the gym. He kind of liked the body dream John had. Muscular like a gymnast, instead of his less than impressive body.

Getting dressed was simple, fast. Jeans and a T-shirt. His hands paused at the shirt, the famous saying 'This is how I roll' and the d20 staring at him. Remembrance of hiking up Kathleen Lake, of waking up with blue screens pushed at him.

They faded as he pushed away the dream.

It was summer, not mid-May. There was no snow, just warmth and long, lazy days where the sun never set. He didn't walk in on his girlfriend banging another man on his couch. She was right outside, waiting for him…

Oh.

She was in his room now and wearing a lot less than even in his dreams. And rather insistent on impressing on him how much she missed him last night.

***

They did not get much done that day. Lying in bed, staring up at the ceiling, her sweaty body lying on his, and warmth radiating through their pressed flesh, he could not help but smile. This was good; this was nice.

What is, is.

The words rang through his mind, and for some reason, the mantra — the reassurance that had gotten him through some hard days — rang off. Instead of reassurance, it felt wrong now, as if a bell had been rung, but he could not hear it, just feel it in his bones.

It tore him from his contented reverie and made him antsy. He rolled her off him and resolved to get moving.

By the time John managed to drag them out of the apartment, they had to have a second shower and change of clothes, and it was late in the day. Since it was a Thursday, that meant the farmer's market was open. Rather than drive over, the pair decided to walk over, arm-in-arm. The walk through the greenway leading to the river before hitting the Millennium Trail was as beautiful as always. Peaceful. Yet, every once in a while, John would look around, his body tensing as he spotted a squirrel, a nesting bird, or, once, a fast-moving red fox. To his surprise, Luthien never mentioned it, just leaning into his arm and blabbering on about her job as a retail worker.

It was a nice walk, a peaceful one, and the farmer's market was as he remembered it. Sparse, with only about a dozen or so tents set-up. Nearly half of them were local farmers, getting rid of their produce, the other half mostly consisting of food vendors. Nothing spectacular, of course, but it was a relaxed evening out.

"Richard! Grab hold of Howard, will you!" The voice was so familiar that John was turning towards it already, his mouth opening as he got ready to call out to her.

And there she was, a buxom redhead in plaid shirt and blue jeans, as curvy as he remembered with that smile on her lips that made most men melt and kept the area in front of her farm's produce table filled. Beside her, rushing to pull back a bouncing, happy Husky, was another redhead, thinner, freckled, but with quite the grin. In moments, he was engaging in conversation with the young lady that Howard had 'accidentally' run up to.

"Richard…" Not the female redhead but the man was who John focused upon. He remembered the smiling youngster, the way he seemed to handle the Apocalypse so well. His last glimpse of him, just before he had rushed off, his face furrowed in concentration as he fired his shotgun, holding the line.

"Hey!" An elbow in John's side. He looked down, only to spot Anne glaring at him. "Stick your tongue back in. No flirting with the boys without asking me first."

That was a surprise. He didn't recall telling her about his interest. Not that it ever really came up, except once in a while. Most people, most men, just weren't that interesting. Physically, they just didn't do much for him — not unless there was something else beyond the physical. He didn't recall telling her, but the look she gave him was all too knowing.

"When… I…" John spoke, hesitantly.

"I'm not dumb. And it's okay, he is kind of cute. Though I saw the way your eyes lit up on Lana. You want to buy from them again?" A smile, playing on red lips, teasing.

"We've bought from them? …" Puzzled now. He did not remember that. In fact, he did not remember buying much from the farmer's market at all. When they first arrived, it was towards the end of the season, and then winter had come and it was gone. And then, the System had arrived and…

No.

There was no System.

John shook his head, letting her lead the way. He could not help but stare a little, but Lana seemed more than used to it. She barely even paid attention to the dumb and mute Chinese man watching her as his girlfriend bought kale and radishes and tomatoes.

Why would she? A pale and thin programmer man wasn't exactly anything to write home about. Especially for someone who obviously loved the outdoors and the farming life like she did.

Then they were done, and with one bag of vegetables that they were not likely to cook before at least half of it went bad, they wandered off into Shipyard's Park to find a place to eat. The flat ground with the single hill where kids ran around screaming was beautifully lit, like Yukon summers can be. Warm. Just warm enough that if you lay down on the grass and closed your eyes, you could nap.

"Fish burritos?"

"Yeah, sure," John said, smiling.

This wasn't a bad life, not at all. A little slice of heaven. And maybe on the weekend, he'd go hiking somewhere with Anne. She did like hiking.

Didn't she?

***

Anne had rushed off, having seen one of her friends that she gamed with. She was speaking with them, waving a hand around, obviously happy. Probably talking about their campaign. What was it they were doing? Some weird homebrew mix of cyberpunk and magic with multiple Classes? And they were on some stupid, quixotic quest to answer a question.

John shook his head, dismissing the thought. Better off to stay here, seated in the sun, enjoying the warmth. Which was why he was surprised when the voice spoke to him, breaking his lazy, summer thoughts.

"Chocolate?"

"What?" John frowned, staring at the young Japanese woman. One of the tourists probably; she had quite a heavy accent. Standing next to her, carrying a baby, was her husband from the looks of it.

"Chocolate." A hand offered him a solid bar of the aforementioned goodness.

"I… I'm okay." Still confused, but he took the chocolate on reflex.

"I find it makes me less angry." Her hand retracted, and she smiled at John. The family looked happy, though the kid was tugging on the mother's dress.

"I'm not angry."

A considering look, one that turned down to his left hand. John followed it, only to realise that he was clenching it hard.

"Baka."

It took a force of will to force his hand open, to massage at the aching fingers, the wrist that throbbed because he'd overused it. By the time he was done, she had wandered off, not even waiting for him to thank her, leaving him with a chocolate bar. One that said *The Galactic Council.*

Weird name for a chocolate bar.

It tasted pretty damn good though.

***

Lazy summer evenings. Blink and they disappear, and you're back in your basement apartment that is perfectly chilled, under warm blankets with an energetic and enthusiastic young woman. Long, languid evenings even as the sun refuses to set, watching old sci-fi TV shows.

Then, blink again and it's midnight, and John found himself awake again. Rather than wake up the sleeping figure beside him, he made his way to the kitchen, grabbing a drink. Upstairs, across the house where his housemate, his landlord, stayed. Where was he? At the mines maybe?

He couldn't remember. It didn't really matter. It was not as if John ever had paid that much attention before. Before the… what?

Never mind.

Just…

Before.

What is, is.

Jarring, again. His free fist clenched, and his stomach roiled. A part of him wanted to scream, to rage. He breathed, slowly, forcing it down. Stupid dreams, they kept creeping back. Weird that it was the same dreams, same thoughts, these memories that were so obviously untrue.

How insane would it be to stand on the ISS, calling down fire? Or getting eaten by a monster, just to kill it? What kind of person would do that?

Not him.

Breathe.

In. And out.

Cup in hand, John took another drink of pure, alpine water from the tap. Best water in the world, bar none. Other places might think differently, but they were wrong. This place, this time, it was right. It was good.

Right?

His phone blinked, and a name and number appeared on it as it vibrated. John frowned, staring at the name. *Papa*. His father… who never called him.

He blinked again.

And it was another name, his sister. John frowned, staring at the phone and then left it behind. He put the cup down and walked out the backdoor. He'd have to remember to pick it up before his friend was back.

Outside, in the backward, where the hill rose and the public trail ran through the area. In the distance, he could hear someone laughing — probably a late-night summer party. The long summers caught people out at times. The constant light. You didn't realise that the day stretched on without end, the sun never doing much more than spending a short dalliance with the horizon before popping back up again. Just enough to tease darkness before popping back in, its side of the bed not even cooled yet.

A deep breath. A tilt of the head. A fox, scurrying along the ground. John wanted to call out for it, to see if Anna wanted a treat. But she wasn't real.

Or maybe it was him that wasn't real.

The him that stood in this backyard, in a world that never was, no matter how much he wanted it to be. He breathed in. Then out.

Then John spoke. "You might as well come out now."

***

"Impressive."

One moment, he was alone. The next, the figure was beside him, wearing Aiden's face and looking entirely at ease.

"You're not him," John grated out. The anger, that coiled rope inside him that refused to disappear. It was coming back, but he just had to breathe.

"No, I'm not."

"If I asked who you are, would you answer me?"

"No."

John nodded. "I thought I had a Resistance against this." A pause. "Whatever this is."

"You do. But the thing about System-gained Resistances?" Not-Aiden leaned in, grinning conspiratorially. "It only works if you want it to work. And few people are willing to leave paradise."

"This is what my paradise looks like to you?" John said, wry, his eyes flicking around the soft light that suffused the green backyard, the simple two-story house. In his mind's eye, he could see his ex in there. Now that he was awake, memories – real memories – had returned. And strangely, he wasn't even angry at her.

Then again, it had been eight years. And a lot of bodies.

Hard to stay angry at the dead.

Not when you were putting even more corpses into the ground every other day.

"I think the question is, isn't this what paradise looks like to you?" Not-Aiden said. He paused, then he shimmered and a taller, dark-skinned, smiling elf was grinning back at him. "Or did it include more of this?"

"No." *Maybe.* "So what now?"

Around them, in the distance, the world was beginning to crack. In the corner of his eyes, John noticed flashes of blue that seemed to appear and disappear just as fast. Only once in a while. But it was a familiar blue.

"Nothing. You're already breaking free. You don't have to, you know," Not-Roxley said, smiling gently. "We can work out a better paradise for you. One that you don't have to wake up from."

What is, is.

"Oh, gods. Not that." Not-Roxley rolled his eyes. "What is so great about your reality. You could stay here, in paradise. Any paradise you want. And not just you. Her too…" A gesture, and the Japanese lady appeared with her family. Except she was asleep, in bed with her family, all cuddled together.

John's heart lurched as he recognized her now. Mikito.

"She's not like you. She won't wake up. She's happy here. I can feel it," Not-Roxley said, leaning forwards, invading John's personal space. He smelled of cinnamon and musk — just like the real one. "But she's linked to you, you know. If you wake, she does too."

Not-Roxley fell silent now, waiting. The world at the edges stopped breaking apart, losing its vibrancy. Some of the sounds, background noises like the creaking of the houses, the shudder of trembling aspen leaves, resumed.

"You bastard."

A cruel smile. Too cruel for the real Roxley. John made a note of it.

Then he chose.

Blue light, in the corner of his edges, flickered.

And came to life.

***

Mental Influence Resisted
Dreams of the Hunters Resisted
Million Year Slumbering Poison Resisted

John opened his eyes, dismissing the notifications. He looked around, taking in everything.

The desert, sand pink and red rather than brown like those on Earth. The monster that hovered in the air, pulsating. A giant balloon creature all pink and grey, made up of organs and brains, of pheromones and lighter-than-air gasses. So big it might have rivalled the blimps that hung around on game day, but closer. So much closer.

Around him, his slumbering party members. Stirring, a little.

He took in the creature, high above him.

And then he called down the Beacons of the Angels and watched it burn. Maybe he even smiled a little, let its death feed his anger. He would not sleep in dreams.

Because *What is, is.*

And what is, had to be finished.

Even so, when Mikito woke, he would not meet her eyes.

###

The End of *Blue Screens of Death*

Year 9.5 Post-System

This is Harry Prince. I cannot inform you of where we are, nor where we will be. Reports are, as usual, time-delayed to ensure that we may escape well in time.

The Redeemer of the Dead and his party—myself among them—have taken to hunting down those Galactics who continue to interfere with Earth's internal politics. We strike at them in their homes and their businesses, taking the bounties that none else will touch. Each time that we take action, the danger increases.

Though we have gained allies in our quest to rid the world of these corrupt capitalists, noblemen, and all-round pigs, I do not know how much longer we can do so.

Our enemies grow in number each time we act, and our options for safe harbor shrink. We seek refuge in the most unlikely of places, in the depths of contested space and more.

Attached are what little reports I am able to release at this time.

Year 9.75 Post-System

This is Harry Prince, reporting from Pauhiri, the capital of Erethra. We have been plucked from the jaws of death, transported thousands of light years across space and time by the Erethran Honor Guards to serve under the mighty Erethran Empire and their Empress.

The Redeemer of the Dead is the last standing Paladin of Erethra that is easy to access. He has been tasked with training new Paladins, recruits of the highest caliber. Individual Erethrans who are loyal to the Empire and the Empress. Yet, deeper politics swirl all around us and I fear that John will, once again, cock it up.

It is what he does.

Attached in this missive is a firsthand report of the battle for Prax, the infamous pirate station we escaped from days ago.

Broken Council

This is Harry Prince, reporting from Pauhiri, the capital of Erethra.

There is a new Empress Apparent of Erethra and if it is not who anyone else expected, they only have themselves to blame for bringing John Lee into their midst. It is, however, the smallest of matters. For we have been declared rebels against the Galactic Council itself, and we must flee.

The Redeemer has found a thread, a clue to that ever-persistent System Quest, that great mystery of the Galactics. He intends to pursue it to its fullest extent. He has learned deep, dark secrets already, secrets that I can only hint at for the System itself bans its revelation.

I can only say this—there is more to the System than what meets the eye.

We flee the Galactic Council, searching for answers, but escape might not possible, not without sacrifice that we dare not pursue. Our friends and families are in danger and Earth is in the cross-hairs.

Untune that string. And hark, what discord follows!

Forbidden Zone

This is Harry Prince, reporting from the Forbidden Zone in the center of the Galactic Republic. Or what used to be the Galactic Republic. They did not heed my words of warning, and now, chaos is unbound.

The Council is broken, fighting amongst themselves. Another group, a shadow council, stands partly exposed. Lies were laid bare during the last Council meeting and violence flowed from the revelations.

For all that, John Lee, engineer of destruction, sower of discord, cares not. He follows the thread of truth revealed to him about the System, searching for the ultimate answer to the System Quest. Knowing that others, so many others, have traversed this very same pathway.

And were slain for it.

Once more, I attach a recording of the events at the Council meeting. Watch it. Or not. Be warned—truth can kill.

System Finale

This is Harry Prince, reporting from within the Forbidden Zone on the planet of Xylargh, home of the dragons and their riders. We have been captured by the Council. The Redeemer of the Dead is a prisoner and will be judged and executed in due time.

Our Quest is over.

All choices have consequences. This is ours.

Rebellion against the true Council has only one outcome.

System Finale Second Message

This is Harry Prince, reporting from Xylargh. Disregard my latest report. It was made under duress. I… I have no words for what has happened.

We are free, escaping from the trap set by the Shadow Council. We are in a pitched battle against individuals of Legendary strength, in pursuit of the completion of the System Quest. The Emperor has fallen. It is unknown how many more will die.

The Swarm are here, on Xylargh. They are contained by the dragons, and here lies the ultimate truth of the System.

We will try to find the truth, expose it.

Or die trying.

System Finale Epilogue

Harry asked me to finish this if he fell. So I will. This is Mikito Sato. You know me as the Spear of Humanity perhaps, or my other appearances.

Here is the truth.

John Lee, the Redeemer of the Dead, is gone. He found the answer he was searching for, the answer to what the System really is. He found the answer to his Quest, and he—**we**—are better for it.

The consequences of his—our—actions on this day will ripple onwards forever. The System has changed in ways that we are only beginning to understand. When the consequences of what happened are widely known, let it be clear.

This was John Lee, a tired, angry, and oh so broken human's doing.

Lay it all on his shoulders. The weal and woe.

He was always able to bear the burdens none of us could carry.

Growing Up - Apocalypse Style

There was something to be said about the Yukon in the summer. Even having visited other cities and provinces, the true North had a charm to it that other provinces like British Columbia lacked. Things like poisonous plants that emanated clouds of carbon monoxide, predatory System-enabled lynxes, and a white dragon and its chicklet.

You know, sudden death and over-Leveled Zones for a trio of Basic Classers.

It helped, of course, that they had grown up in the Yukon after System advent. It helped even more that they automatically got Perks that boosted their overall survivability, though unlike the original generation, they didn't get to pick them.

Then again, unlike the original generation, they also didn't have the mental scarring of knowing a world before the System. A world that—even when watching documentaries and old media pre-System—was nearly impossible for them to imagine.

"Are you monologuing again?" Katie, his sister—younger sister by a whole two years and twice as insufferable—asked as she glared at him. Hands on her hips, slight upturned nose, and tanned skin from their First Nations mother, she had somehow missed out on all of their parent's heights and was barely over five feet.

"I'm not!" Craig said guiltily.

"You should just have become a writer." Katie rolled her eyes. "Now, come on. I want to Level today, and that won't happen if we don't get to the dungeon and clear it."

"You know I hate the Crilik dungeon," Craig muttered, arms crossed. "It's always super cramped in that cave."

"Gremlin shit, Craig. You know J.D. and Turk will get them," Dawn said, arms crossed over her chest.

Craig glanced over to the fiery redhead who, like her father and aunt, had taken to the Beast Master Class with a vengeance. The fact that both of her pets—pure-bred, mutated huskies—had been raised by a Beast Rearer from the start meant the Level 34 beasts were tougher than even them.

"I just don't get why we have to Level in that dungeon!" Craig said, as the group unanimously continued their hike.

"Because otherwise, they'll overflow again. Not that I get why the System insists on porting in Criliks there.... But there you go." Katie said. "Anyway, it's the Crilik dungeon! It's where Auntie Mikito and Auntie Lana and mum and *John Lee* fought together. It's our history!"

To that, Craig could not help but roll his eyes. You could not turn around and not get smacked in the face with stories about the great and powerful John Lee or their mum or uncle or the amazing gladiator Mikito-san or . . .

As though they had done anything more than run around killing a lot of monsters, just like every other Adventurer like their dad. Except, you know, they managed to survive long enough to Level and become Master Classes. As though risking one's lives constantly was something to be admired.

"Oh, come on," Dawn came up to Craig and elbowed him a little, offering him a wide grin. "Don't be a troll. You know you need to hit Advanced before your dad lets you do your thing."

"I know, I know," Craig said. His voice changed as he chose to mimic his father. "*"If you want to play Guide for the Galactics, an Advanced Class is the minimum you'll need."*"

"Exactly!" Dawn said, still full of cheer. "And if you want the Dungeon World Guide premium Class, you're going to have to meet the minimums."

Craig let out another sigh but nodded. He knew she was right. His current Class of Guide was the most bog-standard Basic Class available. He could have gotten a better one, but of course, his parents had chosen to keep him "safe." Which meant he hadn't managed to get any of the prerequisites necessary to get a premium Class beforehand.

"And now he's grumbling about Mum and Dad again," Katie faux-whispered to Dawn.

Dawn let out a little giggle snort, even as she kept her head on the swivel. None of them had stopped watching their surroundings as they climbed the mountain, the slim trunk of alpine trees surrounding the group. Secondary bush was sufficient to block line of sight about twenty feet away, even as the shivering asps high above danced to the persistent winds around the Carcross region.

The occasional snapped branch and quickly ended squeal marked the passage of the pair of huskies as they tore into the wildlife, taking out low-Leveled vermin without bothering the entire group. Thanks to Craig's Class Skill *Guided Tour*, the experience from the kills were shared amongst them all equally even if it was the pups doing all the work.

"At least I'm not *hero* worshipping the Redeemer," Craig said. "It was *soooo* embarrassing when you had pictures of him up on your walls."

Katie turned red and punched at Craig, who adeptly danced away from her flailing fist. "You . . . you . . ."

"As if you and your friends aren't much better, catching all the System-casts you can get of Auntie Mikito's arena battles. Aren't you like, a member of her fan club too?" Dawn said, coming to the defense of her friend.

"Well, I don't daydream about Auntie Mikito." Craig jutted his chin out. "I just think she's cool, you know. Not like you have much better. The

Astronaut, the Explorer, the Gambler, and the Blade are all popular, you know. Just like Humanity's Spear."

The pair had to nod in acknowledgment. The seven—former Champions some, other newcomers that appeared like a comet—had taken over the System-casts and become the major talking points. What their parents had termed "Superstars" or "A-list" celebrities, though they kept changing the terminology such that the kids were never entirely certain what that really meant. Either way, no kid worth their XP didn't have a favorite among the seven.

Or the eighth, as the case may be.

"I never got that," Katie mused. "The others all got Titles—Spear of Humanity or Humanity's Explorer—but the Redeemer never did."

"Redeemer now, eh? Not John?" teased her brother. Then Craig sobered up, as his sister glared at him, instinct born of years of teasing telling him to stop pushing it. "You need to pay attention when Uncle Ulrick talks. Titles are created by the System but also by expectations. And you know the government's done their best to distance themselves from him."

"Politics." Dawn spat to the side with disgust.

The pair mimicked the motion, shuddering at that most dreaded word. Dawn most of all, what with being the niece of Settlement Owner Lana Pearson, also known as the Red Witch of the North or the Red Beast or another half-dozen appalling appellations. Half the time when Dawn had been old enough, she had spent down in Vancouver, learning politics. But even the siblings had dealt with it, both on a local level—via the Carcross Settlement Council and Lord Roxley—and their visits.

Being the children of semi-famous individuals had its own problems.

Dark thoughts crossed over all their faces, even the normally positive Dawn's. There was a reason the three of them hung out together over and above the family connections, and it was mostly because of the way the other children treated them. Not Gen T—Generation Transition; the ones who had lived in the old world but had their lives interrupted—but their generation, Gen A or Generation Advent.

Gen T . . . well, Gen T was just weird. Some were broken, in ways that no amount of System-assisted mental health healing could fix. After all, a certain level—or a lot—of paranoia in a Dungeon World could be considered normal. When monsters could spawn anywhere and psychopaths abounded, paranoia and ruthlessness was probably just about right. Never mind their other quirks.

And if they looked at Gen A with a certain level of pity or cynicism, or at their parents with envy, who could blame them? Especially with their tiny, depleted numbers . . .

Bu Gen A? Gen A . . . they'd grown up through the turmoil; but when the turmoil was mostly settled. Their earliest memories might have been of pain and fear and uncertainty, but they'd also seen the full blossoming of a Galactic Society. And with it, the creation of Legends.

No wonder they envied, they clung, to those individuals—or those individuals close to such Legends—with such fervor. Humanity had lost so much, but their new Legends strode across the stars like the demigods that they were, reshaping humanity.

All of them, even the one who had reshaped it all the most. The traitor, the savior. And if John Lee's story—his full story—was known only to a few . . .

Well, that'd probably be the way he wanted it. If he even spent any time thinking about it.

"Heads up," Craig said, interrupting all their morbid thoughts. The group pulled their attention back to the world around themselves immediately, snapping to full attention like the well-trained Adventurers that they were. A quick flicker over the various detection methods they had laid around them—spells, Skills, and machines—showed no problem.

Well, except for . . .

"Dungeon ahead." Craig finished.

And then they were there. Another dungeon to run, just like the dozens they had done before. Even if this one was a yawning, empty chamber that sent shivers down their spines and made them shudder as they stared into the darkness.

***

The group crept in slowly, a dozen firefly drones no larger than the insects they were named after lighting the way. They moved in easy coordination, flitting upwards to the ceiling, to the floor and the sides of the cavern, and laying down luminescent chemicals that brightened the dark cave before the team plowed deeper within. No wandering into shadow-darkened caverns for this group.

Other, smaller drones, travelled ahead along the tops of the walls, sending out soundless pings to map out the cave and feeding their information back to Craig. *The Adventurer's Guide* had a Neural Link to all the drones running, splitting the data as it came back to him and then redirecting that information to his party mates via another Skill. It kept everyone informed of potential threats and points of interest, allowing the trio and the pair of pets move swiftly through the cavern.

Minor monsters popped up, creatures of shadows and death—toxic mushrooms releasing spore clouds, bounding six-foot insects with shadow-aspected razorblade claws—and were just as swiftly killed by pups and the concentrated beam-rifle fire by Dawn. Only when a hidden monster, something with too many legs and vine-like appendages, had erupted out of the ground to grab at Craig's leg did Katie's daggers come into play.

"Snicker-snack," Katie sung out, her blades carving within millimeters of Craig's own skin; he held very still as she sheared tendrils and arms and sucking mouths away, "went the vorpal blade."

"Not disturbing at all . . ." Craig said as he eased his feet free from the dissected limbs.

Katie's eyes were just glowing as she danced forwards, the pair of blades by her side. The Snicker-Snack Blademaster had uncommonly high Agility even for a Melee fighter, and Class bonuses against monsters that made her deadly even against things a Tier or two higher. That she had somehow managed to Soulbind her pair of daggers to her were just icing on the cake.

"You're just jealous," Katie continued to sing out, dancing further into the cave. She kept moving, so much so that she disappeared from the brightly illuminated portion of their surroundings, into the shadowed recesses.

Which was, of course, when the shadow-aspected Crilik struck.

Three of them, crossing the distance from where they had hidden in the deep shadows. Two went for the Snicker-Snack Blademaster, one launching itself in a jumping lunge, the other loping low and tight to the ground. The third skittered around the woman, engaging J.D. as the puppy turned, hackles already rising.

"Bad choice. Good boy, J.D.," Dawn said, fingers flaring outwards.

Craig saw the way Mana flowed from her hand towards the other, the way the System aided in the casting as the Skill took effect. The momentary buff boosted the pet's Strength, speeding up its reaction times as it lunged and caught a swinging arm in its jaw. A jerk down and sideways tore the

Crilik shifter's balance from it before the monster used its shadow essence to escape the debilitating attack.

Not before leaving a line of blood on the ground, its limb crushed.

Then Craig had no more time to pay attention to the fight as Dawn engaged the Shadow-aspected Crilik while Kirk kept watch over their backs, his own attention focused on the Crilik shifters battling his sister. She had managed to dodge the pincer attack, somehow leaping between the two monsters and leaving a scored line of damage on both, even as she hummed the bizarre poem under her breath.

Pre-System people were strange.

On her feet, she darted forwards, daggers swinging in short, tight arcs around her body to cut and tear at shifting, shadowy bodies that flowed around her attacks. A half dozen swift strikes and only one of them scoring any real damage indicated just how annoying the monster's shadow-aspect was.

"Time to do my part then," Craig muttered to himself. "Easy Prey . . ."

The Skill triggered, washing over the trio of combatants and a fourth, deeper one within. The debuff was one of the mainstay debuffs in his Class, a penultimate-tier Skill, and robbed those targeted of a fixed percentage of their defenses. In his case, with multiple points sunk into it, it removed nearly seven points of resistances, Agility, Strength, and Constitution.

It was, also, unlike most debuff Skills, not a single cast but a channeled one. It was what gave it such a big deduction in even the Basic Class. It would also be a really short-term buff, if not for the fact that his Perk—Mana Battery—helped allay some of the cost. Even if he never became the Mage his parents had hoped of him, their Perk choice was still quite useful.

The Crilik shifter, moving backwards, staggered a little as the debuff hit it, slowing it down just enough for Katie to plunge her dagger into it and then rip sideways. Blood fountained out, and as the Crilik let out a keening whine, she darted deeper within and struck again, lopping off one limb and then another.

"About time!" Katie said, spinning aside as her other opponent tore into her side and leaving her gasping. Even through the pain, she was smiling as she sang. "Come back, come back, jabberwock, the blade goes snack!"

"That's not even the real poem," Craig said, but shook his head as silence fell over the side. He turned to see Dawn giving him a thumbs up as the puppies dealt with a few smaller adds, the woman picking off fliers that his own drones missed.

Turning his attention to the tunnel where he had sensed the fourth monster, he palmed and lobbed a pair of grenades down the tunnel. The first proximity grenade went off moments later, monofilament razors tearing into shadowy skin before they dispersed, flame and heat bursting outwards seconds later as the incendiary grenade followed up.

The Crilik that staggered outwards after that looked a little worse for wear, especially when Craig's lighting drones moved to highlight the tunnel fully, leaving it with no place to hide.

"Thank you, Craig!" Dawn sang out as she targeted the revealed monster with her own beam rifle, firing into the monster and lighting it up.

For a second, the Crilik shifter shuddered before it rushed Craig, choosing to deal with him. Smirking, Craig stood still, waiting until it was nearly on him before he conjured the double-headed axe he used and swung it upwards, half-bisecting the monster.

A gift from Uncle Ulrick on his System-advent. Enchanted, sharpened, and perfectly weighted, the weapon cut halfway through the Crilik shifter even as its claws left a burning tear across his face. Craig grinned, yanking hard, and then booted the monster back, watching it tumble away before he strode forwards to finish the monster off, axe in hand.

Beam rifles and gunfire were good, but at the higher levels, when an individual—or monster—could cross intervening space in fractions of a second, melee weapons were much more important. Better to learn how to fight close now.

Or so Yerrick philosophy held, and there was certain savage glee in tearing up monsters, lopping their heads off and watching the blood splash around oneself.

Wiping his axe clean, Craig did a quick double-check on his team, ascertained no one needed much healing, and sent his drones forwards before glaring at his sister.

"What was that for?" Craig asked.

"They weren't coming out. So I figured I'd bait them out," Katie said, smiling. "Worked, didn't it?"

"And you nearly got hurt!"

She shrugged. "It's just a little blood."

Craig rolled his eyes but left it at that as Dawn walked over, smiling placatingly at him. "It's better than having them cluster and swarm us, right?"

"Yeah . . . but that's my call, isn't it?" Craig grumbled, arms crossing as he dismissed his axe back into his Inventory.

"Yes sir! Your call, sure, sure!" Katie sang out. "We moving?"

"I hate grouping with you all," Craig said, but his drones were moving no matter what he said. Walking after his skipping sister, he smiled a little as Dawn gave his arm a squeeze before moving onwards.

Well, maybe it wasn't all bad.

***

Prodding the broken and shattered body of the Alpha Crilik, Craig shook his head. "That was disappointing."

"Goblin shit. Do you think they were lying to us?" Crouching down, Katie made the body disappear into her Body Locker extra Class inventory before sighing. "Or were they really just that crap?"

"You forget, Katie, they weren't trained," Dawn said, walking around the surrounding cavern and prodding at the egg sacs. The mucus membrane of the sacs shifted and stirred as the larval Criliks were disturbed. "They weren't meant to live in this world. It's why so many of them died. Sometimes for no reason than believing that just because something hurt meant they were dead."

As if to punctuate her point, she plunged her hand into one of the sacs, the skin of her flesh bubbling a little as the acid within reacted. She swirled her hand around a bit, finding purchase on the larva and then yanking backwards, pulling it out triumphantly.

"Ugh!" Staring at the half-formed, hairless creature that weakly thrashed in her hand, Dawn tilted it sideways a few times before extracting the sample collector. Tossing the collector onto the ground and then the larva into it, the force shield snapped on, locking the monster in half-living stasis. Moments later, she had the entire thing stored in her Inventory.

"What was that for?" Craig muttered.

"Side quest from Sally. She says she needs a half-dozen specimens, might be able to get a flow of shadow-aspect potions going," Dawn explained.

"Huh. And you weren't going to share the Quest?" Arms crossed, Craig glared at Dawn.

Grinning, Dawn shrugged as she turned to the next egg sac and repeated the motions.

Rolling his eyes, Craig checked his own Quest—Monster Guide (27)—and nodded. It was three-quarters done, just had to get them back to town and he could complete it. So perhaps they all had their own secrets. Just another day in the System, really.

"Still, this was too easy." Katie bounced to her feet. "Perhaps the Dragon wasn't that tough either?"

Silence filled the cavern, before the trio burst into laughter.

Yeah, they were Dungeon World children, but even they weren't going to annoy a nesting Dragon.

Some things were truly insane.

###

The End of *Growing Up – Apocalypse Style*

**Want to explore more stories in the System Apocalypse Universe?
Continue the adventure in:**

System Apocalypse: Relentless - A survivor in a world gone mad.
www.starlitpublishing.com/collections/system-apocalypse-relentless

System Apocalypse: Liberty - A teacher faces his hardest test yet.
www.starlitpublishing.com/collections/system-apocalypse-liberty

System Apocalypse: Kismet - A different path through the apocalypse.
www.starlitpublishing.com/collections/system-apocalypse-kismet

Let's stay connected!

Be the first to hear about new books, special offers, and behind-the-scenes extras:

About the Authors

Craig Hamilton spends most of his day as a technical sales engineer, translating specifications and talking about IT infrastructure. While writing has been taking up most of his free time lately, Craig also appreciates playing tabletop RPGs or board games with friends. When his inner introvert demands a break from polite company, Craig can be found sprawled on a couch with a good book.

Craig is the author of the spin off series *System Apocalypse – Relentless* and his own series, *Rift Warden Academy*.

Follow Craig here: www.facebook.com/AuthorCraigHamilton

David R. Packer is the author of *The Anubis War* and the forthcoming *Salish Rift* series. He's been a full-time teacher of historical European swordplay, a high-tech wizard, and a security professional. For a few years he was a for-pay bad guy working in police training, which once had him on the run from the entire police force, across the whole city.

Aside from that, he lives a cozy life with two cats and a real-life she-hulk for a wife. He has many books and likes coffee far too much.

David is the author of the completed spin off series *System Apocalypse: Kismet*.

Follow David here: www.boxwrestlefence.com
www.facebook.com/randy.packer

Jason J. Willis is a husband, father, geek, equalist, and lover of art. Gamelit, LitRPG and progression/cultivation fiction. Audiobooks especially are his addiction of choice. Due to a beloved day job that allows him to listen to anything he wants during his entire work shift, Jason spends more than full time consuming the above, plus podcasts, music, and the Great Courses series.

Jason is the author of the spin off series *System Apocalypse: Liberty*.

Follow Jason here: www.facebook.com/jason.j.willis
www.instagram.com/jasonjoneswillis/

Tao Wong is the author of the *A Thousand Li* progression fantasy series and the *System Apocalypse* LitRPG series, among others. His work has been released in audio, paperback, hardcover, and ebook formats, and translated into German, Spanish, Portuguese, Russian, and several other languages. He was shortlisted for the UK Kindle Storyteller Award in 2021 for *A Thousand Li: The Second Sect*. In 2026, the first three books in the *A Thousand Li* series will be republished in hardcover by Ace Books.

When he's not writing or working, he enjoys practicing martial arts, reading, and dreaming up new worlds. He lives in Toronto, Canada.

If you'd like to support Tao directly, he has a Patreon page - benefits include previews of all his new books, full access to series short stories, and other exclusive perks. Tao Wong's Patreon: www.patreon.com/taowong

For updates on the series and his other books (and special one-shot stories), please visit the author's website: www.mylifemytao.com

About the Publisher

Starlit Publishing is wholly owned and operated by Tao Wong. It is a science fiction and fantasy publisher focused on the LitRPG & cultivation genres. Their focus is on promoting new, upcoming authors in the genre whose writing challenges the existing stereotypes while giving a rip-roaring good read.

For more information on Starlit Publishing, early access to books and exclusive stories visit our webshop.

www.starlitpublishing.com/

You can also join Starlit Publishing's mailing list to learn about new, exciting authors and book releases.

https://starlitpublishing.com/newsletter-signup

For more great information about great LitRPG series, check out the Facebook groups:

- GameLit Society

  www.facebook.com/groups/LitRPGsociety

- LitRPG Books

  www.facebook.com/groups/LitRPG.books

- LitRPG Legion

  www.facebook.com/groups/litrpglegion

To learn more about LitRPG, talk to authors including myself, and just have an awesome time, please join the LitRPG Group!
www.facebook.com/groups/LitRPGGroup/